Search for

Xerena

SERENITY K. ORR

Trail Media

San Diego, California, U.S.A.

Printed in the United States of America
ISBN-13: 978-062444924 (Trail Media)
ISBN-10: 069244920

Cover design:
Danielle Keltner of *Dannie Ann Photography & Designs*
http://dannieannphotodesigns.com/

Interior art: Serenity K. Orr

DEDICATION

To my wonderful son, whose imagination inspires mine, and to my mother, whose determination has seen our family through many years.

To God be the glory.

CONTENTS

ACKNOWLEDGMENTS

In my Journey, I have come to realize that nothing is done independently and so I want to express my gratitude to those that have helped me.

I thank my God for the talent and support He has given to me. Without His saving grace I never would have started this process. I want to thank my family for putting up with endless editing, for allowing me the freedom to write, and for supporting the whole process.

To Trail Media, I want to say thanks for believing in my story enough to help it become a tangible book.

A big thanks to all my friends and all their comments. The slightest statement or question can help so much with the story, with the ability to communicate.

PREFACE

I am Siira, daughter of the chief, and this is my story. I was born the second child of the chief. My older brother Siiraq was perfect: brave, strong, and smart. But the Mighty One took him to Xerena, a place of rest beyond this life, in a landslide. I loved my brother and though I was only five annuals I felt his loss deeply.

As most children do, I recovered from my grief quickly, especially after my mother announced that she would soon have another babe. I remember watching her belly enlarge, watching it move on its own. I would tell myself that the Mighty One had sent a replacement for my brother that I lost; another Siiraq grew inside my mother.

But it was not to be. For when my mother went with the women to the birthing pools neither she, nor my new baby brother, returned. Again the Mighty One took loved ones from me to Xerena. I was lost and alone. Grandmother tried to console me with stories of Xerena, of the bright blue sky, so different from our own gray one, of the fields of flowers that never died, of the joy in the Mighty One at the return of one of his creatures to his home; but I couldn't see that. My mother and both of my brothers were gone.

My father grieved his loss, but as Chief he had others

that depended on him. I overheard a conversation between my father and Grandmother that at the time I did not understand, but soon would.

"You must continue on; you cannot upset your people, our way of life. You cannot disappoint your great fathers, by losing the line because of selfishness. You must take another." She had said.

"I know, Mother, but I cannot love another."

"I said nothing of love, I speak of duty."

"If it is duty you speak of, then I will do my duty. I will bring a successor before the council."

At the next meeting my father took my hand and led me into the midst of the people. I stood in front of the story fire, its heat burning into me, causing my uncertainty to boil like Grandmother's forgotten stew.

My father addressed the council, "My fathers have led the people since we left the forgotten valley, and though I do not intend to take another woman, I have a child, a child that can be trained to follow me."

A confused murmur swept through the people. I understood my father's words as well as I would understand the chattering of a bushy tail. How could I be trained to follow him? I am a girl.

"Your daughter?" Boku, an elder and great hunter, asked.

"She can be trained to be a man. She can take the testing so that her sons will be my heirs."

And so it was decided. I was to become a man. I could no longer play dolls with my friends, I could no longer sing the laughing songs, and I could no longer stay comfortably in the cave. I had to follow my father on scouting trips. I had to learn to trap and hunt. In time, I learned to even enjoy my adventures.

But I am becoming a woman, full of female emotions and woes. Will I ever be at peace?

And I suppose that this tale, my tale, is about the

journey of a girl who is told to be something she is not, something I am not.

TO BE MAN

1 A LESSON

I struggle in the world of half waking, trying to make sense of the sounds around me. A rustling of coverings, a soft patting of feet, a rubbing together of skins. Then I remember Father must leave us today. It is the first hunt of the annual. The men will be gone for several days, even with our longer days giving more light; the work of killing the mammoth, cutting the beast into manageable pieces and then hauling the food back takes much time.

I pull the covers down, exposing my face; cool air tickles my cheeks. Rolling over onto my side, I spy on him. He wraps long, thin cords around his knee-high boots, the boots that I had made for him during the time of snow. I try to commit his face to memory. Ever since I have forgotten my mother's face I have tried to imprint his image on my heart and mind. I never want to lose him. I alternate between watching him and closing my eyes, calling up the image in my mind.

His jaw-length dark hair, black as night, is straight and gathered by a cord at the base of his neck. His eyes, the color of the early dawn, focus on the laces he is tying. His broad face, though stern at times, has known much laughter, the evidence in the wrinkles at the edge of his lips. I continue my ritual until I am satisfied that I will remember.

Father stands and stretches his muscled frame to full height. He is about average among the people, although the muscles in his arms are much leaner than most of the men. He is wearing the traditional skin leggings and sleeveless tunic of the people. A cord hangs loose at his throat, his token dangling from it. He wraps a wide belt about his lean waist, securing it with a knot, and then grabs a large square pouch from a small hollowed log by the back of the tent. In the pouch there is much meat powder, a mixture of dried berries, fat, and meat that is pulverized; this will provide him with strength on hunts. All the men carry it. He tucks the cords of the pouch around his belt before grabbing his coat, a jacket made from mammoth skin by my mother, long ago. Grandmother had made him a new one, but he only thanked her and then gave it to Balek. Somehow, I can't see him in any other jacket; it must be this one, with its dark stained skin and shiny elbows. The hood hangs in a triangle at his back; it is waterproof and will keep him warm in all weather.

Father leans over, smiles at me, and tugs at a strand of my hair long, loose hair.

"Sleepy one, soon I leave for the hunt, but I expect you to be busy while I am gone. You are to train with Balek again today, practice your dart throwing and trapping. Maybe you will even bring another jumper for some stew."

"Alright, Father. Good hunt, may the Mighty One bless you with safety and much meat, so that you will return to me and provide for the people." I quote our traditional farewell, one I had learned long ago from my mother. I truly mean every word.

"Thank you, my child."

Before he leaves our tent, he grabs his darts and throwing stick. Then he lifts the flap, eases himself out, and is gone. Although the men do not always use them to kill the great mammoth, they always take them because of the blade-toothed cats and the grizzly claws. These ferocious beasts will smell the kill and quickly try to claim it for themselves. This contest for the meat often ends in injuries and deaths for both sides, no matter what precautions we take.

Once Father leaves, I breathe in the cool air. Now that the time of snow has passed, we only worry about a nightly fire, and so Grandmother has let it turn to coals. I stretch, sending blood flowing and circulating through my body. Today I practice, much as I do many days. The only times I do not prepare for my testing is when I am plagued by the time of the women; it is then that I question my father's wisdom the most. Although I do not suffer every moon as most of the women, I am only plagued two or three times an annual, it is enough to be discouraging. I want to please Father, but I am growing into a woman, capable of bearing children.

"But that is what your father wants," Grandmother would remind me, whenever I would bemoan my plight. "He wants a son, and you shall give him one."

"Then why go through all of this training? I can have children without being a man."

"Yes, but then your son would be your man's and not your father's. It is our way. And so you must be pronounced your father's heir in order to give him an heir."

I crawl out from under my furs to prepare for the day. Pulling on my mammoth skin leggings, I tighten the drawstring around my lean waist, muscles rippling as I breathe. The tunic comes next. It is supple and moves easily over my torso. It is sleeveless, like my father's. I stare at my arms. They are long and lean, so that I can see the small muscles twist and turn with my movements. I frown, wishing for the graceful and full arms of the other women. But my training has set me apart.

I grab my boots then settle on the ground. I tug them on, and then tuck my leggings into them. Finding my cords, I wrap them securely up to my knees. I slide into my skin jacket. It hangs loosely around my lean, hard body. Last, I run my wooden comb through my long tangled hair, and then tightly bind it in a tail with a cord. I grab a handful of dried berries and grizzly meat and leave the tent.

As I walk to Balek's family tent, I toss berries into my mouth one at a time, trying not to notice the looks that the women give me. I do not know what their looks mean, but they make me feel uncomfortable, as though I had eaten some bad meat. I am the chief's daughter, of course they watch me, I tell myself, trying to calm my nerves.

I run a hand along the cave wall, feeling the damp grittiness, as I turn toward Balek's family's tent. All of the dwellings are arranged in a semi-circle around the story fire, which is the center of life here in our cave. My family tent is in the center of the arc of tents, near the back of the main room of the cave, and Balek's is off to the strong side.

Beyond the main room are smaller rooms, used by newly joined couples, and beyond those are mysterious winding caverns. I have never ventured beyond the main room though. I have never had the need.

Most family tents have two rooms. A main room takes up three-quarters of the space. Here the family gathers around the fire pit to eat and talk; this room is where the children sleep. The parents have a separate room, divided by a skin wall stretched and hung from a pole at the top of the tent.

I arrive at Balek's tent. His father, Boku, has left with the men, but I watch his mother talking to Bela then she disappears into the tent. Bela, Balek's sister, remains outside on a stool. She has a large pot and a stone. She is working the stone up and down, probably preparing some meat powder. Her long black hair is braided in two braids, the custom of the unclaimed girls, and they swing with a rhythm that matches the rhythm of her pounding the powder. Her soft skin glistens from the effort of work. I wish that I could stay and join her. I wish I could wear two braids, instead of the long tail of hair down my back.

The men wear their hair jaw length and tied with a cord at the base of their necks. Though I have acquiesced to tying my hair back as the men do, I insist on it being long hair. It trails to my waist. I wish I could just stay with Bela, prepare food, and sing the laughing songs of our people and talk of nonsense, instead of pretending to be something I am not.

"Hello, Bela."

Since she does not seem to notice me at first, I repeat myself and speak up.

This time she looks at me. Her eyes, the color of soft earth, seem to be focused on a place far away, but slowly she focuses on me.

"Something wrong?"

A reluctant smile plays at her lips, "It's just, well, Siira. I have been dreaming about this hunt and I am afraid that something will go wrong."

"I am sure that everything will be fine. Your dreams don't always come true."

"True, but, oh well." With a shake of her head, her braids swing again. I think of a time before I had to train, a time when Bela and I would run to the meadow and pick the little blue flowers that grow there, a time when Bela and I were friends and Balek was an annoyance. Now things have changed.

"Is Balek here? Father says that we are to train this morning."

"No, he has gone to the tree to wait for you. I think he wanted to surprise you."

"Why?" I tear a piece of grizzly meat with my teeth and chew.

"Seriously, Siira, sometimes I think you are the most oblivious person. You are almost fifteen annuals."

I try to think of what it is that I am missing. What am I not noticing that everyone else must be? I don't like the

7

feeling, the feeling of being talked about, the feeling of being left out of some secret.

"Siira, I think that Balek . . .," she pauses as if to think, "favors you."

"That's ludicrous. He's like my brother, and you are like my sister." I toss a berry at her. "I have to go." I spin around, trying to act as though her words have no effect on me, but in truth I had begun to notice some changes in Balek's behavior.

If Balek is developing feelings, I can't encourage them.

I pass the story fire; it is small in the morning light. Seated on a low log is Grandmother, surrounded by children too young to be of any use, yet too old to be strapped to their mother's backs. As the Keeper of the Stories, she spends her time telling the tales of the great fathers, passing on our past to those who are the future. I wave and smile.

Picking up my pace, I begin to jog to the mouth of the cave. I stop on the lip and breathe in the sweet, cool morning air. Our valley lies spread out below me. My home. In the distance, I see the dark shimmer of the Great Salt Water. Feathered flyers, like tiny black specks, fly in weaving dances over it. The tan, sandy beach outlines the water, creating a border between the water and the meadow.

The tall green grass of the meadow bows in the wind. Off to my strong side, a forest of trees goes on for many spans before coming to the unseen high river. In the grass, directly before the trees, is the lookout rock. I see young Tiras sitting on it, a horn clutched in his hand.

Where the grass stops, tall berry bushes grow, making a border between the meadow and our preparation camp directly below me.

I rush down the steps that are at the large opening of our cave. These stairs were first cut by the great fathers during their first winter here.

I race through the preparation camp, paying no attention to the women who are smoking and drying our food. I come to the berry bushes that run rampant, prickly and wild. I know the path and race through it, feeling alive at the movement of my body as it twists and dodges the thorns that reach out and try to snag me. Once beyond the bushes, the land is flat and tall grass reaches to my knees. By the end of the hunts it will be as tall as I am.

The meadow is full of life: flutterbys flit from grass to grass, from flower to flower; fleet feet mothers lead their fawns in grazing and drinking; long-eared jumpers hop, chasing each other in games. I veer to my weak side. The animals pay me no mind as I race by on a well-known path, well known to me and Balek.

There is only one tree in our meadow, a giant tree at the farthest end of the meadow, unseen from the cave. Its boughs stretch out many spans, providing shelter from the torrential rain that comes several times a moon during the season of hunts.

I had first seen it on a scouting trip on my tenth annual. I was with my father, Balek, and Balek's father. We were tracking a herd of fleet feet, hoping to catch a female and her fawns, so that we could share her milk. We almost had them when the sky opened and poured rain on us.

Balek's father, Boku, spied the tree, like a green hill rising above the grassy meadow. We rushed to it laughing, in spite of having lost our quarry.

In its shelter, we stayed dry and listened to Boku tell ancient stories of the forgotten valley. The forgotten valley had been home to the people before the great hunter had begun to conquer and force men to work on his temple. My great father led the people following the mammoth to this land that we now call home. But I am not running to listen to stories; I am going to train with Balek.

I see a leg dangling from a low branch in the tree and I slow my pace, assuming my cat-like steps. My father says that I could sneak up on a grizzly claw and cut his hair if I wanted to, but I, of course, have never tried it. As quiet as a blade-toothed cat, I creep up behind him. Silently, I climb onto a branch that is above his and peer down, trying to decide how to make my presence known. I study him as he is engrossed by something in his hands. He is carving a small flower onto a piece of white wood. The flower is a common one in our valley. A small five-petal flower. The people say that its scent can bring remembrance to those in Xerena.

I don't want to think about those that I have lost, so instead I begin to pluck leaves and let them flutter down onto Balek's head. I watch as the first one lands in his shiny black hair, unnoticed as it sits there. I drop another and it falls to his lap. He is so intent on his work, he does not notice. So I break a twig off and throw it at his bare muscled arm. He waves it off as though a flying insect is bothering him. I throw another and it hits his nose. Then another that goes down the neck of his tunic. He wiggles and loses his balance. He reaches out to a branch to steady himself, but as he grabs onto the branch, he drops the carving.

I watch it fall and break on a rock below.

Balek lets out an angry grunt and jumps to the ground.

"Sorry," I say.

His head jerks up, his eyes locking onto me.

"Siira, I was working on that all morning."

I drop soundlessly next to him.

"I didn't think that you would drop it."

"If you were a boy, I would hit you right now." He scoops up his broken carving.

If I were a boy. Well, I almost am. I am something in between, I suppose, not really a boy, but neither am I a girl. The comment hurts for some reason.

"You mean I am not a boy, I train like a boy. I can out run and out hunt most of the boys my age."

"Yes, but you aren't a boy, you are . . . Siira, the chief's daughter."

Rage burns inside me. I want to fight him, to prove him

wrong. I can't be a girl, a woman. My father has taken that from me, so I must be a boy. Impetuously, I lean back and kick him in the stomach.

He stumbles back, but easily recovers. "Siira, come on, you don't want to fight me."

But I do. I try to remember how the men wrestle in the cave. How does it start? Usually the bare-chested men shove each other.

I stand in front of Balek and shove his shoulders back.

"Alright, if you insist, but if your father asks, it was your idea." He drops the carving, a teasing smile on his lips.

Before I know what is happening, Balek's rock-solid grip clamps onto my shoulders, pulling me off of my feet. Fear rushes through me and I feel the blood drain from my head. He is pushing me backward until I stumble, and we fall to the ground. Instinctively, I tuck my chin and grab his arms, hoping to break the fall a little. He pins my shoulders down. A glint is in his eyes, the corner of his mouth lifts in a half smile.

"Are you done yet?" he asks as though I am a petulant child. He is amused by all this. I wriggle and move but his grip remains firm. As the smile grows on his broad face, my rage grows, burning in my stomach. I am trapped. He is so much stronger than I am; he only needs his two hands to hold me down.

I have to think, to remember, how do the men get out of this? They use their brute strength and just shove the attacker off, but I can't.

Suddenly, the memory of a boy wrestling his father flashes in my mind, and I know what I can do.

I pull my legs up between his massive arms, planting my feet on his chest. I push as hard as I can. His fingers slip off my arm and he rolls to the ground. I have done it, I have broken free. I scramble, like a frightened bushy tail, but I do not get far. I feel his rough hand grasp my wrist and twist my arm up behind me, pulling me to his chest. I feel him breathing, calm slow breaths. He is not really trying, yet I feel that if he used any more strength he could tear my arm free from my shoulder.

Enraged, I throw my head back as hard as I can, hoping to cause enough pain to weaken his grip and break free. I hear a crunch and a grunt. I refuse the impulse to turn and see how badly I have hurt Balek. I refuse to give into the compassion rising in my mind, and I scurry away some distance before I turn to look. Catching my breath, I see that blood is streaming down his face from his nose; I know that I have broken it. The pain in his eyes turns into determination, determination to teach me a lesson. He seems to grow into a giant as he lets his pain turn into rage.

My options are limited. I have to knock him down and maybe then I can manage to sit on him until he calms down. Lowering my head, I run straight at him charging, like a woolly one horn. But he leans over me, wrapping his arms around my waist. He raises me off the ground. The world turns upside down. My feet kick wildly in the air trying to do something, anything. Balek jumps, catches my head between his thighs, and then drops us to the ground.

Blinding pain surges through my head. I crumple in a pile as though my bones have become breakfast gruel

Struggling to stay awake as the world around me spins in blurry circles, I can't move. Balek has defeated me. I have learned his lesson. No matter how I try, no matter what I learn, and no matter if I can throw a dart better than any man: I will never be one. I will only ever be something in between.

I hear Balek stalk away, apparently satisfied that I have learned my lesson.

At first I cannot move, I can only whimper like a hurt pup. Noises from the other side of the tree tell me that Balek has not left me alone. I want to be alone, and yet at the same instant I don't. Curling onto my side, intent on hiding my emotions, I focus on the far horizon, as tears begin to overflow, streaming down my face.

Lost in my thoughts, thoughts of uselessness, of self-doubting, I do not notice when Balek sits behind me.

"How's your head?" His voice is soft, as though he speaks to a child.

I remain silent, choosing not to talk to him. He has humiliated me. The fight has proven what I always knew to be true; I can't do as my father wishes.

Yes, I excel at all areas that I am given. In truth, sometimes I enjoy the target practice or the tracking of the animals; I enjoy running free among the trees, but I am a girl. A girl, I want to scream it.

Balek taps my back with something. "Look at me, Siira, please. I am sorry. I didn't want to hurt you, but you are so, so incredibly stubborn." I hear him fidget with something. "I was making it for you. See, it is the small blue flowers that you are always taking to the salt water for your mother and brothers."

I roll onto my stomach and turn my head toward him, slowly, noticing that somehow he has staunched the flow of blood from his nose. I did get in one good hit, I think, although it is little consolation for the throbbing in my head.

"So do you like it?" As he holds up his broken handiwork, I notice a crimson streak on his tunic.

"It's beautiful, or would have been." Another tear trickles down my cheek. How can I become a man, if I can't fight? How will I ever be able to prove myself to be just as good without being able to fight them?

"How's your nose?" I mutter as I pick a blade of grass.

"It should make for a great scar." He runs his hand under it, making sure that the bleeding has truly stopped.

"No, just a crooked nose." I manage to grin.

He sprawls out in the grass next to me.

"How am I supposed to do it, how can I be Chief?"

"Maybe you won't be, maybe you will have a son to follow your father." I look at him; he is tracing something in the dirt.

"Balek, men are expected to fight and wrestle. I lost horribly."

"Of course, what did you expect, Siira?"

"I don't know, but a headache was not it." I scoot up into a sitting position. "All of the men will be stronger than me, how will I lead them as my father wishes?"

"Well, maybe I will fight them for you." His grin, broad and white, proud and confident, does little to dispel my fears.

"Maybe," I say as my head throbs.

2 A PLACE TO PRACTICE

We stay at the tree until the Great Light begins to dip in its journey. Our empty stomachs become demanding, forcing us from leisure to the berry bushes to gather food. When Balek's pouch is full, we return to the cave.

During the time of the hunts, when the weather allows us to roam the meadow and forest, the people must gather as much food and wood as possible. The time of snow is long and dark; without the mammoth I don't think we would ever be able to collect enough meat to satisfy the stomachs of our people. We number thirteen families, eighty-six people total, with the number expected to increase soon as several of the women are with child, although we may lose as many as we gain due to the unforeseeable tragedies.

The Mighty One, the great creator, is supposed to bless those who follow him, but I have seen the good die as quickly as the bad. My mother was one of the most devoted to him and yet he took her along with my innocent baby brother. If I am called upon to lead the people in faith as Chief, I will do the actions, but I know that my heart will never be in it. I have lost too much.

"Will you join us for the evening meal, Siira?"

"No, Balek, I must spend time with Grandmother. She is to teach me the story of beginnings tonight. I am to recite it for father when he returns."

I begin to climb the stone steps, Balek follows me. As I near the mouth, my nerves are on edge; something seems out of place, but what?

When we enter the cave, all is silent. The usual sounds of children playing and women talking, busily preparing the evening meal, are absent. The story fire, that is usually ablaze by now, is cold. I see no movement around the tents, they seem abandoned. Fear creeps through me. Then I see one of the men, Pire, rushing to us. Why is he here? The men should not be back yet.

"Pire, what is it? Why are you back?" Balek asks, as my voice seems to have disappeared in uncertainty.

"Blade-toothed cats, they ambushed us and," Pire fixes his eyes on Balek, "Boku is injured."

I watch as the color drains from Balek's face.

"The new one is tending him and he needs water." He holds up a large water skin and rushes toward one of the cisterns near the mouth of the cave.

Tamuq, the new one, had joined the people a couple of annuals ago. He and his son, Maruq, had wandered into our valley after many moons of traveling. They came to us at the time of snow. All of the people were in the cave because of the weather. I had been helping Balek with the watch that night. I remember that it was around dawn, when the sky turned purple. Balek stood near the torch, carving a doll for Bela, when he noticed them. He had pointed out into the dimly lit horizon.

"What is that?"

I looked, watching for several moments. Two fur covered men were walking and a large wolf pulled a sled. I couldn't keep my eyes from the wolf. I had never seen it's equal. Its head came past the men's elbows; I would not need to kneel to look it in the eyes.

"Men, of course, what did you think?" I answered, a smile on my lips.

"I don't know; men aren't stupid enough to go out in the snow."

I didn't answer him. I grabbed the torch and began to wave it, hoping to beckon the strange men and their wolf to us.

Balek quickly came to my side, "What are you doing?"

"Inviting them in, they must be cold."

"Stand back, I will do it." He snatched the torch from my hand and thrust the doll at me. I watched transfixed as they climbed to the cave's mouth.

When they stood before us, I studied them. There was nothing of their body visible, not even their eyes. Their hoods were pulled firmly down on their heads and they wore skin masks with small slits for their eyes.

The taller of the two removed his mask first. His features were finely carved, as though the Mighty One himself had carved them and set the man down onto the earth. Without looking at me, he said something to Balek. His voice was sweet and melodic, like honey that we have in the time of the hunts. His words sounded vaguely familiar to my ears; and yet I did not recognize them at all. I remember that Balek's posture became stiff as he shook his head. The man slowed down, and repeated himself, but it did no good.

He turned and tapped the other man's mask. Once his mask was removed, I saw that he was much younger than the first man, maybe an annual or so older than Balek. He listened as the older man spoke to him. I watched as though in a trance. I had never seen a boy so beautiful. His hair, the color of clear honey, seemed to shine in the torchlight. His features more finely crafted than any of Balek's wood worked dolls. His eyes were blue, bright blue.

As I stared at him, he must have felt my gaze, for he shifted his gaze to meet mine. I couldn't help myself. I stared back. I felt that if I could but stare into those eyes, I could forget all of the pain of loss that I could even find a little bit of Xerena here on earth. I could see the remembrance flowers in his eyes. I could see the cool rushing river. I could see the skies of Xerena. I had never seen eyes that color. Balek tapped my shoulder as if to awaken me.

"Go. Get your father, Siira."

I nodded. When I moved to leave, the great wolf snarled. I had forgotten about it. But at the reminder I froze in my steps. The blue-eyed boy gave a short command to it and the wolf sat and perked up its ears. But I was shaking. He took my hard, callused hand with his long, graceful one; and ever so gently lifted it up to the wolf's muzzle.

I do not know why I trusted this stranger to do this, but I did. The wolf put his nose, the size of my palm, into my hand. It was cold and wet, but pleasant. I smiled.

The boy let go of my hand and I ran off to get my father.

My father had accepted them with open arms, allowing them to become part of the people upon completion of the testing. Although Tamuq and Maruq have proven to be beneficial to the people, teaching us new methods of healing, they are still the new ones.

I follow Balek to the healing tent. I see that all of the people are gathered, silently waiting for news of the great hunter, Boku.

I search for Bela in their numbers and see her standing next to the tent, separated from the rest of the curious onlookers, wrapped in Pol's arms. It is no secret among the people that Pol loves her. Once Bela comes of age Pol will claim her as his own. It seems that they have been in love since Pol saw Bela as a babe.

"What happened?" I ask as I approach. He turns Bela out in order to face me, but keeps a protective arm around her.

"Boku and I were keeping watch while the men began to set up camp for the night, when a male blade-tooth crept up behind me. Boku saw him and cried out a warning, knocking me to the ground to attack the beast. I was able to sound the alarm, but by the time the rest of the men came, Boku had," he glances at Bela, "been injured."

Bela's head drops onto Pol's shoulder, as if its weight is too much to bear. "It's all my fault, Siira, I asked him to watch, to keep him safe."

"From what?" I ask.

She raises her eyes to meet mine. I look into them and recognize the tortured pain.

"Was it your dream?" I ask.

She nods.

"It will be alright," Pol tries to console her.

"Yes, Boku is strong, I am sure he will pull through, that the Mighty One will not take him yet."

As if to confirm my assertion, I hear Boku's strong, if strained, voice roaring from inside the tent. "Where is Tomu? I do not want this stranger tending me."

"Calm down, my love." This voice is Natiq's, Balek's mother. "Tamuq knows what he is doing."

"Boku, you are to allow Tamuq to tend you, he is not a stranger. He has become one of us, having passed the testing." My father's voice is steady and determined. At his command, Boku must have obeyed for I hear no more outbursts.

As time passes, mothers begin to take young ones to their tents to sleep. Soon Pol, Bela, and I are left alone. I move away from the couple and sit with my back against the cave wall. It is cool and reassuring; the wall has been and always will be here, it can be depended upon.

The day's trials wear on me and soon I am dozing.

I feel a hand brush against my shoulder, something sniffing at my feet, and then a calm, melodic voice, softly accented, calls me out of my sleep.

I extend my hand to the pup at my feet. He sniffs it with his wet nose. I lift my head and stare into the bright blue eyes of Maruq. I fight the urge to keep looking into them, to get lost in their cool depths as I had so long ago. I drop my gaze back to the pup. I run my fingers through the warm fur.

"You can do nothing here. Why not go keep company with your grandmother?"

"I am waiting for my father."

"He will be leaving soon. Boku is doing fine. Come, I will take you."

He stands before me, offers a hand, and waits. I look up at it and take it. He pulls me up to my feet, more quickly than I expect. I lose my balance and step on the pup. He yelps and scurries between my feet, knocking me forward into Maruq's chest. In that moment, flutterbys are freed in my stomach. I feel nervous and ill. Heat rushes to my face. It is wonderful.

As he sets me back onto my feet, separating us, I feel a strange loss, as though the slightest distance between us is unnatural. He gathers the frightened pup into his arms.

"No, thank you, I know the way," I say.

I leave him, almost running to my tent. I stop at the tent flap to gather my emotions which are threatening to spill out. Chancing a glance backward, I see that he is standing where I left him, watching me and scratching the pup behind its ears.

As I enter the tent, I see Grandmother sitting by the fire pit. Her back is toward me, a long white braid in a single cord dangling down her back. Her soft skin dress rustles as she moves, rocking back and forth in a prayer. I assume it is for Boku.

I don't wish to disturb her and so I enter and sit by the fire pit without a word. Eventually she opens her eyes.

"Siira." Her voice rasps my name in surprise. A crooked smile spreads across her wrinkled face. "Are you hungry?"

My stomach growls.

"I will take that as a yes." She pushes herself up, moving to the large pot that sits on the warming stones. Using a wooden spoon she scoops some stew into a small wooden bowl. "How is Boku doing?"

"Maruq says that he will be fine."

"Maruq?" She arches an eyebrow.

"Yes, he woke me up and told me to keep you company."

"A wise youth," She says, and her smile broadens.

I feel that she is teasing me.

I eat my stew in silence. Once my bowl is empty, I set it next to the stone washing basin. "I will get water for you."

"Not now, Siira, let's pray for Boku."

Inwardly, I cringe. I don't want to petition the Mighty One for anything, he never answers anyway.

Just then my father enters the tent.

"How is he?" I ask.

"Fine, fine." My father's voice is quiet and slow.

"Let me get you some stew." I reach for his large bowl and fill it with the warm food.

"Thank you, my child." He raises the bowl to his lips and slurps some down.

Grandmother then asks about Boku's injuries.

"He has lost his strong hand and good eye, but he will live. Tamuq is a wonder."

"I am glad." She closes her eyes, probably sending a silent praise to the Mighty One. When she opens her eyes, the smile across her face smoothes some of her wrinkles, making her seem younger.

"How was your training today, Siira?" asks father.

My training? Was it really only this morning?

I don't wish to answer. I've never given him a bad report before. Usually I can tell him that I bested Balek at a foot race, or that I caught more game than he had, but that is not what happened today. Today was a calamity.

"That well?" Father lowers his bowl, giving me his undivided attention.

"Father, I just . . . I couldn't . . . Father, Balek is so much stronger than I am. And I know that I will never be stronger than he is, or any of the men really. I can't do it, I can't be a man." Once I begin, the words rush out, like the water in the river when the snow melts.

"Siira, listen to me. The Mighty One never gives us a job without giving us the ability to do it. One day you will be a man, you will lead the people, and so I believe that the Mighty One has given you what you need to lead. You are courageous as a grizzly, as smart as a fleet foot, and as quick as a cat. I think we can figure out a way for you to beat any opponent."

Although I am uncertain, although I still have many fears and doubts, I try to trust him.

"Tomorrow, I must rejoin the hunting party, but maybe before I leave I can show you a place to practice."

The next morning, as soon as the light reaches the meadow, Father is leading me to a place of seclusion, surrounded by boulders and tall green trees.

"I call it the arena. I would come here as a boy, playing games alone, pretending that I was a great hunter, fighting imaginary beasts and enemies." He starts to point out trees and rocks. "There I learned how to leap as softly as a cat as I fought a giant grizzly claw." He points to a boulder.

I watch as he climbs it so much more slowly than I would. He stands at the top and deftly leaps to another boulder. He then turns his back to me and jumps off of the rock, doing a full twist in the air before landing, not so gracefully, on his backside. It does not look very cat-like to me and I laugh.

"Well, I am a bit older now, but I think you get the idea."

Yes, I do. I can train here getting faster and more agile, learning tricks that no man has ever attempted, but how will that help me fight?

He must see my confusion. "They can't fight you if they can't catch you."

"I suppose."

"Good. When I return, I expect a confident fighter, not a defeated one."

"I will do my best."

"That will be enough." He wraps me in his arms, holding me for a long moment, before pulling me back and studying me. I grow uncomfortable under his appraisal. "Sorry, my daughter, there are times that except for your cat eyes, which mirror mine, you look exactly like your mother.

A rush of pleasure runs through me at his words. I hug him to me fiercely and then back up containing my emotions. I recite our farewell. He smiles and then leaves me alone in my new training arena.

"I wonder how Balek will like it." I muse aloud.

3 THE GREAT LIGHT CELEBRATION

The new moon comes and with it the Great Light
Celebration, the longest day of the year, the day where there
is no night. The men have returned from a successful hunt
several days before and the preparation of the two
mammoth kills have consumed all of the people's time. Now
we are eager to celebrate and have a break from work. But
for me it is only semi-sweet, for soon Balek will begin his
testing.

Balek had indeed liked the arena. I took him there a
couple of days after Father left to rejoin the hunters. I
showed him what Father had shown me, the twisting flip off
of the boulder. Of course, I had practiced it alone before I
showed him so that I would be able to impress him and not
humiliate myself again. I was not disappointed, for he
looked awestruck.

"Can you do two flips before you land?"

"I don't know; maybe if I jump higher."

And that is how it began. I would accomplish one trick
and he would come up with a new challenge. Within seven
days' time I was able to spring from rock to rock, flipping,
twisting, and landing almost as though I were a bushy tail.
These small creatures scurry up trees and rocks without

effort, bounding and jumping gracefully.

One afternoon, Balek said, "I could launch you into the air."

"How?"

He locked his strong hands together. "Run at me. Put your foot here, then I will throw you."

I was uncertain, but curiosity burned inside me. I wanted to know if I could do it.

He knelt down, twining his fingers together, grinning expectantly. I ran at him, full speed. I knew that he would have no problem throwing me into the air, so I charged. I stepped into his hands, and simultaneously he stood, pushing me into the air. I shot high above him. I leaned my head back and spotted the ground, bringing my legs around to land, but the momentum was more than I anticipated and I fell on my backside.

"You alright?" He crossed to me. His brows knit in concern, offering me a hand up.

"Let's do it again." I grasped his hand and sprang to my feet.

By the end of the day, we were running at each other. I would step onto his knee, up to his chest, and, using his forward movement, launch myself into the air. The feeling took my breath away. I could fly.

I understood what Father meant. If I could out maneuver an opponent, I wouldn't need to out muscle him.

Today, though, is no time for pushing myself to physical limits, although I would prefer to be at the arena.

We are all gathered at Sacred Point for the sacrifice that begins the celebration. It is midday. My father, the chief, stands at the edge of the precipice facing the people. I don't look at him but at what is behind him. As far as my eye can see, the Great Salt Water moves, alive with life. White flyers circle above it, floating, almost dancing in a ceremony unknown to us, above the turbulent silver-blue water. In the distance a great fish surfaces and spews water from a spout high into the air, as if to shoot at the flyers. I watch until my father's deep voice intrudes.

"Today, we celebrate the Great Light that gives warmth and life to all that we hold dear. To the mammoth, to the fleet foot, to the many herbs and flowers, that all give us sustenance. To the melting of the snow that gives us clean water. To the ability to venture forth from our cave and breathe free. We thank You, Mighty One, for the light.

"During the time of snow, when we lose the light and have only our story fire, we learn what it is to dwell in darkness and therefore we become more grateful for the light."

I try to pay close attention, to engrain every word into my memory, for if I am ever called upon to be Chief this duty, the sacrifice, will be mine, but worry constantly distracts me.

He steps forward and reaches his strong hand out to Tamuq, who leads a young curly horn ram, our sacrifice. The animal is oblivious to its fate. Only this morning, I am certain that it was grazing freely on meadow grass, content with its herd, until Tamuq and his son entrapped it. Now, its fate is beyond its control. It is being sacrificed for our purposes and not its own.

Tamuq lifts the young curly horn ram onto the sacrificial stone, a large brown stone with a flat, declined surface. At the edge of the lower end a small groove has been worked into it, to allow the blood to drain into a basin. The blood will be buried in the forest, as is our tradition, and the animal roasted for consumption.

My father lifts his stone blade high. The black blade has been polished and sharpened to a bright sheen. It only takes one swift, clean motion, a flick of my father's wrist, and the ram's life leaves it, trickling down the stone and into the basin.

"Mighty One, we thank you."

A shiver runs the length of my body, beginning at the

base of my neck, traveling down my arms and legs and out my feet and hands. Next year will be my testing, and, if I pass, one day I may well be slitting the throat of an innocent curly horn.

Each one that is sent out on his testing must return with a token kill. The bigger the beast the greater the man, or so it is thought.

"Tonight," my father continues, "we will celebrate life and tomorrow we will send our young men off to their testing. Balek, son of Boku; Sinaq, son of Naqu; and Kumal, son of Malu, may the Mighty One guide you in your testing."

My eyes find Balek. He is standing in line with the others, his expression aloof and distant, as though he does not care that his life may soon be lost. In the morning, Boku will take him deep into the forest and return alone. Balek will have to live by his wits, hunting, trapping, sleeping under the clouded sky. I know that he can easily do this, but that is not the end of the testing, for he must kill a token. It can be anything really, but no one wants a jumper as their token, so the larger animals are always sought for. Anything from the giant long tooth that gnaws on trees to the fearsome grizzly claw.

I know that Balek will choose something more dangerous though as proof of his courage, his worth. I just hope that he stays away from a blade-toothed cat.

After the ceremony, the people move to the preparation camp, below the cave. We eat and dance, enjoying the long day. Eventually I sneak off to the cave and my bed. I awake to silence and know that the celebration has given way to weariness. Silently, I leave my bed and look for Balek to wish him luck.

He is keeping vigil at the story fire. He sits on his feet. His black hair, shining in the light of the flames, the reflection like the great snow lights that play across the sky, is loose, brushing his square jaw. His round eyes are closed in what I can only assume is prayer for the trials ahead. He looks strong and courageous, already a man.

I creep up next to him and whisper his name. He does not start but merely opens his eyes. As he comes out of his trancelike prayer, a smile blossoms, beginning at his mouth and moving into his eyes and eventually his whole being seems to be smiling. I signal for him to follow me away from the fire. He quietly follows. His step is almost as light as mine, but not quite, probably due to his size.

The meadow is full of early morning light and shadow. I stop at a stand of young trees, turning to face him.

"I wanted to wish you well," I say.

"I am glad; I wanted to see you before I left." In the early light, I see an unfamiliar gleam in his eye, a gleam similar to the one I have seen in Pol's eyes when he looks at Bela.

Don't encourage it, I tell myself. Just give him the traditional farewell, and so I begin. "Be careful, Balek. Good hunt, may the Mighty One bless you with safety, so that you will return . . . " I pause, because the next words, to me, do not seem appropriate, so I leave off the rest of the saying. "You don't have to show off, just come back."

"Siira." His voice falters as he appears to struggle with the next words. "I want you to know how important you are to me."

"You are important to me too, Balek." I don't want to hurt him, and yet I don't want to stir up any feelings, especially not now.

"Once my testing is complete, I want to ask you a very special question. Will you promise to listen to me, to hear me out?"

A rock seems to sink in the pit of my stomach. I am certain that I know of what he is speaking, but I don't want to hear him say it. After Siiraq died, Balek was there, and in my mind and heart, I believe that he replaced my brother. He knows my weaknesses and accepts me, not expecting more than just me. But I feel that he wants something more, and I am not sure I can give it to him.

"Please, Siira, promise me. I don't think that I could face the challenges without that hope."

As he says this, his eyes light with a fire, an intensity that I have never seen in them before: desire mingled with hope. Hope, can I give him a false hope, a hope that I am not sure will be fulfilled. Can I not give him the hope? Sometimes, in desperate situations, hope in something can mean the difference between life and death.

"Yes, I will hear you." I try to smile, try to feel lighthearted, "but you must return." I playfully punch his solid stomach.

He clasps my hands in his. "Good."

I force myself to look into his eyes and smile as brightly as I can.

He lets go, seeming ready, almost eager to begin his journey now that he has my promise. I stand alone by the trees. Most of the people will gather to send him and the others off, but I can't watch, so I disappear into the woods and beyond to the meadow. I make my way to the tree and climb high into its safety. I feel that I am soon to lose a friend, one of my only friends. I don't want things to change between us, but that is what life does. It changes. Even if Balek returns with his token, he will be a man, and I fear that he wants me to be his woman. And what is worse, I feel that the chief and the elders will agree with him.

Don't borrow trouble, Siira, perhaps you are just imagining things. Balek is your friend and he always will be.

4 TAKING A STAND

The days pass, the night-less, sleepless days. I spend most of them in the arena or with Bela. She has collected needles from a spike cat to decorate a pouch for Balek. These small cats eat plants but you don't want to disturb them unprepared because their needles once inside your flesh are not pleasant to remove.

The needles are hollow though and, once dyed and cut into small pieces, the women use them to decorate their handy work. Bela makes a pouch for Balek. I help her gather berries to make the dye for the beads to soak in, turning them bright blue and red. The work is easy, mindless, relaxing. With both of us working the pouch should be ready for his return.

As I work, I remember a day shortly after I showed Balek the arena. He had been so excited about my new tricks that he decided he wanted to try one.

"Show me that flip again."

I climbed up to the rock and easily threw myself backward and landed almost without a sound on my feet.

"Now, you watch me."

I did. He climbed up to the top of the rock and positioned himself as close to the edge as he could manage.

30

My father used to do these things so perhaps Balek could as well, but then again Balek is a quarter span taller than my father and his shoulders are broader than most of the men's.

He jumped high into the air and managed to throw his legs up over his head, but the motion was not fast enough and he landed on his knees.

I heard a pained groan escape.

"Did you break anything?" I rushed to his side.

"No, just my pride." He stood, dusting off his leggings.

"It was only your first attempt."

"Yeah, but I don't know if I want to try a second." An easy smile spread broad across his face.

"Are you scared?" I teased him.

"No, I am smart."

I laughed and raced up the rock to do another flip.

Balek is smart, I remind myself as I place another bead in the pattern, fastening it with a thin cord. Then another memory, a more recent memory assaults me. Balek standing before me hope blazing in his eyes. I don't want to join with Balek. I don't want to join with any man. But that is not my choice.

I reach for another bead, but my action is clumsy and I tip the bowl, sending it end over end into the dirt. I curse under my breath.

Bela looks to me as I kneel to gather them.

"Having trouble focusing?"

"Maybe." I gather the tiny dyed pieces into my hand.

"I know how you feel, when Pol went for his testing, I don't think that I ate the entire time he was gone."

I settle back on my feet and gaze at her incredulous. "Do you think I am pining for Balek?"

"Aren't you?" She settles her work in her lap and stares back at me, almost challenging me.

I think over my feelings as I pick through the dirt, gathering the beads. I had only felt uncomfortable at Balek's insinuations. I love him yes, but not as anything more than a brother.

Before I can answer her, I am bowled over by a big fur ball. As I lay on the ground, the wolf begins to lick my face, covering me in slobber.

"Qitaq, come boy." As I hear his accent, my pulse races. The wolf instantly leaves me, obeying his master. "Sorry, Siira, he got away." Maruq grins, a lop-sided grin, tapping his hand on his leg.

I sit up, wiping some of the residue from my face. Maruq is about five spans from me. He ruffs the errant wolf's neck and then loops a cord around it.

Relief and regret compete inside me.

No I don't want to join with Balek.

As I return to gathering the beads, I hear Bela mumble something.

"What was that?" I look up at her.

"Nothing," a playful gleam in her eyes that makes me think that she has definitely said something. "How long does it take to gather up those beads?"

I shrug.

On the final day of the testing, Bela and I sit on stumps by a tree in the preparation camp. I stitch the final beads into the intricate flower pattern, thinking of the carving that Balek had been working on. Soon Balek will return a man and I will no longer be able to spend hours with him training, working on fighting or hunting.

"Who will work with me now?" I think aloud.

"What?" Bela asks.

"Nothing." Then I change my mind, deciding to let Bela in. "Once Balek returns he will be a man, who will I train with?"

"Tiras." The mischievous gleam in her eyes tells me that she is not serious. At the thought of the young sapling of a boy I laugh; he knows less than I do.

"Well, I wouldn't have a problem wrestling him to the ground."

A commotion among the people draws our attention. Cheers and whoops echo through the valley. Is it Balek?

No, Sinaq has returned, a young long tooth resting across his shoulders. These animals fully grown can stand as tall as a man and can topple trees with their large front teeth. The one that he carries is about half as big as me. A good token.

We return to our work, agitated and expectant for the next man to return.

About midday, another shout of triumph interrupts our work. Kumal arrives, a ram around his shoulders.

Shortly after Bela and I have finished the pouch, we eat our evening meal as we wait for our last man to return. A hand rests on my shoulder. I turn to see my father's cuff, shiny yellow metal encircling his wrist. This treasure has been passed down from Chief to Chief since the time of the forgotten valley. Three strange four-legged creatures race across the front of it. I never can decide why they are running, but they look magnificent. Lean legs, heads raised high, hair flowing behind them. One day I may wear it.

"I am sure that he is fine." Father's voice is soft and comforting, almost as if he coos to a babe.

I try to rest in the knowledge of Balek, his skills, his determination, but I can't shake a feeling of foreboding.

I decide to go to the arena, to exert some energy, but on the way I am distracted by a strange shape laying in the grass, a large lump of fur. I cautiously draw close. The fur looks like a grizzly claw but it is not moving. Then I notice the hand, a man's hand.

Balek. I rush to him.

"Balek! Balek!" I cry out, frantically. I lift part of the heavy skin. His body is covered in wounds, his tunic is shredded. Blood mingled with mud is caked on him. A large ragged gash runs across his cheek, from his ear to his jaw.

Panic rises. I look from his face to his chest and watch it rise and fall in a steady, if shallow, rhythm. He is alive, but barely.

"Balek, open your eyes!" My words sound strangled. Balek is dying.

At the sound of my voice, he attempts to move, to open his eyes, to move his mouth.

"No, don't." I find his water pouch and trickle some down into him. Panic rises in me. "You stay here, I will get the men." I run like a blade-toothed cat, bounding and jumping over all my obstacles, trying to cover the distance back to the cave as quickly as possible. Once within hearing distance, I begin to shout.

"Help! Help, Balek! I have found him! He is hurt." My words coming in short bursts, punctuated with ragged breaths. Boku is the first man I come to. His injuries have healed, but he is left with only one eye and one hand. I grab his hand and tell him to get the others, that we must help Balek. But he does not speak. His one eye darts from me to the distance; he seems conflicted.

"My son must complete the testing by coming to the preparation camp," he rasps out, his gaze resting on the ground.

"He has fought a grizzly. He has lost much blood. He is dying." I am desperate to impress upon him his son's need.

"Then he will die well." Boku seems resigned to his son's fate, his expression becoming hard.

"We can save him, help him."

He shakes his head.

I have no time for this foolishness, Balek is dying. I sprint off to find someone else.

My father has heard me. He is there, worry etched in his features.

"It's Balek."

"Good." He seems to relax at my words. "Soon all our boys will be men."

"He needs help, Father." His tawny eyes look at me in confusion. "He has fought a grizzly for a token, and it has nearly killed him. How he managed to skin it, and bring the skin, is beyond the skill of any man I have seen." I explain, "He is near the arena. Surely he is a man."

My father closes his eyes, as though asking the Mighty One for an answer. What is wrong with them? Balek is dying. Why don't they rush to his aid? Why all this balking?

"Father, I know where he is; come on, follow me."

"No, Siira, Balek cannot pass his testing with any help from another man."

"According to what law? Tradition? He has survived the appointed time. He had taken a token. He is home. He is a man."

"It is the way it is. No man can help." My father drops his hands to his side as if they hold a weight too heavy for him.

"Then it is good that I am no man." Rage rises inside me. How can they do this to Balek? Is being a man so important?

I run into Bela on my way back to Balek.

"What is it?"

"Balek is injured and the men won't help him."

"So what are you doing?" Her eyes are bright with the question.

"He needs help and I intend on giving it to him."

Bela stares at me as if I am a strange creature.

"What is wrong with everyone? Is tradition that important? More important than a life?"

"I will help too." She reaches for my hand.

"We don't have much time. The Great Light has almost finished its journey."

We gather some dressings and herbs then begin back to Balek. I must help him finish his testing, help him become a man. He must make it to the preparation camp in time.

Bela calls to all the women that we pass. Most of them follow us and soon we are all gathered around Balek. He is unconscious, unaware of what the women are doing for him.

"I will bind the wounds," Bela says.

"We will make a sled." I signal the women to follow me; all but one does. A young girl, Malukim, stays with Bela.

Once his wounds are dressed and cleaned, we begin to pull him and the grizzly skin back to the village.

I take the lead proudly, proud to be one of the women, even if only for the day.

As we pull Balek into the preparation camp below the mouth of the cave, the men at first refuse to look at us, until my father joins me in pulling the sled.

Slowly, one by one, the men take over for the women. Lifting him off the sled and high onto their shoulders, they carry him up the stairs to the healing tent.

Since there is nothing more I can do for Balek, I leave to help the women with the grizzly skin.

On my way to the preparation camp, I see Maruq by the mouth of our cave. He stands surrounded by his wolves. His father is speaking to him, but he appears to only half listen, as he looks out across the camp. His eyes follow my progress toward the stairs and I grow warm under his perusal. I stop at the top of them and look across at him. He nods at me and smiles.

Would he have helped me with Balek? I don't know.

I find a group of women in the preparation camp working on scraping the fat from the hide. I sit next to young Malukim. Next to me, she is as fragile looking as a feathered flyer.

I hold a large scraping stone in my strong hand and the grizzly's neck in the other. I push down in short, quick strokes, taking care not to tear the hide, and watch the fat separate from the skin.

"Why did you do it?" The small, sweet voice asks.

"What?" I look at Malukim. Her black braids frame large round eyes. In them, I see everything I want to be, but cannot. Meekness, compassion, even quietness.

"Why did you do what the men would not?"

"Why did you go?" I counter her question.

"I thought to myself, what if it was Kumal?" Her answer is barely a whisper. Kumal, one of the others tested today, is her brother. "What if he was so close to home and dying, but I do not know if I would have stood against the men."

"I am sure that your love for your brother would have given you the courage."

"So then you love Balek?"

I did not answer at first, but then, "Yes, as you do Kumal."

She smiles, and I think I see a glimmer of pleasure, of hope at my answer in her dark eyes.

I listen as the women talk.

"What shall we make the great hunter from his prize?"

"Some boots?" another offers.

"With a kill like this we could make all of the people boots," says another.

"How about a great cape?" Malukim quietly suggests.

The women all nod in agreement.

"A cape then."

I can't help but think that all of their planning may be for nothing if Balek doesn't survive.

Eventually, we have scraped the entire hide and stake it out for curing.

As I make my way to the story fire to wait for word of Balek, Boku emerges from the healing tent and approaches me. "Thank you, Siira, for doing what I could not."

Before I can answer, he turns and leaves. I sit amazed. This man, so bound by tradition that he almost let his son die, has humbled himself to a woman. Well, not really a woman, to his future chief.

5 A QUESTION

The time of snow is upon us by the time Balek's injuries have healed. Although his body is covered in scars, the only visible one is the one on his face. Instead of diminishing his beauty, it seems to add to it, giving evidence of his character.

The men quickly accepted this brave hunter, marveling in his feat. None of the people had seen a grizzly skin equal to the one he had brought home. It seemed that Balek had fought the great grizzly, father of them all. The cape that the women made from the skin added to his stature among the people. Malukim had devised a way to make the grizzly's massive head into a hood. Whenever Balek wore it, all eyes watched the great grizzly claw.

Today, I stand guard at the mouth of the cave, I am alone. The duty requires only enough skill to sound an alarm with the horn that I hold in my hand. I watch as a light snow floats down from the sky. In the torchlight, the flakes turn a bright yellow. I hear a soft tread from behind me. Turning, I see the great grizzly claw approaching.

"Why did you choose a grizzly, why not something easier, a fleet foot or something?" I ask over my shoulder as he comes to stand next to me.

I turn to face him. He is so tall that I have to lift my chin, putting my neck in a painful position, to look into his face. I do not remember him being so much bigger than me. He turns his face to mine. The ragged scar that runs the length of his cheek has healed well, and given time will fade a little; but it will always be a reminder of his near death. I look into his dark eyes, black as night, except for the light from the torch. I watch the flame flicker in his eyes.

I wonder if Siiraq, my long dead older brother, would have been such a man. Balek is brave and strong, the best of the men, but he is also a wonderful friend: kind and fun, full of confidence in me.

"I had to have a token worthy of you." His voice is throaty and full of emotion.

"Worthy of me?" I do not understand, or rather I do not want to understand.

"You are the chief's daughter, any man would be privileged to claim you, but you are more than just his daughter, you are his successor."

Understanding blazes in my mind; Balek had killed the grizzly in order to gain favor, approval. I feel a gamut of emotions run hot in my veins. He had nearly died, and why, because he felt he needed to show off, to claim a prize, me. I am confused, overwhelmed, and outraged.

"Balek, you almost died!" I yell, losing my temper, and shove the horn into his stomach, causing him to exhale all of his air.

"But I didn't."

"Because I found you."

"Yes, and I praise the Mighty One for you." A fire from within him now blazes in his eyes.

I do not know what to feel. My feelings would be the same whether he had brought back a jumper or a fleet foot. He is like my brother. As I realize the depth of his feelings, sorrow courses through me. I do not feel the same for him.

He reaches out a tentative hand, daring to run it along my cheek.

"Please, Siira, you must know how I feel. You are my other half."

I want to be anywhere but here. I want to run, to climb high in the tree, to be in the arena, practicing my twists and turns. I look outside; the snowfall has become almost a blizzard. The light reflecting from it makes me wish for the warmth of the hunts.

He puts a finger under my chin, turning my face to him.

I can't, I can't love him the way he wants. Yet he has risked so much in hopes of making me his. Would it be so bad? To be bound to my best friend for life?

I study his face. Even with the bright scar, he is handsome. His strong jaw, his high cheekbones, his dark eyes, all work to make him the most desirable of the people. I have heard others praise him. But right now his eyes are afire with an almost tangible hope. Hope that I will deem him worthy. Worthy to be my man.

Regardless of my feelings, my desires, which I am learning count for nothing, I don't want to disappoint him, but I can't say yes.

"My man will be decided by the chief, Balek, not by me. He is the one that must choose, for my man must be willing to give up his future, in order to ensure my father's line."

"I am willing."

I know what it means to give up my life for another's will. I would not wish it on an enemy, let alone my friend.

"I would go to your father. All I need is your approval."

My approval? My heart sinks, although I love him with all my being, it is not the kind of love he wants.

6 AN ACCUSATION

Voices at the story fire draw my attention away from Balek. I welcome the distraction, eager for a reason not to answer him, to move on from our current subject.

"What is that?" I walk toward the sound.

"Sounds like father," Balek says, a sharp edge to his deep voice. "Go. Find out, I will keep watch."

He takes my place at the entrance, leaning his strong shoulder against the cave wall and training his eyes to the snow. I place my hand on his shoulder, grateful for his understanding, and sprint off to the story fire.

I come closer, moving to take my place next to my father's great chair.

"There is not enough!" Boku bellows the story fire ablaze behind him.

"What would you have us do, Boku, go out into the snow and hunt? The mammoth have all left moons ago." My father's deep voice is as patient as water wearing away a stone.

The hunts, though successful ones, had only given us five mammoth. But an unexpected raid by cats had cost us an entire mammoth.

I remember that day. It was near the end of the hunts,

most of the men had left the cave. Most of them followed my father hoping to find a herd of fleet feet, a stray long tooth, anything to supplement our supplies. Others went to the Great Salt Water to fish. The women were left to work in the preparation camp, drying berries and smoking the previous kill.

I was left to watch at the lookout rock with young Tiras, a boy of thirteen annuals, who was constantly skipping rocks across the boulder. It was about midday when I saw them, a group of five female cats. They came up over the hill calling to each other. I could tell by looking that they were hungry, hungry enough to fight our women for the meat. I lifted my horn and sent out the alarm.

I did not know if the men would hear it. But I had at least warned the women. As soon as the alarm went out, I saw the women stop their work and look up. I waved at them, trying to signal them to go to the cave. I saw Natiq standing tall by one of the smoke fires. She raised a hand to her eyes and looked. She must have seen the cats for soon she was herding the women up the stairs to the cave. I continued to blow the horn but no help came.

All I could do was stand on the high rock and watch.

Now, I listen as Boku rants and worries our people about something we cannot change.

Grandmother's unhurried voice answers the frantic cries of Boku. "We will survive, Boku. It will just be a leaner time, we have done it before." She sits at her usual place, surrounded by children. As the Keeper of the Stories, she is also a revered member of the elder council, greatly beloved by the people.

Boku, though, is not satisfied, and paces, before speaking again, directly addressing my father, who sits in a great chair. As much as I love his two children, I have never cared much for their father.

"My chief," he continues in a calmer voice, leaning on his staff, "I have information that leads me to believe that the attack from the cats could have been prevented, or at least stopped. For some of the men were scouting nearby when the alarm was given, and failed to come to aid."

"That's not possible," My father's words echo my thoughts. I look at Boku. His missing eye is covered with a skin patch. His stump arm is outstretched in emphasis. His injuries have healed well, but there must have been damage to his mind. No hunter would ignore an alarm.

"My chief," he drops his arm and points at the people with his staff, "Why should we all suffer for the callousness of a few?"

"What are you suggesting?"

"I am suggesting that there are those among us that must be punished, as our trust has been broken."

At his accusation, the people become silent, silent at the thought that one of us could be so selfish.

"Go on." My father settles back in his chair, pushing into the dark furs that line it. He places his elbows on the arm rests and weaves his fingers together, resting his head on them, as though the weight of it is too much. I have often heard him bemoan his duty of presiding over the people in judgment. His face becomes a mask, as full of emotion as one of the boulders in the arena.

"On that day, the day of the cat raid, most of the men were hunting a great distance from here, beyond Sacred Point, too far away to hear the horn that had been sounded. Others of us, myself and my son included, were by the Great Salt Water catching fish. But I have just discovered that two of us were on our very mountain."

"Who?" My father's tawny eyes narrow into slits. And he leans forward.

"Tamuq and Maruq."

No, surely Boku has heard wrong. These two men may be strange, but they are not heartless.

I hear murmurs travel around the story fire.

"Where are the accused?" The chief calls out.

43

I see people begin to part, making a path for the accused. Tamuq comes forward, his head held high. His wolf is at his heels. Maruq follows with his wolf, and her pups. He appears unconcerned with the accusation.

Once they are in the center of the gathering, Maruq's attention is fixed on the wolves that surround him. He kneels down trying to settle the young ones that are yipping and playing among themselves. I try to discern the one that toppled me over, but I cannot.

Once he settles all of them into sitting positions, he stands next to his father. His stance is relaxed. He seems unconcerned with all that is going on around him. His wolf nuzzles his hand then sits next to him. Maruq runs his long fingers through her soft fur carelessly.

"Is this true, Tamuq, were you on the mountain?" My father asks, drawing my attention back to the matter at hand and away from Maruq.

Boku moves a span away from Tamuq, staring at him, daring him to deny the accusation. Boku appears dark and broken next to Tamuq. Tamuq is long and lean, fine and chiseled, as though he had been made directly by the Mighty One and then set on earth.

He and his son are part of the people, and yet they are still apart from us. They choose to hunt as a team with their wolves, instead of with the other men, using their strange weapons, instead of our throwing sticks. Truthfully I wish that we would use some of their methods. Their wolves are truly useful and their bows launch darts much farther and faster than a throwing stick.

"Yes, we were on the mountain." Here Tamuq's melodic voice pauses as he looks at his accuser. "For the morning, but we moved down to the mammoth corridor later that day."

"The corridor is still near enough to have heard the alarm." Boku thrusts his staff into Tamuq's chest. Tamuq's wolf snarls at Boku, ready to pounce. With a flick of his wrist, Tamuq quiets the beast.

"We heard no alarm."

"No? Surely, the sound would have traveled to the corridor."

"It may have, but my son and I were inside the corridor."

"Inside?" Boku's mouth gapes.

I stare at Tamuq. No man has gone into the corridor, at least not to my knowledge.

"Yes, we heard a young mammoth cry in pain and so ventured to find it, to help if we could."

"To help a mammoth?"

"Yes, we help all who need it." As if to remind him of his own need for help not too long ago, Tamuq's blue eyes hold Boku's dark ones. "We ran the length of the corridor and found a calf with its mother near the other side. The mother was desperate to get her babe out of the predicament that it found itself in. Its foot had somehow gotten stuck in a hole in the corridor. Maruq and I worked the rest of the night to free the animal. We returned the following day."

I thought back, trying to remember the next day, trying to remember if I had seen Maruq or his wolves. I had been helping clean the preparation camp, reordering the tattered mess left by the raiders. I remember that as I took bones to one of the woman, I saw Maruq's lean form emerge from the trees in the direction of the corridor. I watched as he moved as gracefully as a fleet foot across the meadow. He was whistling to one of his pups that appeared to be chasing a flutterby.

"There now, you see, Boku, your fears and accusations are groundless. They could not have heard the alarm where they were."

"But we only have their word that they were helping some calf." He spits out his distrust, like the venom of a serpent.

"Yes, and we will trust that." My father fixes a stern,

immovable look on Boku. His eyes as hard as the tawny cuff on his arm. I know that look, I have seen it often, and that look means discussion is over.

"If food is a concern Boku, my son and I can set traps in the snow, once the storm has passed." Tamuq says.

I look at Maruq. Would he truly follow his father into the dangers of the snow? I did not see him flinch in the slightest at the suggestion. His tall lean form, slightly taller than his father, remains relaxed. His long, skillful fingers lazily stroke his wolf's fur. His peace is not disturbed. I wonder if anything can disturb it.

When I had first seen Maruq, two annuals ago, I thought that he looked as if he had come straight from the Mighty One's hand. And now that he is a man, a fine hunter, he is even more beautiful. His features matured and finely chiseled, not like the other hunters whose flat features appear to testify of time spent on their stomachs waiting for prey. The firelight highlights his honey-colored hair that he keeps shorter than the other men do, so that its thick waves stay out of his eyes with no need of a cord.

As I study him, he looks up from his wolf. His peaceful blue eyes lock with mine as though some unheard voice has told him that I am watching him. He flashes an endearing grin at me and my heart begins to pound. I try not to look away first, but I am unaccustomed to having someone study me so unabashedly.

At the sound of my father's voice, I turn my head, trying to appear as though I do not care he is watching me. "As Chief, I appreciate your offer, but, I am sure that the Mighty One will provide. I consider this matter closed."

My father stands dismissing the people. He watches as most of them disperse. I stay by his side watching with him. Perusing over the tops of heads, I look to see if Maruq has finished studying me. He has. He turns to follow his father, but as he calls the pups to him, I notice that he looks at me again, a smile playing at the corners of his mouth.

The story fire is quiet once again. Only Grandmother and the very young stay. She shakes her head and begins to tell another story to the children.

Father turns to leave and I catch his hand.

"Father, I don't understand. Why would Boku do that, in front of all of the people, to someone that saved his life?"

He looks from my hand up into my eyes. "Siira, if you become Chief and need to sit in this chair, you will learn that men are first selfish and proud. Boku, though a good man, is both."

"But Tamuq is kind."

"Boku is afraid, Siira."

I think of Boku's tone of voice and facial expression. The hard accusing looks he had given Tamuq. He did not look afraid. "Why would Boku fear him?"

"It is not Tamuq that frightens Boku, but change."

Change? Tamuq and Maruq have been here for two annuals. There has been plenty of time to adjust to them. A thought leaps into my mind.

"But if I become Chief, our ways will change."

"Will they?"

"Yes, a woman as Chief."

"No, Siira, not a woman, you will be a man. Remember that. The only reason that the elders have allowed my wishes is that you will be a man."

"Yes, Father, but is being a woman so bad?"

"No, women are the softer part of us. They keep us from becoming savage, but your path is not to be like them. You are not like them."

I want to argue, to stop this foolish talk. I am like them. I will never be a man, not completely. I will always be a woman. I can't wipe away my hopes, my dreams, my emotions. I can't stop feeling.

My father seems to read my thoughts. "I am not asking you to become stone, Siira. A man feels, but he chooses not to show it."

7 THE WATCH

The snows are heavier than I have ever known them to be. The preparation camp below our cave is completely buried by the end of the first moon. On my watches, I look out onto the vast whiteness that reaches out to the Great Salt Water. During the short times of light, the glare is almost blinding.

As our stores deplete, the chief has allowed Tamuq to take a few of the men on several trips to set traps for jumpers and other small animals to supplement our stew pots. Tamuq and Maruq teach the men how to use the wolves. Using them to pull sleds loaded with supplies, the wolves make the trips out of the cave less dangerous. The wolves can fight off wandering animals or give needed speed to outrun a storm. The snowstorms give little warning, turning from light flakes to large blizzards in a moment. If a man is caught outside the cave in a blizzard, his death is almost certain.

Today, I sit with Bela working on a gift for her father. I listen to her prattle on about Pol and what her life with him will be like once they are joined. The tent they will share, the children they will have, the things she will make for him. I politely listen although I am not interested in her hopes, because I do not want to encourage any of my own.

I feel eyes on me and look up. Scanning the immediate area, I see Maruq. He is watching me. He lags behind his father and the wolves as they walk in the direction of the mouth of the cave. I guess that they are going out on a hunt or to set traps. Our eyes meet and my insides churn. A smile pulls at the corners of my mouth, as I hold his gaze. A wolf howls for him and he looks away, hurrying to catch up.

"Did you hear me?" Bela's voice brings me back to my task.

"What?" I look back at my work.

"What are you so interested in?" Bela asks as she scans the area around us.

I feel flames rise in my cheeks, "Nothing."

"Really? Your cheeks tell a different story. Did you see something? Someone?" She draws out the last word, with a playful gleam in her eyes.

"Bela, it is nothing."

"Come on, I tell you everything."

"Yes, but you are a girl," I say, trying to stop her probing. I don't want to delve into matters of the heart.

"Alright, be that way." Bela places another bead on her needle, focusing on her work.

We continue to work, but I make little progress. I do not realize that I have been watching for him until I see him pass again. Maruq's stride is long and quick, purposeful. I want him to look at me, but he does not. Except for his wolf at his side and her almost fully grown pups trailing behind, he is alone. I find that odd; he and his father are practically inseparable.

Finding it impossible to work with my mind conjuring images to distract me, I leave going to my family tent. As I approach, I hear voices inside, male voices.

"Maruq, your father is the best tracker and trapper among us. I am grateful for the help you have both provided."

"We have done nothing special." Maruq's voice sounds

like a tranquil melody, like the slow movement of the river at the end of hunts.

"I think so, so do others; you have taught us the use of wolves, how to venture out into the snow. These things the people did not know before. Just think, how would we be able to gather in the time of snow without them?"

My father is right.

I sneak closer, hoping for a glimpse of what is going on inside. A hand opens the tent flap and Maruq's arm and shoulder emerge. He stands half in and half out of the tent as he takes his leave.

"I am to take the night watch," Maruq says. "When my father returns, I will send him to you."

"Thank you, Maruq."

"He should not be much longer. He was just to check some traps by that tree in the meadow." His voice, its sweet accent, is like a song to my ears.

"Good, I shall await him in my tent."

I know that I will soon be found out so I step out from the shadows as if I had just gotten there. My father's tawny eyes appraise me in a strange way, as though he is seeing me anew.

"Siira, I want you to take the watch at midnight, relieving Maruq."

Excited fire runs through me at the prospect, time alone with Maruq. Then, just as suddenly as the feeling rose, I suppress it. I cannot afford to think that way. My match is not in my hands, and I am certain I am meant for Balek. I look at my father, deciding to protest, but he has a strange look in his eyes, and so instead I say, "Yes, Father."

I enter the tent, going into the room I share with Grandmother, intending to take a nap before I have to assume my duty. But I hear a few more hushed words. My ears try to distinguish between my father's voice and Maruq's. But all I hear is the yapping of Maruq's wolves. Eventually, I hear him and the wolves leave, slowly turning, and then running off until I can no longer make out steps.

I awaken, and by the lack of sounds in the cave I believe it to be near time for me to relieve Maruq. Grandmother has left two pots of stew near my gear. I assume one is for me and the other for Maruq. I quickly gulp mine down. Then I place a flat wooden lid on the pot for Maruq, I tie a carrying cord around it. Gathering my gear, I try to silence the excited flutterbys in my stomach. I light a torch, and leave for the mouth of the cave.

Maruq stands alert at the cave's entrance, his back to me. Yet even here actively watching and guarding, his stance is relaxed. He seems to have no cares other than the present. I long for that ability, to have no thought of the future or past, only the present. His wolves lay sleeping at his feet. He focuses on the blizzard of snow outside, apparently unaware of my approach. His torch is settled in a hole in the wall. As I draw closer, he turns. Torch light highlights his features, but his bright blue eyes seem clouded, as if our gray skies threaten his soul. His fingers play with the string of his bow that is slung across his shoulder.

"Grandmother has sent you some stew." I hold out the pot to him by the cord. It sways slowly, while he appraises it. His eyes flit back and forth between my face and the proffered stew.

He takes it, keeping it in his hands.

My mind races for something to say, "Aren't you hungry?" I ask pointing at the pot.

He doesn't answer my question; at least not with his voice. He looks at me as though I should know the answer. As if I can read his unspoken signals like his wolves. I try. I force myself to hold his gaze, to study him. His posture is relaxed as he is leaning against the cave wall, but his hand is actively plucking at his bowstring, never stopping, but continually plucking. His jaw is tense, I can see the cords of it ripple as he clenches and releases the muscles. His head is tilted slightly as if he can hear better that way.

Now, I see that he does not want to be here guarding, waiting for his father. It is torture to his soul. He is worried and wants to be out doing something. Not waiting.

I have my answer: no, he is not hungry.

I shift uncomfortably next to him, longing to comfort him but helpless to do so.

"I am to relieve you."

"I know." His fingers rest on the string. He makes no movement to leave becoming as still as a long-eared jumper waiting for danger to pass.

"If you can't eat, at least sit. While this storm is going, your father will have taken shelter somewhere."

His eyes seem to tell me that he wants to believe that his father is safe somewhere with the wolf. I see that he has been telling himself the same thing all night, but he cannot bring himself to fully relax.

"You and he have traveled in the snow before," I say.

He looks at me and nods. And as he does, he smiles, the light returning to his eyes.

"You survived then," I continue, "I am sure he is fine now."

He looks outside quietly observing the whirling white.

I know that he and his father are close, the only survivors of a people now long gone. Perhaps he feels that in him, he can still hold on to his old self, his old people, but without his father, how would he hold onto the past, as fragile as a dried leaf. The thought strikes me as odd because I would never have thought him concerned with the past. He seems so content with what the Mighty One has done, so at peace with his life.

"Let me help you watch, at least while you eat."

"You are right."

Maruq leans his back against the cave wall and scoots down to the floor. He takes up the bowl and unties the cord. Scooping up some stew, with his two first fingers, he eats. I cross my legs and join him on the floor. We talk; actually I do most of the talking, and he listens. Eventually, his wolf awakens and comes to him, laying her head in his lap. He pets her. And I continue to talk.

Around most of the men, I tend to remain quiet, as though I have to remain silent to prove that I am not a prattling girl. There are a few, very few, with whom I can talk and not grow uncomfortable. I am surprised Maruq is one of them.

I tell him of my mother, my brother, my arena. I tell stories from my earliest memories, when my life was merry. I stay away from sad memories as I try to cheer him, keeping his thoughts from the possibility plaguing him outside the cave.

He smiles at me, listening to my every word. Intently focused as though I tell one of Grandmother's amazing stories and not just my life's story.

Near morning he leans his head back against the wall and closes his eyes. When I see that he is breathing steadily in and out, I move away to let him sleep in peace. I find myself constantly studying him, as I do my father, not wanting to ever forget what he looks like.

As he sleeps, the black sky clears of the white snow, but my torch light illuminates little beyond me.

Just as light peaks above the horizon, casting a purple gleam across the snow, Maruq opens his eyes. For a moment our eyes meet, those wonderfully blue eyes focus on me, and he smiles. "Good morning."

A warm feeling rushes through my stomach. I want always to hear those words, to see him smile at me in the morning, every morning.

"The snow has stopped," I say. "Soon, your father and his wolf will return."

Maruq jumps nimbly to his feet. Hope is born in the morning, Grandmother would say if she was here.

I can see it, an expectancy that lights his bright eyes.

"Thank you for staying," he says and helps me to stand.

Heat rushes to my cheeks, and I smile.

"Your father sent me, Siira." I hear Balek's voice boom from behind me like a thunder clap.

I drop Maruq's hand, as though I hold a forbidden object. I turn to Balek and smile at my friend.

"Good, I am tired." I gather up the bowl that Maruq had used and quickly leave the two men at the entrance.

I rush back to my tent like a giddy child. I raise the flap and see my father and Pilaq, one of the elders, sitting around the fire in hushed discussion.

"My chief," I say as I enter.

"Ah, Siira," he says. "I see that Balek relieved you."

Although Balek's appearance had in no way relieved me, I assure my father that the cave is guarded.

He returns his attention to his guest and they continue in hushed tones for a while. I move into my room and drift to sleep, dreaming of bright blue eyes.

8 SEARCHING

My dreams are interrupted when my father shakes my booted foot.

"What is it?" I ask and yawn.

"Siira, I would speak with you."

I bring myself up into a sitting position, stretching and easing some of the soreness in my back. I settle opposite him, drawing my legs up to my chest, wrapping my arms around them, hugging them closely to me.

He sits with his legs crossed in front of him. His body seems relaxed as though he is about to tell me an amusing story, but his eyes are alight with concern and doubt. And that look unsettles me.

"Is something wrong?"

"No, no, I just need to discuss the future with you."

"The future?" I didn't realize I got to discuss my future, I thought that he had that all planned out. I would be a man and join with a worthy hunter, and then produce an heir to follow in our family line, so that we could continue to lead the people.

"Yes, in specific, your man."

Conflicting thoughts rage in my mind like the great blaze of the story fire at the Mid-snow Celebration. On that night, we build the largest possible fire and praise the Mighty One who is about to grow the light again from its smallest to its full glory. My blazing thoughts grow stronger, loud in protest, as I stare into my father's eyes.

"Someone has asked for you." He continues, "He is an honorable hunter and I believe a perfect match for you. I would be pleased if you would agree to it."

Balek. I suppose that I shouldn't be surprised. I had told him that the choice would be my father's, not mine.

My raging emotions burn in anger at Balek, who had done nothing more than what I told him to. I become so infuriated with him, I feel as though the blaze has set fire to my body. I jump up out of my furs and cross to get some water out of our water skin.

"I haven't even gone through my testing yet and you are already giving me away."

"You are of age this coming Hunt Celebration."

"Does that mean that I am going through the ceremony with Bela? I never thought that I would join her in that ceremony." A hope flickers, cooling some of my rage, a hope that I would be acknowledged for what I am, a woman and not a man.

"No, that is not what I mean; you will be tested as a man." And with his cool laughter, my hope dies.

"If I am to be a man, will I not need a woman to join with?" I say derisively. "How can the future Chief take a man? How can I be expected to obey my man when I am Chief?"

Frustration burns in his eyes at my comments.

"Do not be absurd, you will be proclaimed a man, you will be joined to a man, and you will provide a successor for the line." His voice is hard, determined. But as he stares me down, his look slowly softens. "I am sorry, my child. It is hard, but anything worth doing is hard."

"No, Father, I am sorry. I know that you only do what you think is best." I reach a hand out to his arm, giving him a reassuring squeeze.

His voice becomes very tender. "Do you not wish to join with a worthy hunter?"

I do wish to join with a worthy hunter, one day. Someone that loves me the way my father did my mother. Someone that I can love in return. But there is no one like that, not yet. "No, not now, cannot we wait until after my testing, please?"

Confusion flashes in his eyes. "I thought that you . . . do you not want to at least know who asked for you?"

"No, Father, I do not." I stand and leave the tent.

I wish that the snow was gone, that I could seek solace in my arena, but I cannot. And so I go to the story fire and watch it dance, the bright oranges and reds, jumping and twisting, casting light onto the black ceiling of the cave. The smoke swirls and spins up to a small crack that runs along the ceiling. When I was young, and would sit at Grandmother's feet learning as the other young ones, I had asked about it. She told us that the crack had always been there and that is why the story fire was placed here, so that the smoke could escape. I want to escape as the smoke, to float off to the gray sky above. I do not want to struggle any more. I want peace.

I hear rushing feet, voices of men hurrying to my family tent. My curiosity is piqued, but before I can go to satisfy it, Balek sits down next to me.

I know that I should not resent his presence, but I do.

"What is that about?" I ask, watching the men.

"Tamuq has not yet returned. Some of the men want to go look for him."

In my mind's eye, I see Maruq as he was when I joined him last night, concerned and agitated. I ache for him, I want to comfort him, but I know that I cannot.

"Will you search?"

"Yes. It is a man's duty." But something tells me that Balek only does it for duty's sake. There is no great love between him and the new ones.

"I am glad." I put my hand on his strong arm, deciding to forgive him. I feel the muscles ripple under my hand.

"Then I will be among the first of the searchers." He places his massive hand over mine. I begin to feel uncomfortable and want to run again.

"Let's go join the others then." I leap to my feet.

We go to my family tent. All of the men are there, except Maruq. I assume that he is preparing his own search without the men.

"We can go for short searches in groups of two or three, during the light of day, but I want no one out in the dark. Is that clear?" My father tells the men.

They agree.

"Now for the first party do I have volunteers?"

I hear Balek's deep voice behind me.

"Good, so first we will have Malu, Kumal, and Balek. Then Iruq, you take Sinaq with you tomorrow."

"What of Maruq? He will want to search." Balek says.

"Yes, where is Maruq?" My father asks. Everyone looks around, but he is not there.

I slip between the men and head to Maruq's tent, hoping to find him there preparing a search of his own. It is an average tent set apart by several spans from the nearest neighbor. I have heard some of the women complain of the scent that comes from the wolves. But where else are they to be kept?

I hear the pups yapping as I approach.

"Maruq?" I call out.

He steps out from his tent, momentarily looking in my direction, pausing in his work. And then he shakes his head as if to dismiss me in pursuit of his preparations.

"Nal, come." His wolf obeys. Her ears perk up and her tail wags.

"Where are you going?"

He doesn't stop his work, and he doesn't answer.

"You can't go out by yourself. You will die."

He ignores me.

"At least wait until light, when the others can go with you. You can go every day that way. The first search party leaves at first light. Balek will be going." I ramble things out desperate to make him see some reason.

"Balek?" He stops, and then turns to me.

"Yes, you know the hunter with the scar on his face."

"I know who he is." He states flatly and stares at me, as though trying to divine a secret.

"The chief will not allow any searching without the Great Light, you cannot go right now."

"Yes, I can." He challenges me, his blue eyes hard, determined.

"Not if the chief says otherwise." I press the point, just as determined.

"And if you were Chief would you forbid me?"

"It is not safe." I plead with him.

"No, but my father is out there." He drops his head, focusing on what is before him.

I move next to him. "Please," I take his hand, "please wait for the others."

Nal howls, a long imploring note, eager to be doing something. Maruq does not look at me. He looks at my hand. It seems an eternity before he answers. He runs his thumb across the back of my hand, and then says, "Yes, Siira, I will wait."

Over the next moon, searches are made whenever the weather permits. But Tamuq is never found and he never returns. By the time of the Mid-snow Celebration, all hope is gone. Even Maruq no longer wishes to search; he merely takes more turns at the watch. He does not even join us at the story fire for the celebration.

My father sits in his great chair and I stand next to him,

watching the dancers spin around the fire. It is monstrous, flames that reach almost to the ceiling, licking it with scorching tongues. The heat is unbearable, but no one leaves the circle. The great fire is to remind us that the light will conquer the darkness, but with the loss of Tamuq, I feel as though the dark is winning. What is there that is light?

I want to help lighten Maruq's burden, but I have nothing to do it with. The pace of the drumbeats slows until it stops. The dancers leave the circle. They are drenched in sweat, as though they had been swimming in the Great Salt Water.

Grandmother shuffles into the center. Tiras brings her a stump to sit on.

"Thank you." She smiles and sits.

She is to tell of the birth of the Great Light. I have heard the story every annual since I was born, and so it has lost its luster. As she begins, I sneak away to the mouth of the cave.

"I brought you some water." I raise my water skin as proof of my errand.

Maruq raises his eyes to me. They have lost their peace. "Thank you."

I hand him the water skin.

"Shouldn't you be with the others?"

"Probably, but it is so hot over there." I smile and fan at my face with my hand.

"I see." Maruq feigns a smile. Nal stretches out next to him and yawns. Her pups are no longer pups, but young wolves.

I kneel down and pet one of them. "They are so big."

"Yes, they will get bigger." His voice has no emotion, no joy, no sorrow. The melody is gone, frozen like the water in a pool. I want to help, to bring it back.

I nod and settle down allowing the wolf to lie on my lap.

"What are the others doing?" Maruq asks, never looking at me.

"Grandmother is telling a tale."

60

"I like your grandmother's stories."

"This one I have heard so often I could probably tell it in my sleep."

"Will you?"

"Will I what?" I ask, looking up from the ball of fluff in my lap.

"Tell me the story." His voice softly pleads, pulling at my heart.

I do not know how to answer.

"Please." He looks fragile. His eyes are so sad, so unlike their brilliant, bright blue, that I nod agreeing to his request, hoping to bring back some of the tranquility that he used to possess.

"Once a long time ago," I start, noticing Maruq relax slightly, his long fingers stretching through Nal's fur, "the Mighty One decided that he wanted to show his power to all, and so he decided to create light. Before this there was nothing but black darkness, as dark as the center of our mountain. 'But the darkness is so very thick,' the spirits would say to him. The Mighty One however paid them no mind. He began to rub his great hands together. He rubbed them faster and faster. The spirits could feel the heat from his hands begin to overcome the cold darkness. Then the Mighty One blew into his hands and a spark shot out, igniting the air around it. The darkness was chased away. Everything was light." I close my eyes, trying to picture the story in my mind.

"'It is too much,' the spirits protested. The Mighty One laughed, 'First you tell me that it cannot be done and then you tell me that I have done too much.' The spirits shrank back from the Great Light that engulfed them. 'Very well,' the Mighty One said. 'I shall gather it into one place.' And he did.

"Now as we watch the Great Light travel across our sky, we see His power. We know what He can do. For the Mighty One did not leave the light overwhelming the darkness because he wished to remind us that he is the only one strong enough to make the light that overcomes darkness."

I finish the story and look to Maruq. His serenity has returned. He no longer looks sad and fragile, but strong and handsome almost like he had a moon ago before all of this turmoil.

"Thank you, Siira." The melody having returned to his voice.

I nod, but I do not know what has affected him so.

9 THE TESTING

Now, I stand at Sacred Point with the others awaiting the sacrifice that precedes our testing. Instead of Tamuq, this year Maruq brings the curly horn. He looks at me as he returns to his place among the people. A light has returned to his eyes, a light that had been extinguished with his father's loss, a playful warmth.

A smile pulls at my mouth, but then I remember where I am and the smile disappears.

My father slits the ram's throat, vigorously, as though he cannot wait for my testing to begin. Today is the day that he has prepared me for and he wants to prove that his wishes were not as crazed as a raging mammoth.

I believe that he is crazed. Dismissing my doubts, I measure myself against the boy on my strong side. He is a full two hands taller than me and close to twice as bulky. I feel slight and insignificant next to him.

Among a group of girls my age, I stick out like a sore finger. I am a hand taller than most of them and lean and muscled instead of soft and smooth. I feel as though I am lost being a nothing, a something in the middle that is neither one, nor the other, but both at the same time. How will I do this? I chance a look to the people gathered. Do they think that I will return from my testing? Or like me do they think this is folly?

Balek's broad, confident smile draws my attention. I know that he has absolute confidence in my skills, more confidence than I do.

I focus back on my father; somehow I have missed the presentation of the sacrifice and the prayer and now watch as the innocent ram's blood drains down the stone and into the basin. I feel akin to the poor creature, helpless to do anything about the situation I find myself in.

All of us are presented to the people. I try to assume an indifferent expression, or I hope I do, for fear is playing in my mind.

I barely eat the stew that is placed before me at the fire. It is thick and seems to stick in my throat and, once swallowed, sits like a rock in my stomach, so I drink much water. The chatter and happiness around me grates and I leave as quickly as I can.

I walk down the steps to the preparation camp. The small work shelters are empty and quiet. There are a couple of the men tending to the meat that is drying. I nod to them and pass beyond to the lookout rock, then climb to my arena.

I climb to the top of a massive boulder and sit.

"I shall miss this."

"Why? You will come back." Balek's strong voice startles me.

"You almost didn't." I say back to him.

"True, but I am not Siira."

I grin and pat on the boulder next to me. I have missed my friend. He has been too busy as a man to spend time with a nothing like me.

He manages to pull his hulking frame onto the boulder. He is definitely the finest of the men, easily worth twice any of the others. Pride swells in my chest, the pride of a sister.

"Here," he says and holds up a beautiful beaded

necklace. I catch it in my hand and study the pattern. The medallion is the size of my palm, a beautiful bunch of blue remembering flowers is centered on it. "It's from Bela."

"Tell her thank you." I pull it over my head and tuck it close to my heart.

"I will."

We stare off into the distance neither of us talking or moving, just waiting.

I can feel when the time is nearing and stand to go find my father. Balek catches my strong hand and slightly tugs on it. I look down at him.

"Remember, you don't need to show off; you just need to come back."

"Don't worry; I am not foolish enough to fight a grizzly." I smile and trace the scar on his face with my finger.

I stand, then jump high into the air and soar doing several flips before landing on the ground as softly as any cat.

"Show off!" I hear him call after me as I run to join my father. He stands on a hill at the edge of the valley.

I carry nothing but my water pouch, flints, and a small rock blade. Men must be able to survive without anyone, and so we must be able to make our weapons and traps.

Without a word, I follow my father. He takes me high into the hills and trees away from everything familiar. We pass tall needled trees and berry bushes. I try to memorize the route and direction of the Great Light, so that I will easily find my way home.

We walk so far that I begin to believe that even my father must be lost.

"I know that you can do this," he says.

I am less certain.

"When returning, follow the light."

I nod. He turns to leave, but something stops him and he slowly turns back. Looking into my cat-like eyes making certain that I listen, he speaks.

"When Siiraq died, your mother and I talked about this very day."

His statement surprises me.

"Yes, even then I brought up this possibility. She urged me to consider carefully. She tried to make me see it from a woman's view. I do not fully understand what you are going through, and I know that what I ask of you may seem impossible, but I also know that women are in fact stronger than men because their hearts are larger."

Tears brim in my eyes as his words journey through my ears and lodge in my heart.

"You can do this."

Now, I know that I must.

I continue on, keeping the light to my back until I find a small cave formed by a grouping of three small boulders with a slab neatly placed on top providing a roof. Dutifully, I thank the Mighty One for his provision, and perhaps he will bless me for my respect. I have to duck to get in, but since this place is mostly for sleeping that won't matter. Once inside I find an old fire ring made of large rocks near the back of the cave. Perhaps, another child became a man here. Perhaps it was my father.

I see evidence of a former sleeping mat and I decide that this is a good sign. I begin by gathering leaves and other vegetation for a bed. Now for the fire. Not far from the cave I find a branch that has fallen, perhaps from the weight of the snow that was piled on it so recently. Since it is splintered it is not too difficult to break off some larger chunks that will make my fire burn longer. Although the weather is warm now, I still need the fire to help keep away unwanted guests. If a grizzly decided that my cave was his, I would have a difficult time arguing.

Once back at the cave with my firewood, I sift through

the leaf pile, gathering the dry ones into a pile in the fire ring and tossing the green ones at the entrance. I strike my flints together and begin to create sparks. A spark catches on one of the brown leaves and I place my twigs into it. Enjoying the sight of the growing fire, I place some of the larger chunks from the branch over the small fire as though creating a tent for it and a comfortable blaze quickly warms my cave. I watch the flames dance, pulling out the necklace that Bela made for me. I study it, thankful for my friend and then tuck it back into my tunic. Exhausted from my lack of sleep, and from the adventure of the day, I easily drift into a light slumber.

I awaken with a start at the sound of leaves crunching and shifting. As I become more aware, I realize that the noise is coming from the front of my cave. A young long-eared jumper has decided to munch on the leaves that I had discarded for the fire.

Content to watch the furry creature, I lay still, trying not to think of the trials ahead. A memory surfaces as I watch him.

"Siira, look a jumper." My mother pointed to a bush in a far-off cluster. "Watch, little one."

I obeyed, as though mesmerized, standing as still as a rock. Fascinated by the soft fur, the quick ticking movements, I did not notice when my mother had silently slipped away. I had turned to see if she enjoyed the animal as I did, but she had vanished; before I became frantic she had reappeared very close to the jumper.

Soundlessly, she approached the creature, coming so close that she could have reached out a hand to touch the snow-white fur, but she refrained from doing so. Expecting her to grab it and bring it to me, I waited in strained silence. The jumper merely stared at her, sniffing the air, as though my mother had bewitched it.

From behind her back she pulled out a twig of berries. Gracefully, almost silently, as though she was a spirit able to go anywhere, to do anything, she laid the treats down in front of the jumper. I watched as the jumper moved to the proffered food and began to eat.

Then, magically, my mother ran her graceful hand across the soft fur.

When she returned, I asked her how she had been able to do that.

"Patience is an amazing advantage. Trust must be built. Once a creature, or anyone for that matter, can trust you, you have won. Besides I had a pet jumper when I was young."

"Really?" Enthusiasm at the prospect of having such a pet rose inside me.

"Yes, little one, I found it and nursed it back to health. She just stayed with me after she was better."

The memory fades. I feel as though she has sent me this animal as encouragement in my testing. A grateful smile spreads across my face as I continue to watch. I stay motionless as I watch him eat his breakfast, selfishly wishing that I could get mine, yet not wanting to disturb it and lose the companionship.

The Great Light is a quarter of the way on its journey. My stomach begins cramping in hunger, and I can wait no longer. I carefully sit up, trying not to make a sound, yet his ears miss nothing and he scurries off. Now that he is gone, I quickly go to a berry bush that I had spied yesterday. It is heavy with fire berries, brightly colored red and orange berries, and expertly I gather the juicy fruit from giant, thorny bush.

"Breakfast."

My voice sounds strange in the silent wood and I long for a friend to share the night with.

I eat as I gather, popping luscious berries into my mouth. Eventually I have my fill for the morning and gather enough for later.

My next task is to make darts. I find a thicket. Breaking

off several sturdy branches that are as tall as I am, I use my blade to sharpen them to fine points. Normally I would attach sharpened black stones to the ends but I do not have the time to chip any, and so the sharpened sticks will have to do. The Great Light is high in the sky by the time I have finished five darts.

I decide to search for something small to cook for my evening meal. I carry four of the darts in my weak hand and one in my strong hand, ready to launch it at a bushy tail or feathered flyer. Normally, I would use a throwing stick to give me added power, but again, I don't have mine with me. I will need one though, to take my token, so I decide to make one tomorrow.

I see no small animals, but I find a stream nearby that is full of jumping fish. And it is not long before I have speared three. I take them back to my cave. I coax the coals back to life, and then add dry wood. Skewering the three fish, I roast them on the ends of my dart.

I cook all three fish, but save two for the following day. I eat some more fireberries and soon spy my jumper friend at the leaf pile again. I toss some berries out to him, expecting that he will scurry off, but instead he moves closer to investigate.

Over the next few days, he and I become well acquainted and one evening, about half way through my testing, we share the bed, his warm fur a welcome comfort during the lonely nights. I imagine taking him home with me at the end of my testing, not as my token but as a pet. I can't see my father approving of him though, unless he was a furry hat.

"Would you like to come home with me, Jumpy?" I ask on the tenth day.

He wiggles his pink nose and his whiskers jump almost in joy.

"I'll take that as a yes."

I fall asleep that night imagining the looks I would

receive coming home with a jumper faithfully following me: my father's confusion, Balek's amusement, Boku's shock, and Maruq's quiet smile. A smile creeps across my lips, as I fall asleep.

My testing is nearing its end; I must start to hunt for my token.

"I must leave you for today, Jumpy. I must make my kill to prove myself to the men, and my father." I grab all five of my darts and loop my throwing stick through the two middle fingers of my strong hand. I had taken great pains to carve it, wanting to keep it if I ever made it home, even planning on having Bela paint my token onto it. I look for tracks, tapping my middle fingers on the palm of my strong hand, causing the stick to bounce on the back of my hand and forearm as I walk. At first I begin to look for a trophy, something that Father would be proud of. But after a day of searching for tracks and finding none, I return discouraged to my cave.

"No tracks at all. No fleet feet, no rams, no grizzly claws, no anything." Settling next to my fire ring, I toss some berries into my mouth, more out of necessity for nourishment than a desire to eat.

I start to think of others that had tested before me.

"You know, Jumpy, I used to think that the others that never returned had done so because they had died, but perhaps they did not return because they could not bear the disappointment that would be found in their father's eyes if they returned with no token."

He twitches his ears.

"If I can find no token, perhaps I will stay here with you in this cave. What do you think?"

His ears twitch again.

I start early the next morning. Only one more day, I must have a kill today in order to dress it and carry it home. A gruesome thought flashes into my mind.

You do have a token, Jumpy. A long-eared jumper is better than nothing.

A shiver runs up my spine. I would rather stay alone forever than kill a friend.

About midday, I decide to return to my cave for some food. Along the way I spear a fish from the stream. Its slippery, wriggling body shines at the end of my dart. I toss it to the shore and then I see it: a track, larger than my hand, buried deep in the soft mud at the edge of the stream, the track that I had dreaded finding, the paw print of a large male blade-toothed cat.

I scan the area looking and listening for evidence of his presence. When I am satisfied that he has moved on, I go to the print and I reach down my fingers to check it for freshness. It had to have been made shortly before I had come to the stream. He is close.

Fear sends my heart racing. Few men dare attempt an attack on a male cat, and, judging by the size of the print, he is a monstrous cat. In order to take him, the first dart would have to hit with precision the side of his neck, cutting the main vein and bringing certain death. For if my dart misses and merely injures the cat, there may not be time to attempt another throw.

But my father would indeed be pleased, no, ecstatic, with such a token, one that would definitely set me above the men that I will eventually lead. And right now I have no other option.

I decide to track the cat. Leaving the fish where it lands, I look for another track. I have only gone a few spans when I hear a noise from the direction of my camp, a noise that cuts the silent woods with its sharpness, a high-pitched, long squeal of terror, a sound that Grandmother had told me of, but I had never heard until now, the terror shriek of a long-eared jumper.

"Jumpy."

I don't think, I merely react, running as quickly as my legs will move. Leaping over bushes and rocks, like a panicked fleet foot, I move with one thought in my mind. *Save Jumpy.*

As I reach my camp, I reign in my pace, stopping near the fireberry bush. The cave is in my direct line of sight. Out of its entrance a strong blade-toothed cat stalks. His muscles ripple under his tawny hide. I set my dart into the notch in my throwing stick. The movement draws his gaze. He licks his bloodstained mouth. The blood of my friend steels my nerve, heightens my senses, and chases away my fears. My eyes focus on his neck. He stretches high to cry in triumph, in rage, or perhaps challenge, but it is a mistake. For before he can make a sound, my dart has found its mark. Enraged, he shakes his head and paws at the dart, until, to his doom, he pulls it free. The blood flows freely down his neck. As his life drains from him, the contents empty from my stomach.

I have killed my token. I have avenged my friend, but no joy, no triumph, courses through me, setting my blood on fire as I have heard the men say it does. Instead a sick feeling settles in my stomach. I am a man.

10 THE HUNT

I bury what is left of Jumpy by the fire ring in the cave, saying a silent farewell. I have lost a friend. Cold rushes across my body. Gathering wood, I begin a fire to warm me. I stare out at the blade-tooth's carcass and try to decide how to get my token back to the cave.

"I may be able to manage the skin."

Taking my small stone blade, I slit his throat, down his shoulder, and side to the hind leg. Removing the cat's jacket takes me the rest of the afternoon, for he is a large and heavy cat. Once he is free of his coat, I muscle the carcass into the woods in an attempt to keep scavengers away from my cave.

I am covered in blood and mud. I want to wash in the stream, but first I must scrape the fat from him. Pulling the large skin into the cave, I sit next to the fire ring and set about scraping.

The Great Light is low in the horizon when I finally make it to the stream. I submerge, fully clothed, into the water, scrubbing the grime from me and my clothes. The water is cold, numbing. Shivering from the water and exhausted from the day's waves of emotion, I return to my warm fire and sleep. My dreams that night are riddled with conflicting images. Maruq smiles across from me in the early light. Balek holds me down while he laughs. Bela works next to me on a pouch. Jumpy dies squealing. The blade-toothed cat lies in a pool of dark blood.

I awaken with a start, staring at the token stretched out across from me. Even though he had killed a friend, I find myself regretting that this great king of the woods will no longer roam free.

I fold his skin as best I can and wrap a cord around it, but it is much too heavy for me to carry all the way back to the great cave. And so I must make a miniature sled to carry it. The sled takes much of my morning, searching for wood and binding it together before I can set my token on it. The Great Light is high above, shining down on me, as I set out for the people's cave. Constantly walking toward the light, I pull my token home.

When I reach the preparation camp, the light is resting on the tops of the trees. The people whoop at the sight of me. The men stare in wonder, probably having written me off shortly after midday, and the women beam in triumph, most likely because I have proven to be capable. My training has accomplished the incredible: a girl is now a man.

I walk with my head high, pulling my sled to present my token to the chief. I pass the men: Kumal, Iruq, Sinaq, Pol. Each stares and smiles. I see Balek standing behind my father, looking like a proud papa grizzly in his great cape. I smile.

I stop in front of the chief. I see tears glistening, threatening to run down his cheek.

"You are well."

"Yes, Father." I say gruffly, emotions hidden carefully.

"No injuries?"

"None." Not physical ones, anyway.

"Good." He blinks and the tears in his eyes somehow vanish without being shed as he inquires of my token. "I see the great skin, what did you kill?"

"A blade-toothed cat." My voice sounds small and emotionless as I speak the words.

"A blade-toothed cat." He repeats, breathlessly.

"Yes, my chief, I killed him with one dart."

"One dart." He repeats in a hush. A gleam of pride lights his eyes as he embraces me. "A cat, she has taken a great cat!" He announces to the people gathered nearby.

The look of wonder and amazement in my father's face is reflected in the faces around me. I hear another whoop and one of the men begins a chant. Soon all of the people are dancing in a circle around me, praising the Mighty One for the cat. Then I am lifted up into the air by strong hands, jolted and jumped unwillingly. I look around for Maruq, but he is not there. Disappointment piles on top of my grief. I am tired and I only want my bed, but the people only see a triumphant return.

The women sing back and forth, telling each other that the story of my testing will be remembered among the people long after I have journeyed to Xerena.

The next few days of celebration blur as the others tell their tales of hardship and success; I do not join in telling my tale. On the last night of the feast, I am presented my token. I had expected to receive a cloak much like Balek's grizzly, but instead my father presents me with a blanket.

He nods to me, as though to give approval to unroll the skin. As I work it out of its tight roll, I am amazed at the warm softness of it, a softness that touches my heart. When I reach the center, something falls to the ground. Clutching the large skin to my chest, I look to see a beautifully crafted belt tightly wrapped around something. Kneeling down, I retrieve the token.

I stare up at my father.

He nods at me, and I begin to unwind the belt. Slowly, as I unfurl the belt I see my true token. My father has fashioned the cat's twin blades into blades for me.

"How? How did you get the blades?"

"I went back to your camp and found the carcass. It took some time and care, but I managed to get them."

Father had polished them and attached carved handles to them, handles that I know Balek has carved. They were then wrapped with mammoth cord for strength.

"They are beautiful."

"Wear them proudly."

All that evening I stare at my token blades. They are wondrous, too delicate to be of any real use, other than as a sign of my ability. I hold one of them out in my strong hand. Watching the firelight play in the brilliant white of the blade, I glide it through the air in feigned jabs. The carved handle fits perfectly into my hand. I bring it back to me, running my thumb across the butt. I feel a raised design. I hold it out to the light. Balek has worked remembering flowers into it.

I look across the story fire and see him standing tall among the others, laughing and making merry. I had thanked him for his work on my tokens yesterday.

"Balek, Balek." The people call out his name demanding his story. Willingly he obliges. Confidently standing in the midst of the gathering, he begins his tale.

I do not wish to hear it, but I remain seated next to the chief. Others follow him retelling their stories, young and old. I listen as long as I can, but I am exhausted. And tomorrow we hunt.

Excusing myself, I wander towards my tent, but find myself instead heading to the back of the cave, where shadow wins over the light. I have lost a friend and gained manhood, losing myself in the process.

I want a place to be alone, to grieve. I slump down onto the floor and watch the shadows shift as the story fire blazes higher. I pull out my necklace, the one Bela had made me, and run my thumb over the pattern. A movement to my weak side startles me, and I crouch into an attack position.

"I don't care for big celebrations either." I recognize Maruq's voice, its melody relaxes me. Crossing my legs in front of me, I lean back against the cool wall. Tipping my head and closing my eyes, letting the shadows hide me.

"I am in no mood for revelry." I say.

I hear him shift on his feet. Nal grumbles at him, as though she is impatient to be on their way. I expect to hear him leave. But when all I hear is silence, I open my eyes.

He stands in shadow, the firelight outlining his form. I see him signal to Nal. Whining, she lowers herself slowly, laying her head on her paws. Maruq settles next to her. I can barely see his hand resting on her head. I notice his token, a simple braided cord wrapped around his wrist. The white medallion attached to it, made from antler, lays on the back of his hand. Firelight dances across it, highlighting the simple etching of a fleet foot.

"Tell me, Maruq, how did you feel after your testing?"

"Which one?"

"You were tested more than once?" I say thinking back to the annual after their arrival. He and his father were asked to pass the testing in order to become part of the people. They had spent half a moon out in our valley alone, both returning with tokens. Tamuq came with a long tooth and Maruq with a fleet foot. I don't remember him going a second time.

"Among my people we are tested on our twelfth annual." His calm voice answers, no pride or boasting in the feat, only his melodic self-assured voice. "We spend a moon alone in our mountains. Hunting, fishing, surviving."

I try to picture Maruq alone on a mountain as a young boy enduring trials and surviving. But I can only see him as he is now. Strong, confident, and at peace.

"I am not sure how I survived, except that the Great Father willed it." He looks up at me, I cannot make out his features in the scarce light, but I feel that he is smiling. "I guess I felt loved." He says finally answering my original question.

Loved? I don't feel loved. I feel the opposite of that.

"We were not required to bring back a token, no strange symbol made us better or worthy. We celebrated the life that had returned. Stories of boasting were not shared, only joy at the strength each one that returned had gained."

He grew silent. The sounds from the story fire find us in the shadows. Loud, raucous laughter, and drums. I contrast the two peoples in my mind. Mine only find a man in one who can return with a great beast, while his was content with mere survival.

As I gather my gear for the journey with the men, for my first hunt, I know that I will come back changed.

Father and Pol had gone out to scout yesterday, and found a herd of mammoth grazing lazily beyond the meadow near the salt water. Several bulls and cows along with young. We only need to take a couple in this hunt, so Father decides to attack the few in the rear.

The hunting party has twenty-three men, including me. We will easily be able to take two mammoth and get them back home in a couple of days.

I lay motionless in the grass that borders the sand. We wait as most of the herd passes by us; patience is a key virtue in a hunter.

Father signals for half of us to circle around to the opposite side of the last two mammoth in the procession. I follow Pire and Pol to a position away from the others, giving us a great vantage for the kill. Once the signal is given, I jump up, my dart in position on my throwing stick; all I need do is launch it.

But instead of striking the mammoth nearest me, I am distracted by the sound of the pounding mammoth feet, returning toward us. The lead mammoth must have been startled by something.

I hear the order to run and instantly obey.

I spy a large boulder about five spans away. I spring to it

and launch myself up it easily, as if I had been in my arena. Looking at the sand before me, I see the mammoth chase the men. The hunting party scrambles, most of the men heading toward the cliff. Balek is the first to reach it and scale to the top. He throws down a strong cord to help the others.

I see my father among those climbing to safety and relief washes over me, as I take a deep breath.

A mammoth's trumpeting behind me draws my attention. Pol and Pire are trapped in a tight crevice near the shore. A bull stands raised on his hind legs, and stomps down in front of them. They are about thirty-five spans away. I have only once attempted a throw so far, and without any accuracy, but it is the only option that I can think of to distract the mammoth and allow the men to escape.

I take aim and steady my footing. As I leap from the boulder to add some force to my throw, I launch my dart toward the mammoth. I watch as it soars high through the air, quivering with energy, and sticks into the mammoth. He rears up again, and then turns, trying to dislodge my dart. The distraction is enough. Pol and Pire escape. When the bull decides that he cannot do anything about his leg, he turns his rage on the two men. I load a second dart and launch it at his neck. It sticks.

Other darts join mine, pummeling the beast, and soon he is lying motionless with a spike necklace of darts.

"Are you alright?" I ask Pol, when he comes to inspect the kill.

"Yes, what happened? I mean we were trapped and then he reared and we got out; why did he do that?"

"Because Siira shot him in the backside," I hear Balek say.

"You saw that?" I ask.

"Of course," he says, smiling as though he has won some kind of wager.

"Where were you?" Pol asks me.

I turn and point to the boulder that I had so recently used as an escape.

"There?" Pol's eyes show incredulity.

"Yes, why?"

"I couldn't make that throw."

"You are not Siira," Balek says, pride obvious in his tone.

The rest of the men have joined us. A few, like Balek, had seen the entire thing, but most of the men doubt the story.

A hunter named Iruq, who is at least ten annuals my senior, boldly approaches me. His every movement challenges me; the hardness of his expression, the folding of his muscled arms across his chest, even the firm stance of his feet, all implies his disapproval of my presence among the hunters.

"So, little Siira has done a trick for us, has she?" His eyes are as hard as stone.

I break eye contact, looking for a friendly face. I find three: Pol, Pire, and Balek. Other faces look confused, amused, or conflicted. My presence is tolerated by most out of respect to my father, but not wanted by all.

"Let us prepare the beast for the return home," I hear my father.

Iruq grunts and stalks away.

At that moment, as I watch his broad shoulders sway mightily away from me and to the beast, I realize that the battle to kill a mammoth is not going to be the hardest battle that I will face. I will be fighting resentment, resentment that will smolder and smoke all my life. And if I become Chief; I fear it will blaze uncontrollably.

11 A DREAM LOST

Pol and Kumal are sent to stand guard as the rest of us begin the long process of dismembering the mammoth. The Great Light sets and returns to mid-sky before we are ready to take the first of the sleds back to the preparation camp.

As I fix the pull cord across my chest and shoulders, I dread the long journey back to the preparation camp. I toss some of my meat powder into my mouth and try to pull. I lean forward, throwing all of my weight against the cord. The sled does not budge. Digging my heels into the sand, I try again, but to no avail; the chunk of meat that I have is simply too weighty for me.

I wish for one of Maruq's strong wolves. The pups have all grown. The male has been trained and is much like its father, protective and strong. The two females are now pregnant. Soon there will be plenty of help to haul the meat, if only the hunters will allow it.

Iruq pulls his sled by me, casting a superior look at me down his nose.

I pretend to not see him and continue in my futile attempts to pull too much. My legs begin to burn and I feel bruises forming on my shoulders under the wide straps. I choke back all of my tears of frustration, longing for the freedom of my arena, freedom to fail without the prying eyes of the men, freedom to twist and turn and feel that I can excel; I try to pull.

Suddenly the sled lurches forward and begins to slide on the smooth wooden rudders. A triumphant smile starts in my soul, bursting forth onto my face.

I can pull, perhaps not as quickly as the others, but I can pull. Then my triumph crashes down to disappointment as Balek jogs up to me.

"See, all you need is a little push."

"A push."

"Yeah. I shoved at the back and got you started. Now you got it."

"Oh," I mumble.

"What?"

"Nothing."

"Good. Your father says that I am to help you, to take over at the hill."

Frustration rises again, he had to help me. I am not strong enough. Unable to control myself, tears begin to roll down my cheeks.

I am certain that Balek sees them, but he does not mention anything. Once we are at the hill, I almost refuse to let him help, but he assures me that the others will be switching.

"No man can pull the entire distance back by himself. Why do you think we work in twos?"

Actually, I am grateful to him for the help. My body is already screaming at me from the exertion of the last few days, the tracking, the lack of sleep, the killing of the beast and the pulling of the sled.

The smell of food greets us once we clear grass of the meadow. Balek is still pulling the sled, but instead of walking beside him, I have been helping by pushing for the last hundred spans or so. He has managed to catch us up to some of the others. I see that Iruq is still pulling the sled much as he had when he passed me. Does he not tire? He should be entirely spent, but he does not seem even winded, although telltale streams of sweat run down his face.

Around me the men begin to smile in anticipation of their women's food and comfort. I hear them brag about their woman's prowess in cooking or in the bed. I remain silent, both embarrassed at their words and infuriated at the way they are discussing the women, making their role sound simpler than it is.

I look to Balek to see what he thinks about their comments, but he only shares an odd grin with Pire and joins in the conversation.

I can hardly contain my thoughts; they keep leaping up in my throat, threatening to escape, and I keep swallowing them, like a bitter medicine.

By the time we reach the village, I have lost my appetite and my patience. I perform my duty, helping Balek deliver the meat, using my built-up frustration to give me energy. Once finished, I run to the tree. Climbing high without any thought of caution, I scramble up the tree, until I reach the uppermost branch many spans into the air. The men have infuriated me with their talk of the women. It seems that, according to their estimation, we are only good for a couple of things: cooking and love making.

"I am no man!" I shout into the clouded sky; dark gray, almost black, clouds threaten, glowering down at me. In response, I receive a long, low, grumbling rumble.

"Why? If you are truly the Mighty One that Grandmother teaches me of; if you truly want what is best for me, why can I not be who I am? I am a WOMAN!"

Woman. The word echoes in my mind. What is a woman? I should be able to define it, but I can't seem to. The men have defined it. Someone placed on earth for their pleasure and comfort, to cook and please them. If that is all we are, why do I want it?

Why do I long to stay with them and not be out having

adventures with the men? Do I want to stay safe at the cave chasing children? To join the women in their chattering? Do I want to cook and clean?

Is that what I want? To be left at the camp and wait for the men to return?

But what do I want? I know what I don't want. I don't want to spend my life proving myself, constantly trying to outdo the men just so I won't lose my place. I don't want to hear their vulgar talk and thoughts, some designed, I am certain, just to goad me.

I slump down on the branch that I am standing on, my thoughts as gray as the sky above me. I don't know what I want, but I do know that this is not it.

I guess I felt loved. Maruq's words echo in my mind. But am I not loved? Father, Balek, Bela, Grandmother. They love me, but I don't feel loved. The people closest to me all ask me to be something. Can't they just love me?

Tears begin down my cheeks, and then rain falls from the sky. The clouds seem to join in my pain and cry with me. Slowly, I work my way down the tree.

I am grateful for the rain as I walk back to the village, for it will hide my tears; men do not cry and I must cry no longer.

I feel pieces of me will have to die in order to walk the path that I must walk, a path not intended for a woman.

"Has Father returned?" I ask Grandmother as I enter our tent.

"There was an accident. He went to help."

"An accident?"

"Yes, there was a landslide beyond the high river. The men went to clear the water way. Balek came looking for you; he told me of your hunt. I am proud."

My voice sounds hollow, empty. "I can't do it. I can't." Emotions overwhelm me, a desire to leave and never come back, warring with a desire to stay and cry on Grandmother's shoulders, even to die -- all these things spin like a whirlwind in my chest, my head, my stomach. I know that after such a day a true man would be triumphing, not having an emotional crisis. And I chide myself for once again not being the man that I am supposed to be.

"Now, now, little one, it will be alright. Trust the Mighty One." She pulls my head down onto her chest. I feel her soft touch on my hair, smoothing down the black straying hairs. "You may not understand what is happening or why. I confess that even I do not like the events, but the Mighty One has his purpose. You must trust him."

Trust him. A ragged sob escapes and I feel the dampness of my grandmother's sleeve as it absorbs my emotional overflow. Why should I trust him, I want to ask her. He has only taken from me. But instead I ask, "How?"

"Be strong, rise to the challenge, and continue on where you are right now. Try to see the good."

The good? I raise my head and look directly into her eyes.

"What would have happened to Pol and Pire if you had not been there?" she asks.

I think back. Yes, I had been the only one close enough to even try to save them. Without me they would have died, trampled beneath the mammoth's feet.

"If you had not been there, they would be gone. Their families would be mourning a passing, not celebrating a grand hunt. But you were there. The Mighty One protected them using you as his instrument -- a woman that is called man."

Yes, I had forgotten, forgotten the two men that had been trapped, the mammoth that I had killed. Yes, the others helped, but the kill would never have happened if I had not been there. All of my misgivings, all of my self-consciousness, seem to dissipate in the fact that I had been there. Perhaps the Mighty One did care and look out for us, and perhaps He did have a plan.

A hope rises in my heart, a small flicker of hope.

"Don't worry, one day you will understand the whys. Perhaps you will even tell your sons and daughters of today."

Sons and daughters, my sons and my daughters. I had forgotten it until now, until she said it. I am to join. That had always been a part of the plan, for me to provide the heir. Balek had asked for me.

"But my family won't be normal." And as I say it, I realize that I want a family. Sons and daughters, a husband who will love me, giving me that love that I can feel. Love without expectations.

"No, it won't. But no family is normal, no family is like another. They may seem to be from the outside, but they are not."

Her words are true, comforting, nurturing to the dream of love in my mind. She tucks an errant strand of hair behind my ear, and fingers my necklace, the one Bela had given me.

She continues, "You are the chief's daughter, his only child. You will have sons, you will carry on the line, but none of it will be normal."

She releases me, and turns to get my evening meal. As the words sink in, a chill spreads in my body, beginning to cool the blaze of hope. No, it won't be normal.

My man will be lost with me in this life of in between; I will never be his woman. How odd it sounds even in my thoughts. I think of Balek. I know that he believes himself in love. But if I join with him, I will be condemning him, a great hunter, to a life of ridicule. Not every man would ridicule him, but there would be enough. I think of Iruq and his dark eyes.

I try to work it out in my mind, to see my future. Usually the woman would stay home and cook, watch the children, teach. What would my man be required to do? Would he still be a man? Would he still hunt? Which of us would watch the children? Would Grandmother be called on to raise my sons and daughters?

How can I condemn a man that I care for to that kind of life? Or even someone that I don't care for?

No, I must give up my dream; I can never allow a joining. But how can I refuse? It is why I have suffered all of this, in order to continue the line.

Grandmother hands me the bowl of stew. I scoop up a portion with my first two fingers and swallow it, as I will have to swallow my fate.

12 OVERHEARD

An annual has passed. My time has been spent trying to fit into a world that I was not created for. I have gained stamina and strength during the hunts and endured the constant boasting and shows of bravado. More of the men see me as a useful addition to their numbers, yet there are still those that refuse to accept me, who constantly challenge me or berate me.

But now is not the time for regrets, sorrow, or grief for what I have lost, for today is the claiming ceremony for my good friend, Bela. Pol will claim her today before the people, promising his undying devotion, his protection, his love.

I am determined that today be perfect for Bela. In some ways, I feel that it will be my only opportunity to experience the simplicity of love, even though it is by proxy; boy loves girl, girl loves boy, and they claim one another, joining in love. When I participate in a Claiming Ceremony, it will be anything but simple; it will be riddled with doubt, doubt about the man's true feelings, doubt about my position in the relationship, and doubt about the wisdom of any of it. Through the joy shining in Bela's eyes, I can imagine that a man loves me as Pol loves her, that I love a man in return, that we will spend an uncomplicated life together. Because of our friendship I want to help her prepare, yet because of my unique position among the people, I feel the need to ask my father's permission.

I make my way through the cave, weaving between tents and excited families; they are obviously anticipating the ceremony at Sacred Point. Many of the women are coaxing life back into fires to prepare large morning meals, probably berry stews with dried mammoth meat.

My father stands at the entrance, listening intently to the small group of men gathered around him. Boku, with his stern lined face and patch over his dead eye; Tomu, who tosses back a mouthful of liquid from a skin pouch periodically; and Miiq, another elder with his white hair blowing in the wind, are adamantly discussing something with him, apparently trying to win him over to their way of thinking.

Instead of boldly approaching the group, I slink back into the shadows hoping to see and hear without being seen.

Boku focuses on my father, his one good eye dark with purpose. The patch of dark grizzly skin does not entirely cover the scar that runs from his forehead to the corner of his mouth; the scar makes his appearance almost ominous.

"My chief, I am afraid that many of the hunters are murmuring about your daughter. They become anxious to have her joined to a man, to begin her purpose of providing an heir."

"Who?"

"The names are not important, what is important is that it is being said. If you would keep your blood in leadership, may I suggest something?"

"Go ahead, Boku, your suggestions are as easily stopped as the overflowing of the great river."

At my father's words, Boku's good eye flashes with rage, but instantly he suppresses the emotion and continues. "If you were to announce her match at the ceremony today, to a strong and well-respected hunter, then perhaps the wagging tongues will stop moving," Boku explains.

Miiq barely let Boku finish before he rushes in, "I agree. If we can announce a match, even in the next few moons, much dissension will be put at ease."

"What you are suggesting seems to be more like an adoption of a son than a match. I am to adopt a son to claim my daughter. Has she no say in the matter?"

"Of course, as all have a part in it, but it needs to be done."

"Yes, Boku, but has she not proven herself capable over the last annual?"

"Yes, she is a capable, my chief, but the sooner she is joined, the sooner we will have an heir."

I am not old enough yet. I have another annual before I come of age, I am only seventeen. No one is joined before then, but I seem to be journeying many new paths.

"I will speak to her of it again; she will be joined at the next ceremony, with the others, after the hunts." I cannot see my father's face, but I know the look that Boku is staring at, the look that says he is done discussing, the look that makes you feel as though you are somehow less than, less than a man, less than Chief, less than he is. Boku does not react to the look, but Miiq seems to visibly shrink before it.

"May the Mighty One make it so," Boku says.

"A strong man for Siira would only help her." Miiq has regained some courage.

"I intend for Siira to take a man, a man that will help her in all her endeavors, a man that will understand her position among the people."

"Plans will be made." Miiq's sycophantic voice curdles my blood.

"You know that in our life very little can be planned ahead. We can merely prepare." My father's voice is as cold as ice.

"Then, my chief, let us prepare," Boku says.

Nothing more is said, Boku and Miiq are dismissed by a wave of my father's strong hand. The men leave, coming back into the cave. I wait until they are well gone before I approach my father.

"They aren't serious, are they?"

My father's eyes at first are hard as flint, but quickly they soften as he looks at me.

"Yes, they are serious, not that I agree with their haste."

"The men honor you; surely they will honor your wishes."

"Siira, little one, you know that some of the men crave power and I believe that those men see an opportunity for advancement by berating my decision and, consequently, you."

It is true, that even after almost an annual of being a man, many of the men do not respect me, no matter how I prove myself in hunting and scouting. I cannot convince them to accept me. Perhaps the elders are right, perhaps I should make a match that would seem to give me what I lack, but I still can't help feeling that my man would not be accepted, but ridiculed.

"Come with me." He holds out his hand to me as he had done when I was a child.

I grasp the proffered hand and allow him to lead me down the steps to the preparation camp. I glance at the meat strips that are hanging over the smoking fire. They are beginning to shrivel and darken. Another few days and the women will collect them and store them for the time of snow.

My father continues to lead me out of the valley and to the meadow. He finds a large rock on a hill and sits. Tugging me down next to him, we stare out at the Great Salt Water. The waves roll in and out. Eventually I relax. The breeze plays with some loose hairs that are around my face. I feel them dance across my cheek and I close my eyes, savoring the simplicity of the moment.

I hear my father suck air between his teeth, and then hiss it out slowly. I turn, looking at him and know that the moment of peace is shattered.

"I seem to have aroused a nest of serpents, Siira. All I wanted was to remain true to your mother. I could not imagine taking another woman to my bed. I couldn't bring myself to make another match. Now, because of my selfishness, because of my love for your mother, I fear that I have only made things unbearable for you.

"If I could go back in time, by the Mighty One, my choice would be different, but, my child, I cannot go back, we can only move forward."

His confession touches me to my very inner being. I press a kiss onto his cheek. "My path is not unbearable, Father. Difficult, yes, but not unbearable."

"No?"

I shrug. Well, a little, I admit to myself.

"You will have to live with my decision. I do not know what the future will bring, but we must think of the people first and foremost. If I had done that when your mother died, you may . . ."

"My chief, I will do as you wish." I say, cutting off his words.

He lifts his hand and brushes my cheek with his thumb. "I could not be any prouder of you, Siira, my child. No more talk of this now." His words seem to erase his previous mood. "Today is special and I believe that you have a friend that needs your help."

"Truly, Father, may I? I wasn't sure."

"Yes, go spend some time with Bela." He pats my knee. I jump up and sprint off, eager to help.

I find Bela with the other maidens in the meadow picking blossoms of blue, yellow, and pink.

"Bela." She turns at my voice and smiles.

"I wasn't sure if you could come."

"Neither was I." I start to pick flowers and drop them

into her basket.

"Have you seen Pol?"

"Just a glimpse, he is as nervous as a cornered fleet foot."

Bela's laugh rings out over the hills. "Good."

The other girls and their friends move on to another hill. As one of them passes, I hear her say, "Can't she make up her mind? Is she a man or a woman?"

The statement cuts.

Bela must have heard her. "Don't mind her, I think she likes my brother and is jealous of you."

"Jealous?" The idea seems as ludicrous to me as a flyer joining with a bushy-tail.

"Yes, you can go among the men whenever you want, you can run free with them, while we are to stay within certain boundaries."

"But it is not my choice to be a man, I was forced into it."

"Yes, but, Siira, would you really be content as a woman?"

"Why not?"

"Really? Siira, I have known you all of your life. Even as children when we would play you, well, were more free-spirited than the others, always running into the woods, discovering paths that your mother would have to scold you about. You got me into so much trouble."

"I got you into trouble? Whose idea was it to rain the berries on the elders?"

Bela smiles, mischief in her warm eyes, "It was funny, though, wasn't it?"

"Yes."

We fill her basket and return to the cave.

"When next you see me, I will be a promised woman."

"Yes, and you will be beautiful."

Bela gives me a quick hug and disappears into her tent.

13 THE CLAIMING CEREMONY

Sacred Point is covered in a rainbow of color, the blues, the purples, the yellows, and the pinks of the early flowers. The women have spent much of the afternoon decorating for the ceremony. The flowers that first bloom promise good fortune to the people, and so we use them in this ceremony, the ceremony of hope and promise for our people, the claiming ceremony.

My father stands at the tip of the point facing the people, much as he does for the testing ceremony. The sky behind him is tinged pink at the setting of the Great Light; it is not its usual gray. The expectant men stand facing him on his strong side. They are all as clean as the fresh streams can make them. Every man takes advantage of the new running streams to wash the stubborn grime from his body early on this day, donning new leggings and a clean tunic. Every man stands ready in masculine splendor.

Opposite them are the maids. Their black hair in long braids down their backs. The flowers that were gathered earlier adorn their hair, woven into the braids. Flower wreaths lay atop their heads and flower necklaces encircle their throats. They are beautiful and blushing at the prospect before them.

Pol stands nearest my father, his well-formed muscular

arms bared, ready to receive the greatest treasure that he will ever receive: Bela, his woman. He will pledge today to save himself for her alone until the end of the hunts when he can take her to be his for life, to care for her and to be cared for by her.

He turns briefly, probably to steal a glimpse at Bela, who stands apart from him by a mere span. The look of wonder on his face reminds me of the feeling of exhilaration I have when, after the long months in the cave, having not felt a warm salt water breeze blowing through my hair, having not tasted the tang of the water on my tongue, having not been engulfed by the waves, I plunge deep into them, diving down past rocks, causing my lungs to burn from lack of air, until, unable to stand the depravation any longer, I turn, kicking rapidly to the surface, only to emerge and gulp in the fresh, glorious air and fling my head back, gulping in life. I envy Bela that look.

As she waits for the chief to place her hand into Pol's, Bela glances up, shyly smiling. Her dress of soft skin, the color of the grass at the end of hunts, is beaded with an intricate flower design. At the neck above her breastbone an antler design is apparent; the fleet foot is Pol's token.

"Friends, we have come to witness the claiming of these young women. Since time unknown we have taken the coming together of a man and a woman as a celebration, a celebration of possibilities. These men are today declaring their intention of taking these women to themselves at the end of the hunt, to continue the blood of their fathers' through having children of their own. The women are declaring their agreement to being claimed, to saving themselves for their man only, and to living and loving them only."

As I listen I finger the necklace that Bela had made me. Everything changes, even friendship.

Last annual, at the Hunt Celebration, a twinge of jealousy passed through me as Bela became a woman, something I could not do. The girls do not need to pass a test, to prove they are worthy, the girls need only be seventeen annuals.

Bela had worn a new tunic with a new belt that day. Her long twin braids trailing over her shapely shoulders. I had watched as she knelt before her mother, Natiq. Natiq had spoken a few words of blessing for her and then Bela untied the cords binding her braids. She gathered her hair into one thick bundle, pulling a wooden comb through it, and then she braided one thick single braid down her back.

In that one braid, I felt my life change. Bela had left me, before I had left her. She had become a woman, and I was still to become a man.

But I had been wrong, our friendship had not really changed then, it is now that our friendship changes, now when she pledges to Pol.

The chief walks to Pol and Bela. He takes the strong hand of each and holding them asks, "Do you claim each other and pledge to be true?"

"Yes."

"Do you pledge to save yourself until the end of the hunts when you will then come together?"

"Yes."

"Then with this cord I bind you to each other."

As my father moves to the next couple, Sinaq and Tirsa, I see Pol lean over and whisper something in Bela's ear that causes a deep crimson to crawl up her neck and into her cheeks.

After the next two couples have pledged, the people light a great fire and begin to dance. A dance of joy.

I join in body; my heart is not in agreement with the movements of my feet. I manage to congratulate Bela and Pol then, unable to pretend any longer, I leave.

The sky has turned from a blushing pink to a promising purple as it awaits the Great Light's disappearance. I meander toward the cave, knowing that I will soon be swallowed in darkness.

I weave in and out of trees and bushes, heading in the general direction of the cave. Then I see a familiar figure silhouetted by the disappearing light. He is silently moving, almost as a spirit walks. I draw closer, catlike in my steps. I believe that I go unnoticed for there is no interruption in his fluid movements. I climb a rock so that I can perch and watch him, dreaming of a day that can never be.

Maruq checks his jumper snares. Nal by his side keeps her nose in the wind, alert. I try to remember seeing him at the ceremony, but although I know that he must have been there, I cannot picture him.

So from my perch I watch his graceful, silent movements, like those of the great fleet foot of legend, the legendary animal that lives a solitary life and blesses any one that can catch it. The great fleet foot is said to grant dreams, any dreams. So I dream. I dream of what it would be like to have Maruq's bright eyes light with excitement as Pol's had today. I dream of what it would be like to hear him whisper in my ear, his breath tickling my neck.

As I am dreaming about the impossible, he turns in my direction. Although I am certain that he cannot see me in the fading light, I duck my head. I grow warm with embarrassment from my childishness.

Nal howls. And he returns to his traps. I curl my legs up under my chin, wrapping my arms around them, making myself comfortable so that I can continue to dream for a while longer. Once he disappears from my sight, I slide off of the rock, heading home.

When I reach the lookout rock, I see a blazing fire at the preparation camp. Frenzied celebrants run and dance around it. I see the newly promised couples sneaking off to the meadow. Balek comes toward me in the dark, although he is not wearing his heavy cape, I know that it is him. He must have been looking for me. He carries a water skin in one hand, but by the way he swaggers and rocks as he moves, I doubt that it contains water.

I lean a shoulder against the boulder and await him.

"Where have you been?" His words slur in his mouth, as if someone had filled his mouth with rocks.

"Why? Has Bela been looking for me?"

"No, I have." He stumbles over a rock about a span in front of me, and then stands erect, sucking in the fresh night air, as if it will cure his foolishness.

"Really, why?"

"I wanted you to come join us." He uses his thumb to indicate the men that are dancing around the fire.

"No thanks."

"Why not?"

"I don't feel like celebrating." I shrug.

"Really?"

"Yes, what else would it be?"

"I don't know maybe you have someone you would rather be with?"

"That's absurd."

"Is it? I have seen the way you have been watching that outsider. Ever since you stood watch with him, you watch him like a doe-eyed girl." As he speaks, he closes the distance between us. I can smell the strong drink on his breath.

"That's ridiculous." I protest.

"Really? Then come with me to the meadow and prove it."

"What?" Now, I know he has been drinking. I have never been, nor do I ever want to go to the meadow with a man, having him lead me like a pet. And as far as I know, he has never been either.

"Come with me." Balek takes hold of my wrists with his large hands. His grip is strong, though not hurting me; I know that breaking free is impossible.

"No." I say, making my voice as immovable as the boulder I am backed up against.

"Come, Siira, we are both grown. There is nothing wrong with enjoying ourselves." The commanding voice is his, but the words sound strange in his mouth.

"You are drunk," I say without fear quavering my voice.

"Maybe." He pulls me in closer. I can feel the heat of his body.

"Balek, let go of me," I order, staring boldly into his dark eyes.

"Very well, but first." Before I can make a motion to stop him, he bends down and covers my mouth with his. I can feel his passion and, instead of exciting mine, it repulses me. He thinks that he can make me want him, but he is wrong. He releases my hands. A smug smile is on his face.

I force all my rage down, burying it deep in my stomach. I control every emotion and my voice becomes flat. "Are you finished? Because I am tired."

My words hit him like a blow to the face, for his broad smile disappears, confusion and then indifference taking its place.

"Sorry that I bothered you." He stalks off to the fire, tripping over a rock.

I begin to walk to the steps that go to the cave, my steps slow and deliberate as if I can slow my raging blood throbbing through my veins. I climb the steps and with each step I feel a weight on my shoulders that I do not want to bear.

At the top of the steps, I turn and look down on the gathered people. The men are stomping in circles, dancing around, almost oblivious to anyone else. Some of the younger hunters are leading girls into the meadow. I shake my head, trying to clear my thoughts.

"Fools," I say out loud to no one.

"Yes, little one, they are." I turn and see Grandmother coming toward me.

"I didn't know you were here."

"Yes, well." She doesn't finish, she merely lifts her

shoulders in resignation.

"Is it only me, Grandmother? Am I the only one that is troubled by my path? Is everyone else content with what the Mighty One asks of them?"

"Look at them, do they look content?"

I study the drunken faces of the men dancing around the fire, the hopeful faces of the girls being led off for a night of pleasure, the lustful faces of the hunters leading them. None look content. All seem to want something, something indefinable, the something that I want too.

Love. Acceptance. Peace.

"No, not really."

"No, little one, none are content. This life is full of strife; contentment only comes in Xerena."

"Then why struggle, why try, why not just die and leave this world?"

"Because in all of us the Mighty One has put the desire to live."

I groan. "So the Mighty One would give us a desire for something that we cannot have until after death and only allow us to find it on his terms."

Grandmother rests a hand on my shoulder. "I know it is hard, little one, but we must trust him."

"Yes, Grandmother, I will try." I say it in order to end the lecture and return to my tent.

TO BE CHIEF

14 THE STAMPEDE

What can be taking the two men so long? Surely, they have been able to frighten the herd by now? I mutter a curse as I continue to wait in the bone-chilling rain.

The rain beating on my hood gives a rhythm to match my growing frustration. Father had spotted a herd of ten mammoth earlier and sent Iruq and Kumal to start them stampeding in our direction. None of our hunts have been very successful since the weather has warmed. The mammoth haven't returned in the numbers that we are used to. So the chief has decided to take a chance and hunt in the most dangerous way known to the people, a stampede. Causing a stampede may be the most dangerous of hunting methods, but it is also the most rewarding. Many mammoth can be killed at once, but many hunters can also be killed in the chaos.

My senses focus on my father, more to distract myself from the rain than from any eagerness to herd a mammoth over a cliff. I see him at the crest of the hill; he holds a red stained skin. Once he waves it we are to spring up and begin to drive the beasts over the cliff.

This was the method that our great fathers first devised to kill the large beasts; on this day, in the cold, bone-chilling rain, I question the great fathers' wisdom.

The ground is now almost alive with sound and movement from the approaching herd. I see the first mammoth's dark head crest the hill; my father is several spans away on its strong side. My eyes lock onto the red skin waiting for it to be set in motion. My nerves are raw, my muscles straining in readiness. My father gives the signal, frantically shaking the skin. I spring up, launching my dart in the direction of a massive bull; he veers to his weak side, toward the cliff and his doom.

I send another dart and another, until I see the bull stumble and plunge out of sight. The herd, behind him, begins to rush some of the men, trying to steer away from the deadly cliff. As I ready another dart, I notice Balek dodge behind a boulder as a cow runs past him, leaving her calf to follow her.

Determined to feed my people, I find another bull and try to force him to the cliff, by again throwing several darts at his feet. My blood pounding in my ears, like the celebration drums of the dancers, does nothing to hinder my next dart; a second bull falls, taking another with him. I only hear the trampling tread of the mammoth as they run to their doom or away from it. As the last mammoth runs away, I rush to the cliff to see how many have fallen. Four: two bulls and two cows. It is enough.

The other hunters begin to whoop in victory. I allow a great smile to stretch across my face. I see Balek in his grizzly cape and hear him begin to order the men to throw cords over the cliff so that we can get to our kills quickly. I look for my father, but he is nowhere.

"Balek," I call out. He turns to me. "Did you see my father?"

Balek pauses in his ordering of the men and cocks his head to one side, seeming to think. "No, not since the signal. He is probably still on the hill."

I nod and sprint to the lookout where my father had

been stationed. As I get closer, my world seems to slow, almost stopping completely. I see no movement, I hear no sounds. Something is wrong.

A fluttering catches my eyes. It is a red blur in the rain. The skin, it must be, but where is the chief?

"Father!" I cry out. Terror fills my soul, my eyes scan the landscape, but I see nothing other than the red skin.

I reach the discarded signal and look down the hill. At the base of the hill, the hill that so recently was alive with the stampeding mammoth, the hill that had been the focus of all of the hunters, the men that were so intent on taking a good kill home that none of us noticed that our chief, my father, had fallen in the chaos and now lay trampled in the rain drenched grass.

"No!" My mind rebels at the sight. My feet stumble as I run to his side, barely managing to stay upright and not tumble down the hill. Abruptly stopping by the bloody and broken body that so many trampling feet had crushed, I crumple onto the grass next to my father as he lies dying.

I place my hand tentatively on his chest. I feel the slow rising and falling as he struggles to breathe. Blind hope rises in my heart and I lay my head on his chest. I listen to the beating of his heart. It is becoming sporadic and sluggish.

I search his face. He is almost unrecognizable. The bruises and cuts distort his familiar features.

"Father?" My tears stream down my face, mixing with the rain.

His eyes flicker open. The tawny color, alive with light and fire just yesterday, are dull with pain.

A strange gurgle escapes his lips; I bring my ear down closer to his mouth, trying to understand his last message.

"My cuff," he sputters. "My cuff."

I reach down to the golden cuff that encircles his wrist. I work the sign of his leadership off of him.

"You are chief now." His eyes focus on my wrist.

My mind fights the confusion, trying to make sense of

his words and actions. As if he knows my struggle, he strains, sputtering out a few more words. "Put it on."

I slip it around my wrist, but it is so large on me that it falls to the ground, splattering mud as it lands.

"It doesn't fit, Father . . . I can't . . . Don't go. Hold on."

He shakes his head, "You are chief," he repeats.

I pick the cuff back up, wiping off the mud. I turn it over in my hand. It will never stay around my wrist. How am I to wear this symbol of leadership?

Impetuously, I push the sleeve of my jacket up, baring my arm. "Yes, Father." I push the cuff onto my upper arm and it fits tightly around my hard muscle.

A light flickers in his eyes. "Good."

I watch as he breathes a last breath, and then he is gone.

Grief washes over me. I am alone. The Mighty One has taken my father and now I must face the men, alone.

"Is he gone?" Balek's deep voice asks.

I stare up at him. I am not certain when he had joined us, but he is here now.

"Yes." I stand, trying to convey calm while inwardly I am longing to scream, to run, to die.

The grief in Balek's eyes at my words weakens my resolve to be emotionless, and I allow him pull me into his arms. I lean on him, trying to gather strength in this moment of solitude, provided by his strong arms. Then I hear the other hunters approaching; and I push away from him, not wanting to look weak.

"We must take the chief's body back to the village and we must prepare our kill," I say.

"I will care for the mammoth; you take your father back to the people."

"So be it." My voice is strange in my ears, void of emotion.

Balek runs back up the hill, shouting to the men, preparing to lead in the work of cutting up our kills for transportation back to the cave. I see two men coming toward me from behind, Iruq and Kumal. They are coming to join in the work, but instead I order them to build a sled to carry our fallen chief.

"A dark day." Iruq says as he looks down on my father's lifeless form.

"Yes." I agree with him, swallowing my fear.

The death boat rocks gently in the water, tethered by a length of cord to a large black boulder. I stare at my father's lifeless body, wrapped tightly in furs, his face covered by the hood of his heavy coat. I watch him, willing him to sit up, to open his eyes, to flash a lively smile at me, but knowing that he will not, that the Mighty One has once again taken from me a love.

Boku's voice drones like the annoying buzz of an insect on a wet day, speaking the traditional farewell to our chief. As the death drums beat, I untie the cord, sending my father forever away, away to the blue beyond, away to Xerena. To the place that lies beyond this life, to peace, and to those that the Mighty One has taken before, to my mother, to my brothers, to a myriad of our people; he now embarks on his last journey.

"In Xerena, the sky is the blue of the meadow flowers. In Xerena, the tall green grass moves in the warm breeze. The forest lives with all of the beautiful and majestic creatures, in Xerena. Every day is a feast at the Mighty One's banquet, everyday full of joy at the Mighty One's side. An eternal life of ease and comfort awaits all." The soft chanting comes from Grandmother. She assures the people that our beloved chief will be at peace. If Xerena is real, that is.

As the boat vanishes from my sight, I turn to find myself alone with Grandmother. All the others have returned to the cave. A groan of pain escapes her lips as she turns to leave.

Wearied by age, her steps are short and shuffled; wearied by grief, I match her stride.

No words pass between us; I have nothing to say.

When we arrive at our tent, the fire is long cold. I sink down to the hard, cold stone floor, allowing the chill to run through my body, letting it creep into my heart.

Grandmother kneels down next to me and reaches her hand out to rub my back.

"Siira, little one." Grandmother's voice is soothing.

Little one? Yes, for one more day I could be young again, a little one to be protected and loved, to be rocked to sleep by a lullaby. I curl around her, longing for comfort from the pain in my chest, my throat, my being. She begins to sing a song that tells of Xerena, a song meant to comfort the grieving, soothing notes strung together, a kind of drug.

"Sleep, sleep, beautiful child,
Sleep, sleep, beautiful child,
Peaceful in the grass of Xerena.

"Dream, dream, beautiful child,
Dream, dream, beautiful child,
Safe under the skies of Xerena."

I allow it to lull me to sleep with visions of unearthly beauty.

15 THE GRIZZLY CLAW

The next morning I dress, fastening my token belt around my waist and sliding my father's cuff onto my arm. I grab my throwing stick and darts, more out of mindless habit than anything else. As I pass the tents, I hear the hushed sounds of men and women exchanging early-morning endearments. Living in such close quarters with all of the families, only having the privacy afforded by layers of fur, leaves very little to the imagination when it comes to intimacy between a man and his woman. I suppose I know less than most, since my mother died when I was so very young.

I descend the worn stairs to the valley floor and follow the trail through the hills to the high river. This river originates at the great ice wall that juts up many hundreds of spans into the gray sky, cutting us off from the rest of the world. The water from the river flows freely at the beginning of the hunts, rushing, too quickly for anything but a grizzly claw to stand in. By the Great Light Celebration it has slowed to a steady current, easily navigated.

A giant boulder juts out from the bank. Here my father

taught me to fish and swim. I lean against the rugged surface and allow myself a moment to miss him. I close my eyes and pull his image out from my memories. I see him as he was that morning so long ago, before I fought with Balek at the tree. He is strong and handsome, fearless and determined. Abruptly I push away, opening my eyes, losing the image. I watch the dark water move: slowly, persistently going on, never allowing any obstacle to deter it from its journey to the Great Salt Water.

I, like the river, must move on. But how?

I gather wood and begin a small fire. Stripping my clothes off, I discard them in a pile near enough to the fire to keep them warm. I remove my necklace, laying it on top of the pile. I keep the cuff on my arm, refusing to remove my father's last gift to me. I dive into the frigid water. At first a shock runs through my body, but as I dive and resurface my limbs become accustomed to the icy temperature, becoming numb. I welcome the sensation.

I plunge again, kicking to the bottom of the pool, scooping up a handful of sand, dropping it back to the bottom as I push myself back up to the surface. My head and shoulders shoot out of the water, throwing my head back, sending water spraying all around me, a miniature rain shower.

I cannot change the past and so I must move on, like the river, but how?

I plunge again, settling at the bottom, sitting there, allowing my lungs to burn with the lack of air. I could stay here. I could just leave it all and end my journey. As I contemplate the possibility, every face of every person that I have lost rushes in rapid succession, followed by a stream of every face of every hunter, every woman, and every child that I will leave. I would be leaving them, like a selfish coward. My father's face comes to me again and I know that I cannot disappoint him. I push myself up again, gulping the air as I surface.

I hear a rustling of leaves near the shore, a low moan. Something large shifts its weight, alerting me to imminent danger. I am fully aware of my utter vulnerability, caught in the pool, weaponless. I hope that my fears do not materialize; I hope it is just a bushy tail, and that my ears are playing games with me, but I am not blessed.

The monster lumbers out, a grizzly claw, as tall as a full-grown man to its shoulder, doubling in height when he rears up onto his hind legs, sniffing the area. I hope that he cannot smell me, but I know the hope is blind. I must get to my darts, before he gets too close.

Taking a deep breath, I submerge slowly, so as not to draw the grizzly's attention. Kicking both of my legs at once, I cross the pool underwater. Once I emerge, he is sure to see me. So, like a sea mammoth, I shoot out of the water and onto the shore. Dripping wet, I run to my throwing stick and darts. I hear the monster begin to charge, gaining speed as he comes around on land toward me. I dare not waste time by looking behind me, so I load a dart onto my throwing stick, then turn to find my attacker. He is too close.

Rushing at me like a moving boulder, dark and broad, he is a mere three spans from me. I look into his black eyes and know that soon I will slip into darkness, joining my father before I can fulfill his desire, producing an heir to his line. The line will die with me.

I close my eyes, drop my weapon, and put my hands to my side, waiting for the death blow. But it does not come.

I open my eyes when I hear the grizzly moan in pain.

A swift, small dart pierces his shoulder, then another. He moans again, rearing up to his monstrous height, turning to face the unseen attacker. I look for the source of my salvation. From the trees comes another small dart sinking deeply into the grizzly's neck, but three darts are not enough. Five more come in rapid succession, clustering around the first, and then the grizzly drops to his front paws, groaning. He lies down and bellows again. The sound shakes my soul. I recognize the pain that produces it, the pain that I feel at the loss of my father is voiced by this dying monster, dying at my feet.

I watch as his chest heaves one last time; the monster can do no more harm.

Stunned by the fact that I still breathe, I stand motionless. My mind races, trying to decipher what has happened. I focus on one of the darts that saved me. It is half the size of one of mine and the ends, that stick out from the grizzly, have three feathers attached to them. Only one man of the people knows how to use this weapon: Maruq.

He emerges from the woods surrounding the river and, without glancing at me, he whistles to his wolf. Nal trots out from the trees, a jumper in her mouth. He and his companion move to the fire; and then squatting next to it with his back to me, he takes a stick and stirs the embers, bringing them back to life. He tosses a couple of nearby logs onto it. I am mesmerized. He has saved my life.

A wind moves my damp hair across my back, sending a chill through my body, reminding me that I am naked. My eyes flit from Maruq to my clothes lying near him. I sneak up behind him, ready to spring to a bush if he turns unexpectedly in my direction, although part of me doubts that he would attempt something so juvenile. I reach out my arm and gather my clothes. Clutching my warm clothes to my chest, I back away to a large bush on my strong side. Concealed behind its branches, I pull on the warm clothing.

When I return, fully clothed, Nal's ears perk up and her head turns in my direction. She appraises me, and then as though I am an insect, she dismisses my presence. Maruq sits next to her, lazily roasting a couple chunks of meat from the grizzly. Settling down opposite him, I wonder how he came to be here when I needed him.

"I saw the fire," Maruq says, his lop-sided grin across his handsome face, and turns the meat.

I stare across at him, astonished that he has read my

mind and uncomfortable under the gaze of his bright blue eyes, eyes that have seen me exposed and weak. The flames dance between us, leaping red and yellow, the reflection in his eyes giving the appearance of an understanding beyond his age, as though his soul has aged well beyond his years, perhaps due to the trials that the Mighty One has piled on him.

The juices sizzle down out of the now browned meat. Grizzly is not my favorite, but I am hungry. Deftly removing the meat from the stick he has used to skewer it, he tosses a warm chunk to me.

I catch it and bounce it around in my hand blowing on it for a while before it is cool enough to eat.

"We should take the skin back to the people, it's good fur," I say, breaking the silence.

Maruq nods in agreement, and then finishes his food. Without a word he stands, turning to begin work on the grizzly.

"Before we begin with the grizzly," I say. He stops, giving me his full attention. "I want to ask you if we could keep the part about my bathing a secret. I do not wish to appear weak in front of the other men."

He looks at me with a question in his eyes, and then, as though understanding has come to him, he smiles, an easy, lopsided smile. "Certainly." He looks at Nal. "Guard."

The wolf lopes a few spans away and sits, alert. She sniffs the air and watches the trees. I find myself wishing that I had a companion like her, a loyal friend to be with me always.

"In my pack," I hear Maruq. He must have asked for something.

"What?" I say looking at him. He has crawled under the grizzly's arm, waiting for me to help.

"My blade. It is in my pack."

I go to the large skin pack that he uses to carry everything he needs while out scouting. The blade is in an outside pouch made especially for it. I grab it and join him.

"She must be a great help."

"Who?" He looks at me, a smile playing at the corner of his mouth as he strains under the weight.

"Nal," I say, looking at her guarding us. "She must help when you feel alone."

Readjusting the grizzly's arm slightly, his eyes flash to her and then back to me. He studies me with his calm blue eyes, his face expressionless, as if he listens to a voice that only he hears, "You are not alone."

His words warm my heart, and I smile at him. I make a long clean slit down the arm and side. Maruq moves to the hind leg and I continue the cutting. We work silently as we undress the grizzly, each one knowing what the other needs and doing it. We never fumble or cross purposes. When he reaches out to pull the skin, I reach for the corresponding piece, pulling it, separating the dark jacket from the hard muscle. I match my pace with his, easily falling into his relaxed rhythm, it seems second nature to me.

By midday, we have skinned the monster without a word. Once the skin is folded and bound with a cord, ready for the return, I glance over at Maruq. He is covered in grime and I know that I am a reflection of him. I lift my chin and turn my gaze to the pool. A smile spreads across my face. I run toward the cold water, full of excitement. Impetuously, I plant my hands on the ground throwing my legs up and over me. Landing firmly I plant my feet and shoot up into the air, flipping into the deep pool.

I surface and find Maruq staring at me. He stands in his characteristically relaxed stance, his strong, lean arms crossed. His lopsided smile beaming. "That was amazing."

"Come, clean off." I say and plunge again, trying to calm my racing heart. It only takes a moment before I see him swim past me, kicking in long fluid motions. Kicking back up, I swim toward the bank. But before I can emerge, I feel a hand close around my foot. He tugs on me as though to ask me to join him. Instantly, I take a breath and dive. He turns and I follow, knowing that with every movement more of the grime comes off of me. No longer able to hold my breath I swim to the surface. I scan the shore and see Nal howling and barking from the bank. I want to stay in the water and forget about the ceremony, but soon the cold forces us out.

As we warm by the dying fire, I savor the moment. The quiet comfort of it. I do not have to be more than just me. Right now there is no training, no hunting, no expectations. I look across the fire and see Maruq scratching Nal behind the ear, affirming her for her job well done.

"Why don't you hunt with the others?"

He looks up at me and shrugs. "My ways are different."

"But you are one of us."

"Not everyone thinks so." He says, his melodic accent a little thicker than normal.

16 LOYALTY

Climbing a large boulder at the arena, the one that my father had clumsily jumped from, I sit, tucking my knees tightly under my chin. The gray sky above me threatens more rain. I look upward, daring the Mighty One to make it rain, soaking Sacred Point, dousing the fire. I hope he will take me up on it, making it rain so much that the ceremony must be postponed. Today, I become Chief.

I rub my bare arms, my hand catching at the cold metal encircling my strong arm, my father's cuff. I stare at it. The herd of beautiful strange beasts rushing forward, their long hair caught in motion, nostrils flaring. Dust billows around their feet. The creatures seem to be running from something.

I want to run, run from my pain, from the finality of the day, away from my future, but I can't. I am now Chief.

The brief joy I had found at the pool with Maruq had quickly faded once we returned to the cave and the reality of my duty greeted me.

I only have one duty, the survival of the people; but it looms large and impossible before me. I pull my legs in tighter, using all of my strength to press them against me. I have only seen seventeen annuals, how am I to lead?

My father's words rush back to me. "The Mighty One never gives us a job without giving us the ability to do it."

If you have given me this job, can I trust that you will help me?

As the wind blows around me, I hear the rustling of leaves, I hear flyers call back and forth to each other, and insects buzzing, but I hear no answer.

The Great Light is high overhead, telling me that soon I will be expected to take my place. I release my legs and stretch up tall. Throwing my arms behind me, I twist my body around and land on the grass.

Back at the cave, Grandmother gathers my long black hair, tying it with a cord at the base of my neck, the long tail trailing down my back. I dress in my best leggings and a beaded sleeveless tunic, my blades at my sides, my cuff shining on my upper arm. I don't feel like a chief, I feel like myself, small and foolish.

I don't know the ceremony to make a successor a chief, and so Grandmother prepares me as we walk to Sacred Point, her voice softly rasping.

"Maruq will give you the curly horn. You have seen your father perform the sacrifice many times, but this time you are petitioning for yourself, not the people.

"Directly following the sacrifice, Boku, as head elder, will lead the procession back to the cave, where you are to take the chief's chair. Look commanding and in control; don't show any fear. Your loyal men will pay you homage of some sort, showing that they stand with you. Boku will then burn the token of the old chief and you will be our new leader."

She dangles my father's token in front of me. The familiar necklace dances in the air. The beautifully carved fleet foot is as much a part of my picture of my father as his tawny eyes. Now, Boku will burn it and so say a final farewell to his spirit.

I take it in my strong hand and lift it over my head,

laying it next to my heart, under my necklace. I nod at her instructions, not really understanding all that she says, almost as if she is speaking in the voice of a bushy tail, merely chattering gibberish at me.

The drums begin, and I give her a quick squeeze of a hug before leaving her comfort. I stand in my father's place by the altar. I see Maruq's eyes, his encouraging smile. I take the beast from him. I go through the motions, although I do not distinctly remember performing them.

After the sacrifice, I fall in step behind Boku. I take a step with each beat of the slow drums. I see the story fire. It blazes, leaping with joy to the ceiling of the cave; the smoke dances, escaping through the crack above it.

The procession continues to my father's great skin chair. It towers over me, antlers decorating the back of it. Once as a child I remember looking at my father presiding over a dispute, the antlers appearing to me to have grown out of his own skull. I had laughed then, but not now. I sit in the skin chair, wondering if any child sees what I had seen. Then, as Boku takes his place in front of me, I feel small and insignificant, as though a bushy tail parades as a grizzly claw. But, remembering Grandmother's instructions, I try to look fierce, chiefly.

Dancers begin to move around the fire, spinning and chanting to the rhythm of the drum, trying to celebrate the life of the former chief, giving thanks to the Mighty One for the new chief.

I try to focus on them, but find myself scanning my people. I am looking for Bela, for Balek, for Maruq. Instead, I catch sight of Iruq and find him eyeing me, as though a plague has been sent to destroy the people, as though I am incapable of anything good, only bound to bring the people to catastrophe. Part of me, that part that has always felt my father was insane for trying to make me a man, agrees with Iruq; but I try to remember my blood line, my father's instructions, and sit taller, glaring at him.

My seat is being lifted high upon the shoulders of four of my fellow hunters. Balek is in the front to my strong side; Pol is opposite. I do not know who is behind. I don't dare look. As they carry me around the fire, I realize that these men have pledged their loyalty to me, lifting me high in honor. These men will follow me in the path that I choose for the people, for their future, a future that I will now direct.

My seat is replaced at the head of the gathering. Boku addresses me.

"Siira, successor to our fallen chief, do you promise to lead the people in the way that the Mighty One has directed, to seek their good and not your own, and to die if called upon in your duty?"

A lump forms in my throat, cutting off my ability to speak. Silence reigns for a moment before I am able to swallow and utter my response. "I so promise."

"Then I proclaim you Chief." He holds out his hand. For a moment, I am uncertain what he is requesting, then I remember the last part of the ceremony is to burn the chief's token. I lift it off from around my neck, pressing it tightly with my fingers as though to imprint my hand with its form, then hand it over to Boku.

He walks to the story fire and drops the antler token into the flames. The drums continual beating stops in silent homage to a great chief.

Boku watches the fire, as though meditating while the token burns. When he turns back he looks boldly at me, and then lowers his eyes to the ground in deliberate submission to my new authority. He kneels. All of the hunters follow his lead and soon all the men are acknowledging me Chief, at least outwardly.

When the fire no longer blazes, when the people have mostly returned to their homes, when I believe I am alone, I step away from my chair. I walk to the embers of the fire and stir them, hoping to see a fragment of my father's token. But it is gone.

"Good journey, Father," I whisper the words, almost a prayer.

"Yes, good journey."

My heart races, startled by the deep rumbling voice behind me, but I turn slowly as though I knew he was there.

"Balek, you should know better." I want to appear indifferent, and so I smile.

He struts forward, a smile playing on his broad face. His torch dances red light in his dark eyes. He drops to the floor next to my chair, fixing the torch in a hole by him. He lies back, reclining on an elbow.

I walk over and join him on the ground, pulling my legs in tightly to my body, resting my chin on my knees. I stare at the story fire, enjoying the comfortable feeling of friendship.

"I wanted to speak to you of the future," he says.

"The future," I repeat, giving the words little thought. My future is not up for discussion, for it has been decided for me.

"Yes, our future."

"Our future?" He has caught my attention.

"Yes, Siira, I want you to be my woman."

"Woman?" Absurd, a woman, I have just been made Chief of the people. I can't seem to control the flood; my emotions spill out, they come loudly out from me in laughter. As I laugh, I find relief from all of the turmoil of the last few days, I feel some control again, and so I laugh loud and long. Tears begin to roll down my cheeks. I reach a hand up to wipe at them.

Then I see Balek's face. In the torchlight, it is distorted, but he is clearly hurt by my reaction.

I calm myself, wiping the tears away. I reach my strong hand out to him and run my fingers through his loose black hair. Resting my hand on his strong chest, I say, "A woman, Balek. I am no woman; I am Chief."

He pulls away from my touch and looks at the ground. I watch as he sucks in a ragged breath. He raises his head and looks straight into my eyes. "I don't give up easily, Siira, you know that. One day you will need a man, if only to have the heir your father so desperately wanted, and I will be here, waiting."

"Balek, please try to understand."

He pushes himself up. In a fluid motion, he takes the torch and walks off, leaving me alone with the dying story fire and my thoughts.

17 THE JOINING CEREMONY

Since my ceremony, my sleep is plagued with dreams, dreams of the past, my father, mother, and brother, of Balek, Bela, and even Maruq. All visit me in turn, taunting me, asking impossible things from me. I wake each night covered in sweat.

No longer can I find leisure at the arena, or the tree. I am Chief and I am in charge. I must lead. It seems that every problem is to be easily solved by coming to the chief. I listen and try to help, but they demand I solve a petty dispute with a word, using wisdom I do not yet possess. More often than not I defer to the elders, mainly to the chief elder, Boku, who seems to relish my dependence.

Today, before the weather confines us to the cave, my new role requires that I lose a friend. Bela is to join with Pol and I am to officiate.

As we had at the beginning of the hunts we stand at Sacred Point, the late blossoms cover the rocks and women. The expectant men appear eager; the promised women look vulnerable.

Pol nervously shifts his feet back and forth.

I nod, signaling that the men are to move, standing next

to their chosen woman. Pol moves to Bela. Kumal moves to Latiqa. Sinaq moves to Tirsa. Each woman is scrubbed as clean as a new baby, pink and rosy. I watch Bela. Her smile, one that would crack her face if it was any larger, beams at Pol as she takes his hand.

The other men and women join hands; each one that pledged has made it to this day, no one was lost during the hunts. None of the pledged, that is.

The drums begin to beat, a slow rhythm that seems to mimic the sound of a heart.

In my hands, long thin skin cords that will bind these men and women wait. They will be bound again, but now instead of only a promise of love, a solemn pledge will be proclaimed by each before their love is consummated this night.

I stand in front of Pol and nod. Pol begins his pledge, "I will be your man, protecting and providing for you until death takes one or both of us. I will lead our family in the ways of the Mighty One, honoring and keeping the traditions of the father's. This I pledge to you."

Bela returns, tears threatening to spill from her eyes. "I will be your woman, serving and honoring you until death takes one or both of us. I will take care of our family in the way prescribed by the Mighty One, teaching our ways to any children in order to keep the traditions of the fathers. This I pledge you."

During her pledge, I feel as though someone has pierced me with one of my blades, cutting deep into my heart. I am losing a friend, really truly losing her. The separation has been coming slowly, in steps and now it is finally complete.

Bela and I have always been close, as close as sisters, yet now she is moving on, joining with a man and beginning a new part of her journey. I have a new path as well, and we shall never be as we were. As I look at her I am certain that she has no thought of me and my cares, she only sees Pol's face, eyes alight with expectation, smile beaming in pride and love for her.

Clearing the emotion from my throat, I finish the ceremony. "Pol, this is your woman; Bela, this is your man. The people will honor this union and help you in your journey. The Mighty One protect you both." I wrap the cord around their entwined hands, joined now for life. "I bind you to each other with this cord, as you have bound yourselves with your words."

I move on to the next couple and listen to their pledges, twine their hands, make the final pronouncement, and smile. These last two joinings are not as emotionally charged for me and I am able to easily smile my approval on each couple. "I present to the people our new families." The people whoop in approval, dancing around the couples. They dance the entire way back to the story fire with the couples lifted high on their shoulders.

I walk slowly, watching the procession. My father's words of promise to the elders come to me. "She will be joined at the next ceremony, with the others, after the hunts."

But I am not among them. Whatever plans my father had, the Mighty One overruled.

I take my place in my chair, newly draped with the grizzly skin Maruq and I had brought back. I watch the people carrying the newly pledged around the fire. I run my strong hand through the dark fur as my mind tries to gain a firm hold on my emotions. I fear that instead of looking joyful as I should I only manage indifference.

Pol and Bela are placed next to my chair on the floor of the cave. Soft mammoth furs are spread out for each of the honored couples tonight. The feast begins with roasted mammoth and fleet foot, dried grizzly, and the last of the fresh berries. Taking a large wooden platter that has been filled for Pol and Bela and lifting it high up toward the ceiling of the cave, I dutifully make a petition of blessing for the couple's first night together.

I look to my strong side, holding the platter out to them. Pol and Bela sit lost in a world of their own, as though all of the noise of the dancing and drums around them is happening in a far distant land, as though they two were loving flyers surrounded by a vast forest of nothing instead of being one of the main attractions of the evening. I loudly clear my throat, drawing Pol's attention, as well as some remarks from the nearby hunters.

Pol takes the platter and offers the food to his woman. Bela eagerly takes some of the meat and begins to feed him from her hand. He then does the same for her. Unabashedly they display their feelings for all but the blind to see.

What would that be like? To be free to lose yourself in the eyes of a man who loves you? I cannot imagine never having to worry about how I appear to the people. To love as Bela loves Pol is to be open, to show weakness. As Chief, an unconventional Chief, I cannot do that.

I offer the other couples their platters and then take my own. The people are in a festive mood and soon all of the sounds are happy ones. Children run and chase each other around the story fire, causing some young mothers to panic. The hunters share boastful stories over some of Tomu's medicine. The women chatter stories back and forth, laughing and caring for their families at the same time. I take it all in, watching each scene in turn. A feeling of awe and dread settles in my stomach as I know that I am to lead them.

Grandmother is sitting on a stone telling a story to the young eager children. I know which story it is because it is the story that she always shares during this celebration, the story of the first people. It is a wonderful story, beautiful and full of hope. The Mighty One, after having made all things, surveyed his world and saw that it was lacking and so he took some earth and formed the man, carefully placing each feature. Then he did the same for the woman, making her a perfect helper for the man. The Mighty One then set them in a beautiful place, much like what Xerena is said to be.

As a child, I would listen intently to every detail. The Mighty One seemed to care so much for the man and woman in this story. I believed that he cared for us, that he had a beautiful plan for us, but then tragedy struck and my belief in that plan waned. It slowly died piece by piece with each new tragedy, as though despair were a beaded pouch waiting for the placement of the final bead to finish the design. The design of despair in my life received its last bead when my father died.

Once the meal is finished and mothers have taken the young ones home, Pol leans over to Bela and whispers in her ear. A flush creeps up her neck and into her cheeks, a flush that I know is not caused by the heat of the story fire. Unable to wait any longer, Pol sweeps Bela into his arms, eager to be alone with his woman. For their first seven days together, the couples retreat to small rooms farther back in the cave; the rooms have been used for many moons by the newly joined. It is the only chance at solitude that they will get here in our large cave. Each man chooses a room, and then he prepares it for his woman, stocking it with food, lining it with furs, and storing firewood for warmth. In this way, the couple only needs to concern themselves with each other.

I can see that all of the couples have already forgotten the people that surround them and only need to physically remove themselves.

A few of the men notice Pol's movements and begin to shout out encouragements, but he only waves them quiet as he departs with his woman nestled in his arms

Others leave the story fire, men and women that want to spend time alone on this night, the night that reminds everyone what it means to be loved, to have one person that you care for above all others, and yet I have never felt so alone. I have no desire to return to my oversized tent, filled only with the sounds of Grandmother sleeping, so I continue to watch what remains of the revelry. I pull on my necklace, fidgeting with the beadwork on it, finding comfort in the feel of it. Iruq, Lotik, and a few others stand around in a loose circle a few spans from my chair. The sound of their deep laughter echoes off the cave.

A lone figure moves toward the group; it is Balek. His token cape makes him appear twice the size of any of the other hunters. He easily joins in with the laughter. Iruq apparently is telling a tale and, although he stands in the center of group, he is no longer the center of attention, for all of the men seem to acknowledge Balek's presence.

This grizzly of a man commands the hunters' respect and attention; they seem to wish to emulate his actions. At the end of Iruq's tale, Balek throws in a deep genuine laugh, followed by everyone else's laughter. As he calms down, he glances in my direction. Our gazes meet and he leaves the hunters and moves to me.

My pulse races as I remember our last encounter and my hopes are that he will not bring up his hopes again.

"It was a fine ceremony, my chief." He pushes back the hood of his cape, exposing his face. The firelight plays across it, casting strange playful shadows that dance.

"Thank you." I remain in my seat. Striving for stoicism, I continue to finger the medallion.

"May I join you?"

I indicate the now vacant fur on my strong side. He removes his cape and sits. A few uncomfortably silent moments pass. And then he breaks the silence.

"You do realize this is a celebration?" He nods at the fire.

"Of course." I can tell by his tone that he is baiting me, setting a trap for me, getting me to do something that I would not otherwise wish to do.

"Then why are you sitting here alone?"

"Maybe I like being alone?" I say, replacing the necklace inside my tunic.

"But do you not think that it is strange for the chief to look like an old sea mammoth during the celebration of her closest friend's joining?" A fire dances in his black eyes.

I raise an eyebrow, as if to tell him that I do not appreciate his comparison. "I am not a sea mammoth."

"No, you are not, so come join the men."

"I do not wish to join in the revelry."

"I know," he pauses, a smile spreads across his face, "but as a man, you must."

I stare hard into his mocking face. Taking a deep, exaggerated breath, I push myself up and stride toward the hunters, forcing my sorrows down as I conjure a smile.

Balek quickly catches up with me and we join the men together. I laugh and make merry, acting the part that has been thrust upon me, all the while wishing I were in my tent listening to Grandmother snore.

18 THE CHALLENGER

On the eve of the darkest day of the annual, the day before the Mid-snow Celebration, I feel restless, wandering aimlessly among the people looking for something to do. But it seems that no one has a dispute, or a complaint. No matters need my attention. And so I walk like a spirit among my people, smiling at those who glance my way.

"Good day, Natiq." I smile at the older woman. I have always admired her, her kindness and wisdom second only to Grandmother's. She raised my two closest friends and was like a mother to me.

"Good day, my chief."

Boku's woman stands by a pot of blue dye.

"Are you making something?" I lean over, studying the contents.

"Bela is with child and so I am starting a gift for my daughter's first child."

"I had not heard that she was with child." My voice betrays my surprise.

Without the slightest pause in her work, Natiq says, "She does not yet know."

"Then how . . ."

"I just know." Her voice full of confidence.

Of all the women of the people, Natiq has assisted more than her fair share of babes into the world, and so I believe her.

"I will keep your secret." I smile and leave her to her work.

I come to the story fire and see Grandmother sitting, telling stories to the young ones again. I find my chair and settle into its warmth.

"Grandmother, what is beyond the story fire?" A curious child points to the back of the cave.

"There are some rooms for the newly joined couples." She rasps, and gives a slight cough.

"And beyond that?"

Grandmother's face becomes very solemn, almost intimidating, and yet in her eyes I see a gleam that gives away her secret. "No one knows, little one, but once when I was a child like you, a strong and brave hunter decided that he would travel to the end of our cave. He packed a large pack and took a great torch with him for light. All gathered to watch him go. I decided to creep behind him unseen to share in his adventure, but as I came to the room beyond the rooms set apart for the newly joined ones, I heard a terrifying scream. The sound of it made my heart thump in my chest and my head swim in circles. I have never heard such a sound of terror since then. But I knew at that moment the great hunter was lost to us forever."

"He never came back?" The child's face is a mixture of awe and fear.

"No, he never did."

I shake my head in amusement, remembering when Grandmother told me the same tale. It was very effective in keeping me from exploring and becoming lost.

I stare into the black unknown at the back of the cave. How far does it go? Our mountain, although not the largest in the range, is much larger than our cave. What secrets are kept in the darkness? I glance over to Grandmother, a fleeting thought of asking permission flits across my mind.

"I do not need permission, I am Chief." I murmur.

No longer will I stay away. I am Chief and the cave is my domain. And so, rashly, I stand and stalk off to my tent.

Because I could walk into the darkness for days before turning back, since no one knows for certain how extensive our cave is, I gather food and water into my pack. Shrugging it onto my shoulders, I test its weight. I grab a charred stick from the fire pit in order to mark my path as I delve into the unknown. I duck out from my tent and glance about for anyone to stop me. I see no one. Then I take a torch from the wall and quicken my cat-like steps to the black unknown.

As I approach the places beyond knowledge, a cold shiver running the length of my spine cautions me, but I ignore it and continue on my quest.

The deeper I delve into the dark, the brighter my single torch becomes, casting red glowing light on spaces that have never seen light, heating areas that have only known the chill of dark. The thought excites me. I feel more alive than I have in the moons since my father's accident, life courses through me born from the adventure.

I reach down and mark my first stone with my marking stick, then turn, following a trail that seems to lead downward into the heart of the mountain. Pillars of stone rise from the floor and hang from the roof, like monstrous teeth in the jaws of the cave. Strange stones sparkle like light on water, shimmering brilliantly.

Mesmerized by the wonder surrounding me, I journey as though in a trance. Eager to see all I can before I must turn and go back, back to being something I am not.

A voice in my head constantly warns of danger, urging me to turn back. Yet, another part of me urges me into the black unexplored region. I mark another stone, quieting the voice that tells me I will get lost.

I hear a skittering of rocks behind me. Is there someone,

something, following me?

I freeze in my tracks waiting for another sound, but after several moments I hear nothing. I turn, searching the blackness behind me for evidence of another light. Reasoning that if someone followed me, he would also need light, but I see nothing.

It was probably. . . I don't offer any suggestion, for all of my thoughts seem utterly preposterous. I decide to remain vigilant but to continue on.

My stomach begins to protest at the lack of nourishment, and so I pull out some of the dried berries I had brought in my pack. Setting my torch in a crevice between two boulders, I survey the room around me. I see more teeth hanging from the ceiling and jutting up from the floor. The rocks here glisten like water in the light. I close my eyes recalling the farewell we gave my father. I see his boat rocking gently on the shimmering gray water. A tear rolls down my cheek.

The sound of dripping water reawakens my curiosity, pulling me into the present. I cannot see it, but it sounds near. I stand, taking my torch, and walk forward about ten spans. Before me is a black pool. I see it now, water drips from the ceiling of the cave into the black surface of the pool. The soft plopping noise peacefully echoes around me, as though the mountain cries, collecting its tears here in this pool.

A desire to touch the water rises within me. I make my way over to the pool, without another thought I plunge my hand swiftly into the water. It is warm. I lift my fingers to my lips, tasting it. The water bites my tongue.

I lean my hip against the stone encircling the pool. Raising the torch high, allowing the orange and white heat to reflect off of the black surface, I look in to see my face.

My broad cheekbones, common among the people, are highlighted by the firelight. My large tawny eyes, eyes like my father's, reflect the heat of my torch, but give off no heat of their own. The corners of my full mouth droop. Every feature, including my hair, long, soft, and black as the cave around me, speaks of sorrow.

I look sad, though I thought I was enjoying myself, but I suppose my sorrow is too deep to be relieved by a mere afternoon's walk.

I have to change my demeanor; if I am unable to control my face, how can I control anything? This weakness must be overcome; a chief of the people cannot be weak. So I stare at my reflection, carefully sculpting my expression, determination replacing the depression in my eyes, my mouth straightening into a hard line, my nostrils flaring defiantly. I work until I am satisfied. I memorize the feel of the muscles in my face. Practicing, then forcing the expression to become as hard as stone, as if my face were a piece wood that Balek carved, working it here, changing it there. I carve a hard look of superiority in each feature, a look that would tell the other men that I know what I am doing, a look that will inspire confidence from my people, a look that I can easily conjure up even if I feel small and weak. Then I set it as though my face were a stone mask.

I turn from the pool, leaving my weakness behind and work my way back into the main room of the cave. The return walk seems much shorter than my descent. Surveying the room, I spy a group of men gathered, in heated discussion. I pull on my mask as I approach them, only to discover that the argument is about me, specifically my ability to lead the people.

"She is the chosen successor of the chief," Pol states.

"Yes, but she is a young woman, barely proven in the hunt," Iruq says, unaware of my presence in the shadows.

I move silently behind him, making sure that some of the men see me before I speak. "Do you challenge my right, Iruq?"

He spins so quickly at my voice that he nearly falls over. Regaining his balance, he puffs his chest out, a gesture I am certain meant to intimidate me. "Not your right, your ability."

"Do you wish to lead the people?" I stare at him with my newly acquired expression.

"I believe that I would make a good leader of the people."

"Are you willing, then, to approach the council with your challenge?"

He looks around him at the men gathered, smiling, as though I had just given him his dearest desire, and says, "Yes."

"Good, come." I say and turn on my heels. I see Balek, his expression showing concern, and I hear him fall in behind me.

Iruq's long stride easily keeps pace with my quick steps. We find Boku in his tent.

"Boku, Iruq wishes to challenge my leadership," I announce upon interrupting Boku's meal. Remarkably, I make the comment sound as natural as the migrating of the feathered flyers.

"I see." Boku glances at me, and then studies the hunter that is looming behind me. "Ah, so, Iruq, you wish to lead the people?" His tone implies that he is not surprised at all by Iruq's bold challenge.

Iruq crosses his arms across his expansive chest and looks down his nose at me. "Yes, I will prove that a woman's place is in a tent with children."

Although I would love to be free to be in a tent with a man that I love, my blood runs hot at Iruq's dismissive attitude toward women, as if we were only put on earth to make his life easier.

"Is this your wish, Siira, to accept his challenge?"

"Tomorrow at the story fire, before the celebration begins, we shall see who is more able to lead the people," I say, concentrating on Boku's one eye. I do not look at Iruq, but I imagine the satisfied look on his broad face as I leave to return to my tent.

Iruq's challenge means that I must defeat him in combat, hand-to-hand combat, no weapons, only my skill against his skill, my strength against his, which in comparison is nothing. If I am successful, he will be unable to challenge me again, unless I prove myself incompetent. But if I do not properly defeat him, someone else may decide to challenge me.

I need to rest, so I return to my tent. I take my pack off and lay it by my bed. I no longer share a room with Grandmother. I have moved into my father's room. I lay down, attempting sleep. I must have drifted off for I am surprised when Grandmother stirs my shoulder in circles waking me.

"You have a visitor."

I smooth my hair back into its tail, and then enter the main room of my tent. I sigh when I see Balek's broad back.

"What do you want?" I ask, perhaps more harshly than necessary.

He stares at me, as if to determine my mindset, as if he can read my mind. Maybe he can, everyone seems to know my thoughts before I do.

"I want to wish you well."

I raise an eyebrow.

"Truly." He looks at me with honest purpose.

"So you think I can beat Iruq?"

"No, that is not what I said, but if I offered to fight him for you, you would refuse, so instead I came with good wishes."

"Well, I may have lost to you before, but I have grown since then."

"Yes, and you do have a few tricks," he pauses. His eyes, as dark as the pool hidden at the back of the cave, fill with doubt. "But what if he catches you, Siira, what then?"

"I won't let him catch me." I snap, pushing down my own fears. "Now, if you'll excuse me, I was taking a nap." I begin to leave, but he catches my wrist in his hand.

"I am sorry, Siira." His deep voice, husky with emotion.

I turn and study his face. I see pain, fear, hope all mixed up in a strange expression.

Letting go of me, he fumbles with his words. "Sorry about your father, about my lack of compassion, about pushing you."

"Balek, you do not need to apologize for anything. I have and always will count you as my friend, my brother." I pat his arm with my strong hand.

A sound at the opening draws my attention. A tall lean figure steps in. His blue eyes lock with mine. They seem clouded with something that has disturbed his composure. His hand rests on his bow string, his fingers plucking at it. Suddenly, the tent seems much smaller.

I move away from Balek toward Maruq worried that something is wrong. The last time I saw Maruq this agitated was when his father never came back.

"What do you want?" Balek's low rumbling voice demands from behind me.

Maruq's hand stills on the bow as he draws in a long slow breath. He looks to Balek. Crossing his arms in front of him, he relaxes his stance, forcing tranquility into his expression. "I came to speak to the chief."

"Well, there she is." Balek grumbles.

I spin around appalled by his behavior, glaring at him. "Thank you, my friend, but Maruq is one of the people as well. And I am Chief. I will see you tomorrow." I say dismissing him.

Balek puffs his chest, crossing his arms, planting his feet, as though he intends to ignore my wish, to stay while I speak with Maruq. Rage boils in me, but I control it, pulling on my mask. I stare at him unblinking and cat-like.

He sighs relenting, stepping closer to me, he bends and places a kiss on my forehead, "I swear, Siira, at times, you look just like your father." His deep voice softly whispers in my ear.

He straightens back up, puts a hard look in his eye and struts past Maruq.

I shake my head. "I am sorry, sometimes he is over protective." I motion toward the fire and the stools near it. Once we are settled, I see that the concern has returned to his eyes, causing them to appear gray. "Now, what is wrong?"

"I overheard some of the men say that you have been challenged."

"Yes, Iruq has challenged me." The gray in his eyes becomes darker, and his hands begin to fidget again. "I face him tomorrow."

"Must you?"

"I am Chief."

He nods in understanding. "Then I will let you get some rest." He stands. "And I will ask that the Great Father keeps you safe."

Although I believe the petition useless, I find that his sentiment warms me, giving me a strange confidence.

I hear the drums start, announcing the beginning of the celebration. The people begin to meander toward the story fire. Instead of taking my place in my chair, I step up next to Boku. Scanning the gathering of the people, I see Kumal, Bela, Pol, Grandmother. I do not see Maruq or Balek. Then I hear a sound behind me on my weak side, a wolf whines. I turn and see Maruq, apparently relaxed except for the drumming of his fingers on Nal's neck. And then Balek moves in behind him, a smile of encouragement of his lips.

"My people," Boku calls out, and my attention snaps back to my task, "our chief has been challenged; as is the tradition passed from our great fathers, the challenge must be met. Siira, do you accept Iruq's challenge?"

I nod, remaining silent, so that my voice will not give

away my fears. I have yet to fight someone using my new technique. I have trained with Balek, but we never had a true rematch.

My challenger steps forward, his bare chest gleams, having been rubbed with oil. Fire dances across his skin as though he is a part of it; he looks fierce, formidable.

"Iruq is it your wish to challenge our chief?"

"Yes." The arrogance of this monstrous man is appalling. I wish to teach him a lesson, the same one that I had been taught by Balek.

"Then let us begin, the winner is decided when only one is left standing." Boku returns to stand among the people, next to Balek.

I keep my chin high, my expressionless mask in place as I approach my challenger. The people move out, forming a circular arena in which the challenge will take place. The drummers beat out a signal, as if to count down to our match. I listen, but when the drums stop, I do not move. I wait for Iruq to attack. He struts about the circle, while I stand still. Some of the men cheer him on, but most of the people are silent, probably thinking it is rude to cheer against someone so obviously outmatched. He finally turns to me, a smug look in his eyes. He charges, lunging forward, massive arms wide, ready to entangle me in a death grip, ready to crush the air out of me, charging headlong like a woolly one horn.

But like a blade-tooth, I quickly, almost in one motion, place the foot of my strong leg on his thigh and my hands on his shoulders, then catapult myself high over his head, flying almost to the cave's ceiling before tucking and returning to land on my feet, silently.

I turn, seeing Iruq kneeling in utter confusion, pushing himself up to his feet. Others around the circle speak in hushed tones of amazement at what they have just witnessed their chief do.

"She flies like a feathered one."

"She is as agile as a blade-tooth."

Forcing the sounds around me out of my ears and focusing solely on Iruq, who is now enraged at being so easily dodged, I await his next move. He again charges, focusing his attention higher, looking me in the eye. I wait until the last moment, then crouch down and roll between his legs.

I hear a deep-throated laugh and know that it is Balek.

I turn to my challenger and see him nervously glancing at the people. A muscle flexes in his jaw as he is determined to catch me, to show that I am unworthy, just a woman. Yet, each time he comes, I am as elusive as a jumper, as agile as a cat. Whatever tactic he tries, I elude him and become more confident.

I cannot simply stay away from him. I must find a way to defeat him and quickly, before I make a mistake, before he catches me. How though, how am I to bring down this hunter? A thought comes to me. If he cannot breathe, he cannot stand.

Deciding to end the monotony of my game, I run at him. Confusion flashes in his eyes. I leap up, tucking into a flip, I land and then place my hands on the ground. I throw my legs up over my head, as I had at the pool. Landing I use all of my momentum to spring up over Iruq and land behind him. I punch myself forward and onto his back. My momentum knocks him forward. As we fall, I encircle his bull neck with my arm, lodging my forearm under his chin. I pull back with my other hand, closing off his air supply.

We hit the ground with great force and the breath that he had in his lungs is forcibly expelled. He thrashes at me with his tree-like arms, but because of his bulky muscles he is unable to reach me. Slowly he loses consciousness. His hands quiet, dropping to the floor. His head lies still, and I loosen my grip. I do not want him dead, and so I listen to his heart. It still beats, slow and strong.

I stand victorious, having proven myself against this challenger. Small and young I may be, but I am able.

19 ANOTHER HUNT

The chill in the air has given way to the warm breath of the time of hunts. The first of the mammoth have returned from their journey back to our lands to have their young and grow fat again.

For the time being, Iruq has conceded to my leadership, but still I feel his eyes watching me and weighing my every move, as though he is a hungry wolf eyeing his prey. But after what happened when he challenged me, he has no choice but to await a mistake on my part.

I led the men from the cave several days ago, but mammoth are scarce. We have not yet seen any. This morning Balek has joined me scouting.

"Have you ever journeyed this far from the cave?" I ask my old friend. I stand high on a cliff. Gusts of wind catch my hair and send tendrils flying in all directions.

"No, but the mammoth have never been so few."

As he says it, I see movement below me. The cliff I stand on extends its giant arms, offering up the level beach below to the Great Salt Water in obeisance. A small herd of eight mammoth meanders below us, grazing peacefully on the sparse grass. Hope swells in my chest.

"We shall bring the men here tomorrow." I watch the unsuspecting beasts, unaware of the imminent danger.

"Are you sure you are ready?" Balek's words are not meant to challenge me, but I glare at him anyway.

"I have no choice, we need this kill." Since Iruq's defeat, my voice has become strange in my ears, terse and clipped, almost angry in every beat.

We return to the camp. The men are restless, some wrestle and some tell stories. Pol and Pire are working with Maruq's wolves. Because of the difficult time I had carrying my allotment of meat, I had asked for Maruq's assistance with some of his wolves. I had hoped that he would come and hunt with the rest of us, but instead he trained a few to work with his wolves so that when we left as a party, he went off on his own with Nal.

Most of the men looked on the wolves as nuisances, extra mouths to feed on the hunt, but as the distance to the cave grew, the necessity of help became clear to all.

Balek gives the report of the herd to the other men and we break camp. Long moons of sitting in the cave, only being able to glory in stories of the past, preparing for future accomplishments, are now over. We have found our prey.

I see Iruq gathering his throwing stick and darts. His pack is heavy with the necessities of the hunt: flints, blades, furs. He is a good hunter and so I choose to give him a role of leadership; in a way, I throw the hungry wolf a bone. "Iruq, I need you and Kumal to guard the hunting party once the kill is taken. I know that cats would love nothing more than to steal some fresh meat."

His eyes focus on me, boring deep, trying to unnerve me. I struggle not to flinch and just stare stone faced at him. "Yes, my chief."

I lay prone on the cliff from which I perched earlier, watching and waiting. Since the herd is below us, I have decided to have half of the men herd the beasts toward the base of cliffs, and the other half will cause a rock slide that will kill the mammoth.

I look back to Balek and the hunters. Each man is positioned with a large pole made from a young tree, angled under a pile of small boulders. When it is time he, and the others, will push on the pole, causing the boulders to plummet to the meadow below, killing the beasts.

I scan the sand for Pol, who is to lead the drive to us. All is ready. I stand and signal Pol to begin driving the beasts our way.

The sound of trampling feet brings to mind the death of my father, but I push down the memories and focus on the task at hand. The men, Balek, Kavok, Sinaq, are pushing, and boulders are raining down to the ground. I run to help Lotik, who is struggling to push down on his pole.

I hear the sound of bones crushing under the weight of the boulders, I hear mammoth cry in pain, I hear hunters whoop in victory; I smell dust, mingled with blood and sweat; I see six mammoth dead, all hunters alive, a successful hunt led by a new chief.

Some of the kill from this hunt will become food for the Hunt Celebration once we return to the cave, a celebration that will give thanks to the Mighty One for his provision during the last annual and looking forward to the new annual, that will proclaim girls to be women, that will remind me of what I am not.

The rest of the kill will be dried and stored for use during the time of snow.

Quickly, our hunting party begins to recover the mammoth and kill the injured ones, who are not yet dead. After I check Iruq's position as guard, I join the others.

The work is hard and my muscles, though strong, soon tire after the inactivity of the time of snow. Yet I push on, for the chief cannot sit and rest, no matter how tempting the thought.

Soon we have freed enough to begin packing the kill back to the cave. Balek wordlessly loads the sleds.

Pol moves toward Balek. I watch the two brothers for a moment before joining them.

"The wolves are a wonderful idea, but Wolf Boy should have come too. I can't seem to get mine to behave," Balek says to Pol neither having noticed me.

"Wolf boy? Do you have a problem with Maruq, Balek?" I ask.

"No, just his wolves." As though in defense of itself or its master, the beautiful gray and white wolf tethered to Balek's sled growls, a harmless threat. I step toward her and offer my hand in the same way that Maruq had shown me when we first met.

The wolf's ears perk up as though to ask a question, then she sniffs my hand. I kneel and begin to rub her ear, then neck and belly. Soon her eyes are closed in pleasure.

"Well, Balek," I look up at him, "if you get to know her, I think you will do alright."

Balek shakes his head at me.

"I guess Wolf Boy is going to need some new friends. Our chief has just taken one of his." Pol says.

"Why do you call him that?"

"What?" Pol glances to Balek and then to me, as if he is unsure what it is that bothers me.

"His name is Maruq."

"It is only a nickname, a joke." He shrugs looking to Balek for help.

I stare at him, incredulously, give the wolf one last scratch, and walk off. Thoughts race through my mind. Only a joke? Do the men have a name for me that is used when I am not present? Do they call me *Man-girl* or *Girl-chief* or some such mocking title? I can only imagine what Iruq refers to me as, but do the others mock me as well?

I find a sled and a wolf. I get to know him a little and then command him to pull. When he easily obeys, I tell myself that at least I am still in control and proving myself the superior to the men, but in the back of my mind a thought torments me. *How long can you continue, Siira; how long can you best the other men?*

As the men and wolves cross to the cave, I see the feathered flyers circling overhead. They cry out to one another, sending wordless messages as though they are the women back in the village. I watch them, wishing I could understand what they say. Are they expressing joy or sorrow? Perhaps they are merely sharing the news of their journeys. They move away, becoming small dots against the gray haze of our sky.

The gray sky opens, pouring water down on us, the first deluge of the annual. The remainder of the trek back to the village becomes muddy, and some of the sleds get stuck and slow our progress as we must stop and help out, using the poles, but with the wolves it is easier.

Covered in mud, struggling to help the wolves with the weight of the mammoth, we enter the preparation camp. The women are waiting for us. They stand under tightly stretched skins that provide some shelter from the rain. The work of the women begins – the cleaning, cutting, organizing, smoking, drying of the meat; and the feeding of the men.

Our arrival brings a lively group of children; even in the rain they are curious to see the kill. Once I give the women my load, the drizzling rain stops, leaving me chilled, wet, and exhausted.

"My chief, looks like a good hunt." Grandmother shuffles to me, giving a cough as she stops.

"Yes, we will have a good celebration," I say flatly.

"Praise to the Mighty One."

20 THE REQUEST

I don't know how far the Great Light has journeyed across the sky when I awaken. I only know that something is tapping at my feet, Grandmother's walking stick.

"The people are awaiting their chief. Are you coming?"

I groan and stretch my cramped muscles before answering, "Yes, the chief is coming."

After the ceremony at Sacred Point, I had returned to the tent for a short nap, apparently I overslept.

The story fire blazes and all the people turn to watch me sit. I attempt to move as effortlessly as a great cat, but I stumble slightly on a rock. Perhaps no one has noticed, but I suddenly become very aware of my every motion, as though my next movement will be my last. The short walk to my chair seems to me to take much longer than normal. I try to calm myself by remembering that all I must do tonight is sit and listen, but the pulsing blood does not slow its pace. It seems to me louder than the drums.

Grandmother approaches my chair. "My chief, I ask your permission to tell the people the story of beginnings."

I nod, and so Grandmother begins the tale. I stare at the flames flickering behind her and so pass through the ceremony without really participating in it.

As we finish with eating and more stories, I settle into my chair and listen to Balek boast. He is telling of his testing and it seems to me that over the past couple of annuals that the story has changed into something that I do not remember it being, resembling the true tale about as much as I resemble my father.

Balek stands tall and handsome in his sleeveless skin tunic and leggings, his creative storytelling adding to the celebratory mood. The firelight bounces off of his muscled arms, his features seem to blaze with a light from within, giving him an otherworldly look, as though a son of the Mighty One has come to visit us.

I am not alone in my assessment, for all of the unclaimed women seem captivated, willing to give of themselves at a moment's notice if only he asked. Their eyes follow his movements, their smiles beg him to notice them. A smirk threatens my mask as I remember his proposal.

Then I see little Malukim. She was proclaimed a woman earlier at Sacred Point, her twin braids becoming one. She sits in silence listening to him, and in her petite face I see more than the bold fascination of the others. I see something deeper in her eyes, like the look that Bela gives to Pol when he is not looking. The look of love, self-effacing love. She doesn't care who notices it because the love is more powerful than any fear of embarrassment. If only I was free to be like that.

I drop my gaze, looking down at my arm cuff. The firelight flashing, dancing, playing on the shiny yellow metal entrances me. A beautiful heirloom from a past that none of us remember, except in Grandmother's stories, stories that tell us who we are and what we believe. Do I believe the stories? Do I believe anything? I try to think what do I believe and I find that I cannot answer the question.

A commotion in front of me draws my focus back to the present. The people are chanting for a story.

"Story, story, story."

The faces are eagerly turned to me.

Boku gives me an accusing glance, but I don't know what I have done that he disapproves of.

"My chief, will you give us a story?" I look in the direction of the voice; it is Iruq goading me.

I have never entertained the people with a story, not even the story of my testing. The personal loss would not be understood by the men and so I only shared that with Bela. But now I am Chief.

Father would easily entertain his hunters around the fire, any fire, whether here in the cave or out on a hunt. Stories came easily to his tongue, something he must have learned from Grandmother.

But can I tell a story? My mind races, refusing to find a story, refusing to give me any tale that I can tell them. As I begin to panic, I feel my stone mask beginning to melt. I stand to regain control.

"Long ago," I begin, "the Mighty One was grieved with the world that he had made. The people had begun to be selfish and hateful, fighting and killing for pleasure." The people hush around the fire as I tell a well-known story to them.

"The Mighty One decided that he would wash away the evil from the earth. He would kill all of the people that did not obey him. But there was one man, the Old Man, that still obeyed the Mighty One and so the Mighty One agreed to save him and his woman. The Mighty One provided a box for the Old Man to hide in and when the rains came, cleaning the earth, the Old Man and his woman were found safe, hidden in the box. As the waters rose, the animals came to the box to find safety. Soon the world was covered and the evil washed away."

The faces all turn to me, listening in rapt silence. I find that involuntarily I am making hand gestures and raising and lowering my voice. Telling the story I have heard so many times proves easy. I feel almost powerful as the children smile or jump at my words. When the Old Man makes an altar for sacrifice and I finish the story, I am energized and exhausted at the same time.

The people do not acknowledge me in any way, but remain utterly silent, paying my story the highest honor, thoughtful respect. Instead of returning to my chair, I find myself walking to the mouth of the cave. It has been a long hunt followed by a long celebration and I want peace.

A lone figure leans against the mouth of the cave, I know this silhouette. Long and lean. Maruq. It does not surprise me that he has not joined in the story telling, but the increase in the beating of my heart does. No matter how hard I try to control my emotions, they will not obey.

"My chief," he says without even turning to see me.

"Maruq." I notice Nal lying at his feet. She ignores my presence.

"Have you come to relieve me of my duties?"

Although it was not my intention, I answer, "Yes."

He turns and a smile spreads across his lips and into his eyes. "Good, I am hungry and the new pups are due to come soon." He slings his bow across his shoulder and walks past me. Wordlessly tapping the side of his leg, he calls Nal to him.

Focusing outside, I watch the dark night. Nothing stirs; every creature must be occupied elsewhere and so the footsteps behind me startle me. I do not jump, but control myself as I turn to see my visitor.

It is Pol.

"Pol, are you next on watch?"

"No, my chief."

"Then what brings you here."

"A request."

"A request?"

"Yes, I want permission to travel with my family at the end of hunts. We wish to follow the mammoth."

I am aghast. Leave the people? No family has journeyed since we rested here, so long ago.

"And what does Bela say?"

"Bela has been dreaming."

21 BELA'S DREAM

The next morning, I go to Bela's tent. She lumbers like a sea mammoth, taking slow careful steps, supporting her enlarged abdomen with a hand under it, as though she cradles the sleeping babe inside.

"Siira, how good of you to come see me."

I duck under a drying bouquet and enter the dwelling.

"Pol brought me those yesterday, beautiful aren't they?"

"Yes. The first of the annual."

"Oooooo," a low groan escapes from her lips, "the baby is moving. Come, put your hand here."

Obediently, I move to her. She eagerly takes my hand, placing it on her abdomen, pressing in on her stomach until a strange pressure pushes back, reminding me of a jumper that I once caught in a sack who struggled against the skin, wanting to get out. Bela beams with pride and excitement, as bright as any story fire.

Inwardly, I cringe, knowing that this is what killed my mother, carrying a new life; but outwardly I smile, feigning amazement.

Bela stops her work and sits down on a stump with a low groan. "Are you in pain?" I ask.

"A little, but that is to be expected. The babe will be

ready soon."

She becomes lost in thought. I stand watching her, until she shakes herself back into the present.

"Did you need something?" Bela's soft eyes look at me.

"Pol asked me a very strange request." I shift.

"Ah." She rubs her stomach in a slow circular motion, a calming motion. I look down at my cuff, attempting to compose my thoughts. Scanning the tent, I notice that Bela has been painting.

"Do you like them?" Bela asks, noting where I look.

"Yes. They are beautiful." I move to them, tracing her strokes with my finger. The red berry juice contrasts brightly against the tan of the tent skin. Bela has masterfully captured a family of mammoth. The father, large and strong, leads his mate and young one toward a large cave. No, not a cave, it is the corridor, the mammoth's way out of our valley.

"You should add to the cave paintings near the story fire," I say.

"If I have time, maybe."

"Bela, right now, I need to ask about your dream."

Bela struggles to stand, using her strong hand to push herself up off of the stump. She walks toward me, her dark eyes somber. She searches my face. I don't know what she is looking for, but she is soon satisfied.

She looks to the painting of the mammoths and traces the form of the corridor with her fingers, copying what I had done just moments before.

She closes her eyes; her voice is a hushed whisper. "I lay enveloped in Pol's arms, safe, secure. The cave floor is hard beneath us. My child, a daughter, begins to fuss, so I pull her to me. As I settle her at my breast, the earth begins to move beneath us.

"Pol awakens eyes wide. He grabs me and propels us through the opening of the tent. We run for the mouth of the cave, but before we get there the mountain has begun to crumble. I see boulders blocking us in and hear the screams of those being crushed behind us. I feel a sharp pain at the back of my head.

"As my child slips from my hands, I sink to the ground. The last thing I hear is her screams. Then I awaken." Tears stream down her cheeks. "I know that dreams are not always forewarnings, but this one I have had every night for three moons. I can only hope that the Mighty One will guide us to a safe place. My chief," she pauses, taking a deep breath, "Siira, my friend, I wish to journey."

Bela wishes to leave, to face a future of insecurity, based on a dream that the Mighty One has plagued her with. "You would risk following the mammoth, journeying to the unknown?"

"To give my child, my daughter, a chance at life, I would risk anything." Bela's eyes blaze with love and courage.

"Bela, cats and grizzlies may be waiting beyond the corridor. Creatures beyond our imagining may be beyond that corridor, troubles the Mighty One would only know. Perhaps death waits for you." I place a hand on her shoulder.

"Siira, death waits for us all. I am not troubled by death, but with the thought that my child will have no life."

"And so you would risk everything on a dream? You don't even know if the child is a daughter. What if the babe is a son, would you risk it then?"

"I cannot explain it to you, but I know with a certainty that this dream of mine will come to pass the next time of snow. I know it, like I know that warmth follows the cold, and I would risk the journey for my family."

I look at her. Everything about her speaks of conviction, of determination, of purpose. "You would risk it all?"

"Love is a risk, Siira. To love a man, to love a child with all of your soul is a risk and I know that one day you will learn that, learn to risk even yourself for the ones you love."

I feel cut by her words, then a flame of anger begins to rise, I do risk. I risk every day for my people. I risk my life to hunt. I have given up my hopes to lead them, isn't that risk? I risk everything for the people. Perhaps not everything; I don't risk my emotions, I keep them carefully guarded.

22 A GIRL

I sit in the meadow, playing with the medallion around my neck, entranced by a beautiful feathered flyer. He is large and dark with a head as white as snow. He soars and floats. He is free, no responsibility, nothing tying him down. I indulge in pretending, pretending to be as free as that flyer. Free to feel the wind, free to travel wherever I choose.

I hear a low whistle and I tuck the medallion into my tunic. My ears prick and my eyes dart across the meadow, to the trees. Then from the trees comes a lean figure, seemingly gliding across the landscape to me, as though he rides a cloud. As though he has discovered the flyer's secret, Maruq comes.

Holding his head high, with his bright eyes fixed on me, he smiles. Something about the smile makes me long to smile back, but I do not. Instead I hold his gaze, wondering which of us will look away first. I do, not because I can no longer look without heat rising in my cheeks, but because I notice that he is holding a sack, and that in the sack is something that keeps wiggling.

I look back to his face. His easy lopsided grin spreads across it. A light gleams in his eyes. At almost the same instant, a question rises in my mind, what is in the bag?

I wait patiently for him to come to me, trying to appear aloof, fixing my expression, yet my curiosity is becoming strong.

"My chief, I have brought you something." When I look at him, I dream of the life that I want, a life where I do not have to hide in the garb of Chief, but am free to be myself.

He sets the sack down on the ground at my feet. The contents again wrestle inside, squirming to be free. I watch his hands, hands used to working knots and strings, deftly loosening the familiar and intricate loops. Mesmerized by his grace, and unable to contain my curiosity, I scoot closer.

Finishing with the cord, he reaches deep inside the sack, carefully pulling the living contents back out. A gray fuzzy tail wiggles in my face, and a small whining sound comes from the other end. As Maruq turns the creature around, a sigh escapes my lips.

"A pup."

Wordlessly, he offers the warm bundle to me, pleasure dancing in his bright blue eyes.

Without hesitation, I gather the gray and white puff ball to my chest. The pup immediately, unquestioningly, returns my affection by nuzzling into me. I lose my heart to this small creature.

"I found her in a trap that I had set for a jumper. My wolves have too many pups for their milk, and so. . ." He does not need to finish his statement.

I stare at the young pup, probably too young to be away from her mother. A panicked thought comes into my mind, how do I feed her?

Maruq again has anticipated me. "Like this." He takes a piece of dried meat from a pouch at his hip and begins to chew it. After it has turned into a soft mush in his mouth he takes it out. Holding it in front of the pup's nose, he allows the wolf to sniff at it. Then a small pink tongue flicks out and licks at the dark mush. Hungrily, the wolf takes the rest of the proffered food.

"She will need to eat often and drink. Milk you can get from the women who tend the curly horns. Do you think you can manage that?" He raises an eyebrow in question.

I choose not to be offended by his insinuation. "Yes, I think so." I laugh as she whines for more. Maruq offers me some and I mimic his actions, chewing the meat then offering it to her, until she no longer whines to eat, but whines to run free.

"Thank you." I say. My eyes meet his. He holds my gaze. In his eyes, there is no defiance and no condescension. He sees me as I am. So I offer him my friendship. "And, Maruq, you don't have to call me Chief, especially when it's just us."

"You are most welcome, Siira." My name sounds almost like a sacred whisper when he says it. The sound puts knots in my stomach, knots that can only be untied by Maruq.

"What shall you call her?"

Pondering the gray sky above me, I think for a moment. "Qim," I reply.

Maruq stands and catches the bundle of fluff up in one easy motion. "Now, Qim, I shall leave you in very capable hands."

He drops her into my lap and leaves. I look into her wise blue eyes, and know that I have found a friend that will have no expectations of me, except of course to feed her.

Over the next couple of moons we become inseparable, Qim and I. We scout, hunt, and train. She rests on my lap as I preside over disputes and when she becomes too big for my lap she stands guard next to me, barking playfully at Balek, growling whenever Iruq glances our way, and silently watching Maruq. We become a team.

She becomes the confidante that I never had, listening to all of my secrets without complaint. I never need fear telling her my secrets for she would never betray me, she would never feel threatened by me or inferior to me. At night, after a long day, when Grandmother's snoring is the loudest sound, I lie on my furs, petting Qim and in hushed tones unburden myself with the day's worries.

Tonight, though, my worries center around one person: Bela. Natiq and Tiqa, Bela's aunt, went to the birthing pools with her in the early light.

"Now all we can do is wait, Qim. But what if her child is a girl? Does that mean that I must move the people, lead them following the herds like we did in the time of the great fathers?"

She returns my stare, unwavering and unworried. I look into her bright blue eyes. They remind me of Maruq's eyes, and that makes me suspect that in her calm there is wisdom.

"You are wise, Qim. I cannot do anything until word comes about the babe." I rub the spot that she enjoys the most, right above one ear, and then I lay down. Soon we drift to sleep.

My dreams are plagued with visions of Bela dying. She dies bringing the babe into the world. She dies in the great quake of her dream. She dies in the high river when a grizzly attacks her. I awake with a start, sitting up. I am ready to confront an enemy, to save my friend. When I realize that all around me is dark and silent, a strangled noise escapes my lips. I think it is supposed to be a sob, but it doesn't develop fully.

Qim moves to comfort me, pushing her soft muzzle between my arm and my side; her head pops out and rests in my lap. "I am alright, girl. It was just a dream." Just a dream; I am no dreamer, and so it will not come true, it will only plague me.

I stand and pace to calm my nerves before dressing. I pull on my summer boots, made only of well-worn skin, carefully tucking in the ankles of my soft skin leggings. I fasten my belt around my waist and place my blades in their sheathes at my sides. I secure my long hair in a tail, the only real visible reminder of my femininity, with a long skin cord.

"Let us go for a walk." I smile and rub her soft fur. I am of no use waiting in the cave with the men, wondering what is happening to Bela, so I decide to go scout.

The days are steadily growing longer. We only have dark for a quarter of the day now. Soon the Great Light celebration will be upon us and I will offer the sacrifice. I am not nervous about killing the ram, but rather that I do not honor the Mighty One. How or why would he honor my people if I do not honor him?

I have never questioned his existence, only his purposes, and perhaps that is enough.

I whistle for Qim to join me. She barks and yips, an excited sound, her tail wagging, eager for the day's adventure. Then she spins, sniffing the air, as though she will lead me. And today, I let her.

We weave through thick greenery and under large trees. I don't recognize the way, but I keep following her, enjoying the small reprieve from leading. My head hurts from pondering Pol's request and Bela's dream. I am already weary of my position. How did father do it for so many annuals?

A flutterby floats by in front of me. I watch it land weightlessly on a fireberry bush. Its wings are pale, almost the color of fleet foot milk. I watch it take what it needs and move on. Why is it that of all of the Mighty One's creatures, people seem to be the only ones that worry?

I hear Qim's quick bark as though chiding me for falling behind. I rush forward through the bushes, my bare arms getting scratched by the sticks. I see Qim, her nose pointing toward a cavern. The black hole, an entrance into the mountain, and though I have never been here before, I know where we are. We are staring at the mammoth corridor. This is where, at the end of the hunts, the remaining mammoth leave us, journeying on until they return after the snow. I stare at it. My empty stomach begins to swirl in protest of going any further today.

"Come on, girl, let's get some food."

She looks back at the corridor, sniffing the air, then howls. She seems to smell something exciting in the corridor.

"Not today, Qim, but perhaps soon."

As I wait for her to join me, my gaze climbs the mountain before me, jumping over rocks, bounding from ledge to ledge in my mind. Then I see the peak. It is covered in snow. I think back to last annual; was the snow on the mountain this long? Have I just never noticed it before?

My stomach grumbles, complaining about the lack of food; but I silence it, running for the high river. It is many spans from here, but I must see the ice wall. I am driven by curiosity.

When I reach the river I am out of breath, my panting quick and shallow, matching Qim's, who is coming to a stop next to me. I walk up the river. After the time of snow, the ice wall always glistens with the new layers of snowfall. But by the Great Light celebration, most of them are gone, melted by rain and the warmer weather.

I stop as I come to the wall. The new layers of snow have not completely melted. What does that mean for us? I seem to be collecting unanswerable questions lately. But I don't know what else to do.

Then a slight motion, as though the ice wall shivers in the cold, begins a small slide of snow from the top. I am close enough that I am showered with powdery snow from the peak. Grandmother once told me of a chunk of ice that she had seen fall from the top of the wall. It was as large as a boulder. She had told me that it crashed down the wall until it landed next to a tree. She had taken me to that tree and shown me the large impression left by the chunk that made it to the ground. Though it had started as the size of a large boulder, Grandmother told me that it had landed only half as large, yet the impression next to the tree was impressive.

Again I see a quivering of the ice.

Is the earth under it moving? I whistle to Qim and we

run home.

Thoughts race through my mind, as quickly and as blurry as the trees beside me. Nothing comes into focus, only vague outlines. Bela's dream, the earth moving just now, the snow not melting. But what does it all mean?

Change. The answer teases me.

"The people do not like change."

No, but whether they like it or not it is coming.

I stop running. My thoughts focus.

"We must."

Qim turns at the sound of my voice, ears pricking as if to try to hear what I had heard. "Well, girl, what would you do?"

She sniffs the air and looks back toward the corridor.

"That is what I thought you would say."

Wind whips through my hair; I must have lost the tie somewhere.

Qim and I enter the preparation camp side by side; most days we are inseparable. I see Pol. He is beaming as proudly as any father would on hearing about his child. I smile and hurry to him.

"Well, Pol, tell me the news."

"My chief, oh, Bela is fine . . . The babe came in the early light . . . She is resting in the tent . . . Praise be to the Mighty One."

I know that I won't get much more from him now, he is too excited. I shall go to Bela.

I climb the stairs and go to her tent without hesitation. I peek through the flaps. Bela is sleeping on a bed of furs, a babe cradled gently on her arms. Natiq quietly prepares a stew.

"How is she?" I whisper only loud enough for Natiq to hear me.

She turns and motions for me to move back, that she will talk to me outside the tent.

"Bela is well, the delivery was without problem. The child is healthy and beautiful, a perfect granddaughter. She is a joy to the people."

A girl just like Bela's dream. I need to find Boku.

23 THE COUNCIL

I find Boku sitting on a stool outside of his tent, chipping at stone for a knife. Although he is no longer able to join in the hunts, he still manages to make weapons. This small knife is made with a fleet foot antler and small chips of stone inlaid into a groove. The people use them for skinning the kills.

He does not notice me until he sees the toes of my boots, directly in front of him.

Slowly, he shakes his head, his jaw length hair swaying. "You were always as quiet as a blade-tooth." His dark eye finds mine.

"I had a good teacher."

"Yes, your father was the best of everything. At times you remind me of him. I think it is a look in those eyes of yours." He sets the stone knife down next to him and grasps his staff, a symbol of his position as elder, to assist in standing. The staff is covered in beautiful carvings, probably done by his son, Balek. "What would my chief wish of the head elder?" His stern expression glares down at me. I feel small, and so I quickly put my stone face on and speak.

"I have a matter for the council."

"Does this have anything to do with the babbling amongst the women about someone wanting to leave?"

"Have the women been babbling?" I am surprised, but then I do not spend my days waiting around camp and listening.

"Well, women always babble about something."

"It does have to do with change, and perhaps leaving, but I wish to confer with the council, before approaching the hunters or the babbling women."

"I understand." He stares over my head as though he tries to read the gray sky. "We can meet tomorrow."

"Good, I shall tell Grandmother to make extra stew."

The council surrounds the fire pit in my tent. I am in my father's place. Boku is settled on a stump to my strong side, his staff rests across his lap. Tomu, thin and haggard, sits next to him and sips from a pouch at regular intervals. Across the pit are Pilaq and Miiq, sitting on the ground talking of the old days. Grandmother sits on her small stool across from me, serenely watching the others. Natiq and Tiqa noiselessly serve us.

The council of elders has helped the chiefs govern since we left the forgotten valley. It is made up of five members, never more, never less. They are chosen among the people for their wisdom and longevity. Boku is the head elder, not that he is the wisest or the oldest, he is just the most outspoken; then Pilaq, who was my father's tutor; Miiq, Pol's grandfather; Tomu, the medicine man; and finally Grandmother. She is not the only woman to have been on the council; her mother was also the Keeper of Stories. When I was a child, before my mother died, I used to pretend that I was the Keeper of Stories, the respected woman on the council. Then I never dreamed I would be Chief.

I need their advice and support, if I intend to lead the people in following the mammoth.

Once everyone has eaten, I stand, calling the meeting to order

"Honored council members, I have called this meeting to discuss . . ." I have seen my father easily discuss matters with these men. I have watched since I was a small girl, hiding under a tent flap, but now that I am doing it I can't seem to breathe. I take a sweeping looking of the group, trying to make my next words form in my mouth, but I am uncertain of what to say or how to say it. "Bela has been dreaming," the words rush out.

I expect the elders to look at me as though I am unstable with unfounded worries, but instead these men continue to gaze at me with no judgment in their eyes. I remember that since Boku's accident, Bela's dreams have become special to the people.

I then relate the story to the elders of Pol's request, of my visit with Bela, and of the partial fulfillment in the daughter that she bore. When I finish, the elders, as though by a predetermined signal, begin to speak at once, throwing questions at me as they would throw darts at a mammoth.

I cannot comprehend any of the questions. "One question at a time." The quiet rasping voice is Grandmother's. "The chief cannot answer you all at once."

I smile in appreciation.

"What of the dwindling number of the mammoth?" The voice is thin. I barely recognize it, Tomu's voice. Once he was a respected medicine man, a healer. But when a landslide killed his wife and daughters, he began to consume more of his medicine than he prescribed.

"What of the mammoth?" I ask.

"Our chief is too young to remember the great herds of mammoth, numbering into the hundreds. It would have been impossible to take too many, but now we must count the kills or risk eliminating them entirely."

"Yes, my chief, the herds were your father's greatest concern."

Were they? I think back, trying to remember. Had my father said anything to me about this? No, I don't believe he

165

had, at least not in particular. He had always made certain that I understood the number of people compared to the amount of meat. Was this motivated by more than just a desire to see that we had enough?

"So if we add the dwindling mammoth numbers, as well as the ice wall, then the need for change grows," I say.

"What of the ice wall?"

"I made a scouting trip to the river and discovered that the snow on the wall has not melted as is normal; it still sits there. And there was something else." I shake my head, uncertain of the information's importance. "Small tremors were shaking snow off of the wall and down to me."

"What is it that you want us to do, my chief?" Miiq asks.

"I am not certain what to do. Pol wishes to travel with the mammoth, following the herds as did our great fathers. I am of a mind to follow. But I believe the people should be consulted, for I am certain that our way of life is about to drastically change." I force strength into my words that I do not feel. I have to persuade them that I am capable of this task, but now that I look at these aged faces, I begin to doubt myself.

"I agree with the chief," Boku says. "Change is coming. I have watched the herds' numbers shrink. I have seen the worry in my daughter's face and asked her about it. She has not confided in me, but Natiq has told me of the dreams." He nods towards his woman. "The chief's observation of the wall is new to me, but then again I don't see as well as I used to." He taps his eye patch with his good hand, and we all smile.

"We need to bring this matter before the people," Pilaq says, "It is their future we discuss."

"Yes, whether we stay or go, the people need to have a voice."

And so it is decided the next evening I will tell the people of the uncertainty we face.

"We have survived many of the Mighty One's testings: earthshakes, floods, and storms in the comfort our cave, our home; but, my people, I fear that change is coming. With the passing of the annuals, where once we wandered following the mammoth, we have learned to live in one place. Now our sustenance, the herds of the great beast that we depend on for our food, clothing, weapons, seems to be waning. Their numbers have been growing smaller each year. I propose that we once again follow the example of our great father's and journey with the mammoth, following them to the warmer lands at the end of hunts. That we find a new home with plentiful herds." I turn to my seat, attempting to control the swirling in my stomach. I sit, enthroned in my grizzly fur chair, waiting for responses from the sea of faces in front of me. Confused faces. Excited faces. Ambiguous faces. Men, women, and children.

Mothers grasp children closer to their breasts, men place protective arms around their women, and children look to their parents bewildered by the somber silence following my words.

Boku stands, an encouraging smile on his face. "We of course do not wish to make a decision before consulting all of our families. So please speak up."

Iruq is the first to speak. "My chief, I too have noticed the mammoths dwindling numbers, but why abandon our safe home? We may lose the mammoth, the fleet feet, the curly horn, but, I say, we have the sea. The abundance of life there will supply our needs. We may have to adapt to new challenges, but are we not people of the cave?"

I rise, meeting his challenge. "No, we are people of the mammoth." I sweep my arm to indicate all of those gathered. "We have always depended on the mammoth. All our stories teach us this. We must follow the herd. We always have. Did our fathers stay in the forgotten valley when the Mighty One tested them? No, they moved, following the herds. We are hunters, not fishers. We have only looked to the sea in dire need, not for sustenance. Do you really think that the sea could support our numbers? If we follow the herd, we will have sure supply of food, as did our fathers."

Iruq continues in a patronizing tone, "I do not propose that we forget the great fathers, my chief, but that we stay in the cave that they left us. They traveled to this place to give us a safe home; none continued on, all stayed here. How can we abandon that home to follow you on unknown paths?"

His eyes meet mine, cold and hard. The challenge is unmistakable. I cannot ignore it; my hands move, ready to grab my blades. "Are you challenging me?" I feel a hot rush begin to surge. I have fought Iruq before, and defeated him. I doubt that he wants to try again.

"No, no." Iruq steps back, confusion in his eyes. "I only want propose a different option, something other than leaving."

He leaves me standing like a fool, the heat flushed in my face.

Boku speaks. "We are here to do just that, Iruq. We are not here to fight but to decide on a path. I, personally, have no wish to travel. Many of us would not survive that journey, the elders and the sick. We have as a people always depended on the mammoth, it is true. They give us life. But we are no longer a traveling people; we have settled and made a home. We do have the sea; it can give us life as well."

As he speaks, I am confused. Boku had not mentioned any of this at my tent. If he did not wish to travel, why not tell me before? Why now? I can understand his wish to stay in the land of his birth. But he must know that is impossible, for if Bela's dream foretells the truth, the cave will not be here past this next time of snow.

Grandmother rises from her place in the council. "There must be other reasons for leaving. My chief, surely you would not resort to such measures merely because of the waning mammoth numbers?" Although she knows the answer to the question, she asks anyway, seemingly to voice a question of the people. The sound of her voice calms my passion, bringing my mind back to the task at hand and away from the suggestion of Iruq and Boku.

"Yes, Grandmother," I reply calmly, "I have also seen, with my own eyes, the ice wall. The wall, which usually has lost much of its newly accumulated snow by now, is taller than I have ever seen it. Very little of the new snow seems to have melted. I guess that is why the river is not rushing as is normal."

A hum of low voices, buzzing around the fire and behind the council, as the people begin to murmur, to question their leader's statement. I see some beginning to nod in affirmation that they too had noticed the lack of the river rushing.

Balek comes forward out of the gathering; he moves around me, standing right behind me. His intention was most likely to back me up, but he only makes me feel small, childlike in comparison to him. I put on my stone face, trying to appear calm, assured, in control.

"Maruq," he bellows, surprising me, but I suppress my feelings. "You recently scouted there, have you noticed what the chief says?"

From the back of the crowd, I hear a commotion. As Maruq slowly makes his way forward, I deliberately turn my back to the crowd and lower myself into my chair, in order to escape Balek's nearness and to hide my flushing face.

I settle in my chair. Qim comes to me and nuzzles my hand, which I rest on her head. Balek moves to meet Maruq in the center of the gathering. Maruq's lean form saunters forward, purposely unhurried, accompanied by Nal. I sense that he is uncomfortable at being singled out. Has he visited the river as well?

Memories flood into my mind, visions of a great grizzly, and of Maruq's lopsided grin. I dig my fingers into the fur that covers my chair, the fur that we had gotten together, as I wait for him to answer. Does he still think I am amazing or is he beginning to think me crazy?

I try to hush the thoughts, the doubts, but I cannot. Maruq ignores Balek and directs his eyes toward me. I can read the answer to my unspoken question in his eyes.

Qim leaves me and goes to Maruq unbidden. She trots right to him and pushes at his hand with her muzzle. Maruq squats down and begins to rub her fur. Nal ignores the intrusion, as if Qim were one of her pups and not an adopted orphan.

Balek shifts on his feet. I think that he is unnerved that Maruq has not acknowledged him, and so he repeats his question. "Have you seen the ice wall?"

Maruq looks up at Balek. "Yes, and the chief is correct, the new snow is untouched. I doubt that the high river will rush for the Great Light celebration."

"Thank you." I say. Maruq nods, releases Qim, then turns to walk back to his place. For a moment, Qim seems unsure whether to follow him or return to me, but she chooses me.

I scratch her head as I stand. Moving out in front of Balek, I address the people again, feeling more confident in my hopes.

"There have also been dreams."

"Who has dreamed?" Balek's low voice comes from behind me, and is echoed in hushed tones by those gathered.

"Bela, Pol's woman."

As soon as I say it, a pain of remorse goes through me. The people need to know but I have not consulted Bela about summoning her publicly. I push past Balek to my chair, suddenly unsure of myself again.

Boku calls his daughter forward. "Bela."

She stands tall, holding her newborn child in her arms, a

long, ebony braid draped over her shoulder. She is confident and beautiful, powerful.

I see no reproach for me in her eyes as she moves forward.

Boku questions her, "My child, how long have you been dreaming?"

"I have had this dream every night for more than three moons."

Boku nods, silently asking for her to tell her dream. She closes her eyes and begins, "In my dream, it is the time of snow. Each family sleeps peacefully in their tents inside the cave. I am sleeping peacefully next to Pol. I awaken to nurse my child, yet I do not get the chance for the earth begins to quiver." She has changed the telling to make it less personal for the size of the crowd, but it is the same dream. "I gather her in my arms. I run from my tent, but before I reach the cave's mouth, the ceiling collapses on us." Bela's body shakes fiercely at the memory. "Then I wake up." Her eyes open, tears threatening to spill out.

Boku nods, dismissing her. The people are aghast. Bela's dream has taken any hope that change was unnecessary, any hope that they could stay warm in their cave. No, the people now know that we must leave our home, or perish.

24 TOGETHER

As thick as the fat layer of a sea mammoth, as oppressive as the smoke cloud from damp wood, a gloom settles over the people. Confused and stunned, they glare up at me, as though I had given Bela the dream, as though I control the things that have led up to this point. Do they think I want to leave?

I don't. I want to stay, to enjoy the comfort of our cave, to leave life the way it has been for a hundred annuals or more. But as I think of the last few days and of the excitement that they have raised, maybe I do want to leave. Maybe I want to leave the grief and heartache, to find a Xerena on earth.

Boku addresses the gathering, "My people, we have much to consider. The grave news indeed requires a change to be made, but what? I implore you to take the next few days and discuss the matter with your families and with the elders, and then we will meet again at the Great Light Celebration and make a decision."

I am tired.

The meeting has left me drained, emotionally, which is always more wearing than physical exertion to me.

"Well, girl." I lean down to ruff Qim's ear. "I need sleep.

Can you watch Grandmother for me?"

As though she understands, she turns to find Grandmother encircled by the young, telling another story.

"Good girl." Qim trots over to Grandmother and joins the circle. The young ones surround Qim and silently begin to pet her without disturbing the rasping voice telling a tale.

Grandmother raises her eyes to mine, and I wave.

As I approach my tent, I hear two men in a heated discussion. Quietly, I come closer, allowing my curiosity to guide me, stopping short, deciding not to reveal myself, but to listen.

"I will not follow a woman into the unknown." The first voice, full of bitterness, is Iruq's.

"She is Chief. She has trained her whole life to be Chief. It was no secret, Iruq." This was Balek, defending me.

"No, she was to learn the ways of a man and then take a man, a man of her father's choice, probably you. She would give the chief a male heir to follow him."

"Yes, but that is not how it happened. The Mighty One has chosen this."

"Balek, men are to lead. A woman's job is to have children and tend the fire."

"Perhaps most women, but Siira is no ordinary woman; she is different."

"Your feelings have blinded you, Balek."

Someone approaches. I peak around the corner. It is Boku.

"Father, tell this man that he must follow our chief, that the decision is one that all will be required to accept."

"It is true, Iruq, we must abide by the council's decision, whatever that may be."

"If the decision is to follow a woman into an unknown land, I refuse." Iruq stomps away.

"Balek, I know that others feel as Iruq does. Perhaps I have a way to persuade them, but I must see Siira about it first."

"I understand."

I leave them, retreating to my tent, expecting Boku to come find me, but he does not. I am alone with my thoughts and the sounds of the argument in my mind.

I did not want to be Chief. I never asked for it. My brother was to live; he was to be Chief, not me. I was to grow up to become like my mother, or my grandmother. I want to be kind and gentle, as she was. I want to sing soft, happy tunes while I stir the pot, waiting for my man, the one who loved me so much that he could barely live without me and I without him.

But my wants were made void when the Mighty One let my brother and mother die. No one ever consulted me about my wishes. It was decided that I would become a man, because my father did not want to join with another. Since he would have no other heir, I was the chosen one, the successor. So a girl became a man, a woman became Chief.

I lie down on my furs and snuggle in, wishing now that I had brought Qim with me. I miss her comfort. I toss and turn, unable to find the sleep, the oblivion from my thoughts. I stand and leave the tent, the cave, sneaking out into the purple night.

I start to run, leaping from one foot to the other, jumping over the brush and rocks that I have jumped over most of my life. Trying to calm the pounding in my head with the pounding of my feet, I rush to the arena. I need to fly.

I stare at the tall boulder that my father had once stood on, that he had shown me how to flip off of, and tears brim, threatening to spill. I allow them. I am alone here; no one is examining me and looking for weakness here. In this place, I learned so much and now I realize that I am soon to lose all of it.

When the people journey with the mammoth, we will not be coming back. Was there a place in the forgotten valley like this place that someone had to leave? A place that held more than just the rocks and trees, but a place that held memories so precious that just the sight of it brought tears flooding into someone else's eyes?

How will I leave?

I climb the boulder. The motion is easy, as only something that has been done over and over can be. In the faint purple light, I cannot see very well but I can feel the edge of the rock. I find it and turn around, my back facing the center. I bend my knees and shoot up into the air, soaring up and throwing my feet over my head, and then landing solidly on my feet. I did not realize that I had closed my eyes, until I hear his deep voice.

"Beautiful."

His sturdy, long legs devour the ground between us. A disarming smile on his lips, Balek struts toward me. His wide round eyes, strong jaw, and muscular form are highlighted by the glowing firelight from his torch. Balek fixes the torch into a crevice on the boulder in front of me and casually leans back against the rock next to it, a mere two steps away.

He stares at me, examining my face. Out of habit I stare back, though my stone face is nowhere to be found.

"You've been crying?"

My hand wipes at my eyes, but I do not respond. With the torchlight illuminating my features I cannot deny it. He shifts uneasily on his feet, as if he is trying to decide how to proceed.

"Siira, once again you have surprised the people, surprised me, with your words."

"Yes, well, it seems that few expect or want me to truly lead." I cross my arms, trying to gain some emotional distance.

"I do. I know you, Siira, you would not wish to only sit and watch."

I look down at my cuff, composing my thoughts, controlling my voice. No, I would not be happy just sitting. I have always been active, running through the forest, searching for jumpers, even when I was young. Balek has known me as long as, and as well as, anyone. Perhaps he is right, but how can he know me when all I do is hide myself, bury my feelings. I stare, unflinching, into his eyes. "Do you truly?"

"Of course I do. You love the people. Only caring for and protecting us, what more should we want in a leader?"

"Oh, I don't know. Height, muscles the size of boulders?" I tap his arm to indicate the solidness of his build.

His laugh fills the silence. "You don't need those; you are perfect the way the Mighty One made you."

The twinkle in his eyes reminds me of a time long ago, of children playing, before all of my troubles, and my chest tightens at the memories, more lost memories.

"What is it you want, Balek?" I retreat back a step, creating more space between us.

"I want you." His voice is husky with emotion as he reaches forward and clasps my hands into his, pulling me to him. "We could be a formidable team, you and I." He rests his forehead on mine. "The people need us to be a team. I believe that we have always been meant to claim each other. You have skill and the blood of the chiefs; I have that height you were talking about. Together we could keep the people safe."

"Together?" I say the word.

"My desire, my hope, has always been to claim you, to lead with you."

"Your desire, your hope, is not mine, Balek. You say you know me, and I believe you. But I do not know myself."

"I have hunted with you. I have watched you through the years. You are fearless, determined, confident, amazing."

As I listen, I find myself thinking of another hunter that called me amazing. His melodic voice echoes in my ears. His eyes the color of remembering flowers stare at me, and a grin that is lopsided warms my heart.

"I love you as I will never love another." Balek's words spark a fire in his eyes; his arms tighten around me, willing me to love him with their strength. While their warm heaviness is comforting, I don't share his desire. I can't be what he wants.

He bends down and covers my mouth with his. I allow him to kiss me, but I do not return his passion. I look up at him, and see confusion in his eyes. He must sense my reserve. "Siira, please, one day you will need a man. Why not me? Surely the Mighty One would smile on our union." His words sound desperate. I know that I have hurt him.

"I am so sorry, Balek, I cannot. I do not know if I ever can."

"Yes, one day you will and I will be waiting."

His love for me smolders in his black eyes, like waiting coals.

"Don't wait for me, Balek. Choose another." I try a smile. "I know of some girls that would be more than willing."

His hold on me loosens. He gives me a mirthless smile and releases me fully. "You are right, as always, my chief. The task that you have chosen, leading the people alone, is great. If you need me, and I believe you will, I shall be there, always."

"Thank you, my friend." I climb the boulder again; stare out at the purple dawn, and then turn. When I land on the ground, he has gone, leaving me alone.

25 TROUBLES

Eventually, I tire, and so I return to the cave. The cave gapes, a black yawn into the valley before me. I breathe in the crisp morning air, filling my lungs with cleanliness, calming my mind as I climb the steps. Leaning my forehead against the rough stone of the entrance, I rub back and forth, trying to roll out my uncertainties and fears. I walk to the edge of the cave's lip. No one is around. I should wonder about who is to be on watch, but I do not. I lower myself to the cool stone floor, pulling one leg in tight to my body, dangling the other over the edge, swinging it like a pendulum. My gaze wanders to the light of the rising Great Light.

Cats, storms, earthshakes, many unknowns await us, but the certainty of the dawn will never be left behind. It will come with us. How can I, a woman masquerading as a man, think to lead these people to a new home?

"Siira?"

I stiffen at the sound of my name, chiding myself for not hearing an approach, for being caught off-guard.

"It's Maruq." His name instantly relaxes me, a sedative to my panic.

Running my hand along the ground, I pick up a handful of pebbles and begin to toss them off the edge, as if I could toss my troubles away. Soundlessly, he deposits himself next to me, and begins to toss his own pebbles.

I scoop up another handful of troubles.

Silently, we sit; tossing our cares away as the Great Light grows brighter, illuminating our valley.

"Have you ever been lost, so lost that you did not know who you were anymore?" I say.

He throws another pebble.

"I know that change is coming. I believe we must leave, but am I right? Can I do it?" I say, filling the silence with my doubts.

Another pebble soars out of sight to the valley floor.

"When my father was alive, all I need do was follow his directions. 'Siira, today I will teach you to use your throwing stick,' or 'I want you and Balek to go to the arena and practice. I will take you to the point to see the herds and show you how to choose one for a hunt.' Now I am the chief. No one directs me, I must direct others. I can't. What if I am wrong and we all die?"

Maruq stands, dropping the rest of his pebbles. They bounce off of the ground and roll to the edge. "I would follow you." The sincere tone causes my heart to race.

He offers me his hand, like a cord to pull me out of the mire, a quagmire of my own making. I grab it, and effortlessly, he pulls me to my feet. We stand silently; my hand in his. Unlike Balek's touch, Maruq's feels right. I never want him to let me go. I look into his brilliant eyes, and feel the peace he has seep into my confused, insecure mind. With him I feel I am no longer the girl who longs for love, the uncertain girl looking for answers, the girl who is afraid of being who she is. I am finally me.

My gaze moves to his lips. What would they feel like? My stomach begins to spin in uncontrollable circles, heat rushing through me.

His thumb runs over the back of my hand, and then, as if determined to put distance between us, he steps back.

"I must ask you something, my chief." The formality of his address, the staccato of his voice, pierces my heart.

I release his hand, ashamed of my thoughts, certain that the feelings that he had stirred in me were not mutual. I pull my stone mask on, resuming my position as Chief.

His eyes search mine and his hand finds his bowstring. "Do you remember the day my father disappeared?"

I nod.

"I stayed behind that day to speak with your father about a match. Although we were a part of a new people there were certain traditions of my people that I felt sacred and that I wanted to honor." His fingers move rapidly on his bowstring and his eyes focus on the wall behind me. "One such tradition dealt with the matching of a man and a woman. Among my people, all matches must be approved by the chief. If the chief approves, he then asks the woman's father." Maruq's eyes return to me. "Then the father names the price of his daughter, a price that he feels is equal to his daughter's worth."

My mind has gone black. Maruq wants to ask me permission to join with a woman. He had discussed a match with my father, who? My heartbeat stops. I try to recall his spending time with or showing any interest in any of the women. But I can think of no one.

"But you have not pledged to anyone in the promising ceremony?"

"No, life seems to have gotten in my way." I think of all the changes the Mighty One has made to our people since that time. He lost his father, I became a man, I lost my father, and then became Chief. I nod.

He closes the distance between us, stepping closer. He looks down on me. "And I have not been able to discover the girl's feelings because of it."

Confusion clouds my mind, as hope blazes blindly. "Who did you wish to claim?"

The moment stretches out. If he wants me to read the

answer in his eyes, he will be disappointed for I cannot. My emotions are in turmoil. He reaches out and takes my hand again, running his thumb across the back of it. His eyes alight with love, but it is not the fierce, desperate passion that I saw in Balek's eyes. It is steady and calm, like him. "You." His voice is a whisper, the sweetest whisper I have ever heard.

Then, without waiting for an answer, as though he knows that I cannot speak, he leaves.

His confession floats around in my mind. He wants me. I allow myself to believe in the impossible, the impossible joining of a female chief to one of her hunters.

My heart soars and dreams come back from the dead. I think back to that night. I remember my father wanting to speak to me of a match. Had it been Maruq he spoke of and not Balek? Did my father approve of the match?

I jog off to my tent, my mind alive with questions and hopes.

Smoothing my hair and quieting my breath before I enter, I reach up, pulling back the flap. My cuff glints in the firelight from within, highlighting the strange and beautiful creatures that run across it. I feel a rush, a certainty that they are running to something, an exciting new future. Not caring about the possible dangers, but embracing the thoughts of a new world. Perhaps the future holds grand and great things for me, the fulfillment of my dreams. A smile bursts forth and I don't hold it back.

Grandmother sits by the fire, stroking Qim's fur. Qim's ears perk and turn in my direction. When she sees me, she instantly comes to my side.

"Were you worried, girl?"

She howls in a low whining response.

"I don't know about the wolf, but I was beside myself. You were gone all night."

"Grandmother, I am fine, and I am no longer a child."

"True. No matter how I wish it differently, you are no

child, Siira. Were you alone?"

I drop down next to her, amused at the parental tone.

"Mostly."

"What is that supposed to mean?"

"It means that most of the time I was alone. I was at the arena, thinking." My mood sinks, like a rock tossed into the river once I remember Balek's words to me. He loves me too.

"I know that you are torn, my daughter. I know that you only do what you have been trained to do, not out of a desire to do so, but in order to fulfill the roll given you by others."

She turns cloudy gray eyes on me. Her sight, though physically ailing, only seems to become clearer with age, seeing things that others cannot.

"Yes, well there is nothing else to do. You must do what is best for the people."

I know that she speaks of the journey to follow the mammoth, but I have other problems that she doesn't know of. Only moments ago, I had forgotten the responsibility I have to my people in order to indulge a selfish, adventurous thought, and now reality makes me long for days when I did not have the weight on my shoulders. I want my father back to guide me and tell me what to do. I want to be tucked into my furs at night, sung a night song, and fall asleep listening to Grandmother busy herself with preparations for the next day. But to wish for simple days is less than useless.

"I miss him, too." She pats my arm.

26 CHOICES

I hike the trail to Sacred Point. I want to see it and rehearse the Great Light Celebration ceremony in my mind, before I am required to perform it. This year there will be no testings; no boy has come of age and so all I must do is thank the Mighty One and sacrifice a curly horn ram.

I close my eyes, picturing my father his graceful and quick motions, and then mimic what my memory supplies me. I feel the wind on my cheek and loose tendrils playing on my neck. The wind is cool and sweet with the smells of blossoms and grass in the meadow.

I hear rocks skid and slip, bouncing down the path, alerting me to the approach of something. Involuntarily my eyes open, my heart races, and I long to crouch behind a rock, but I stand my ground waiting for whatever is coming. I see a black head coming up the path, a rugged face with an eye patch. Boku.

I warily watch as he moves toward me, the conversation that I had overheard rushing into my mind. I had expected him to seek me out sooner, but this is the first time I have seen him since then.

I stay silent, standing behind the altar, distractedly watching an orange flutterby, waiting for him to speak first.

"I hope that I find you well this morning," he says.

I rest my eyes on him for a few moments, and then return to watching the flutterby. "Yes, thank you. I am preparing for the ceremony."

"The ceremony is fast approaching and so is our decision. Do you still feel that leaving the valley is the path that we should take?" He settles on a small flat boulder, his staff in his hand and his stump arm in his lap.

"I do, we cannot hope to stay in the cave."

"No, we cannot, but some have suggested another way."

"I am listening."

"Some feel that we should stay, make sturdier tents that can last in the time of snow. That we should then learn to hunt the sea mammoth."

"And what do you think?" I say, although I find the suggestion preposterous. Live out in the snow.

"As I said at the story fire, I am not inclined to journey, but if my family were to choose to go then I would follow."

"By your family I guess you mean Balek, for certainly you know Bela's mind on the matter. It was Pol that asked me to leave."

"Yes, if Balek and his family were to go then I would follow and encourage the rest of the people to do the same."

Boku's backing on my venture would mean a great deal when it comes to dissenters, but Balek has no family.

"Balek's family, of what do you speak, Boku? Has Balek decided to claim someone at the Great Light Celebration?" My thoughts fly; perhaps he has chosen meek little Malukim.

"No, he has but one desire and it seems that she is reluctant."

"Do you speak of me, Boku?"

"Yes, my chief; agree to take my son and I will side with you about our journey."

"As I have told your son, I am not inclined to do so." I want someone else, but I will never admit that.

"Then I will encourage every man to decide as his conscience calls him."

I stand motionless, allowing my thoughts to process. If I take Balek, Boku and the rest of the elders, no doubt, who look up to him for guidance, will agree to follow the mammoth. But if not, then he will practically break apart the people, break us into two.

I think of Balek. I do not believe that he knows his father's plans, but maybe he does. Perhaps he feels that this threat will force me to take him. But if I agree, I lose the only choice left to me, the choice of who I take, and it is more dear to me now than ever.

I don't want to give up my choice. I want to choose. I want Maruq.

"So then do you agree with those men that insist a woman's place is with children, tending the fire?" I ask.

"I have been married too long to hold that opinion, my chief."

"So then you must think me incapable."

"No, my chief, you have proven very capable, but you are a woman. Some among the people do not want to bend the knee to you, but with my son at your side, who knows? You may soon have an heir as your father hoped. The match would give you all of the advantages that my son offers. He is a fine man. And you will produce a strong heir with both of your attributes. Is this not a wise decision?"

"And once this heir comes, Boku, who will tend the child? Will I stay at home, giving up my responsibilities for my child? Or perhaps I will allow Natiq to nurse the child."

His hand waves in the air as though to dismiss my statement. "Yes, either option would do; Natiq would be more than willing, I am certain, but the final choice would be yours."

Mine, the choice would be mine. No, I would have no choice. Boku and the elders have again taken my future and planned it all out. They would have me take Balek and have children. I would then, of course, choose my child over anything else and so Balek would become Chief. My entire life and work would become nothing. All of the training that I endured, the testing, the losses, everything that I gave up would become for naught.

I do not want to be told what to do anymore and so, because of that, I choose what will appear to be folly.

"Boku, I understand you and I decline your offer. I am Chief and no one will dictate to me. You may act as your conscience calls you."

"So be it, Siira, but remember that I offered. That the people's decision could have been avoided."

"And what decision is that?"

"To divide. Those loyal to you will follow you wholeheartedly into the wilderness, but the malcontent and the aged will embrace a new leader and way of life."

A new leader. The thought had not entered my mind until he said it. Yes, the people may divide. Certainly in the forgotten valley there must have been those that would rather face a certainty, even if it was evil, than chance the unknown.

A new leader. I see Iruq's face, smug and determined, determined to become the chief.

"Certainly the council could prevent this. They could certainly decide that we all stay as one."

"Yes, I think we could, but we must be able to do so without reservations."

Reservations? No, Boku had no reservations, he has a desire. He will not support my plan unless I claim his son as mine, and eventually give him the responsibility of the people. Boku does not want me to be Chief any more than Iruq does.

"I am Chief. I have passed the testing, conquered the challenger, and led the hunters. No one's skills surpass mine. My life has prepared me for this, more than any man. You know this. You were my father's friend and confidant.

You knew his heart, his wish, his desire."

"But his desires were not mine." His dark eye stares into mine and I see what he has always wanted: power. "A woman as Chief." He laughs, the sound grates like the screeching of flyers, "When your father suggested letting you train as a man, I was astounded, but I checked myself, hoping you would prove incompetent, but you quickly grasped all of the skills needed." His eye narrows. "Once you passed your testing and you were made a man, I knew that I would have to press my son's advantage."

I stare at him, my lips pressed together. "What advantage?"

"It was obvious to all, if not to you, that he was in love. I intended that you would take Balek and have children to carry on your father's name. I didn't expect you to be so stone headed about the whole thing. Tell me Siira, why won't you take the best of men to be yours?"

"I do not believe your son to be my match." I say it flatly, hiding my emotion. I know that Balek would not be happy in the life he would have with me.

"Well, I agree with you there."

I raise an eyebrow. "Then why insist I take him as mine."

Boku stands and I see a fire in his eye, kindled by a desire long burning in his mind. "The Mighty One intended greatness for my son and I want him to have it, even if it means joining with you."

Fury, no rage, begins to grow inside me.

"Does Balek know what you would do?"

Boku turns his back and wanders a span away before replying. "No, probably not. My son is love-struck. He believes you to be his other self. He intends to wait for you."

"But surely he will follow me and you will lose your chance then."

"No, Balek will not follow you."

"Why not?"

Boku turns and stares at me, his gaze as cold as ice. "Because it is not my wish."

Involuntarily, my mouth gapes in astonishment.

"So, Siira, I suggest that to lead the people, to keep us as one, you take my son, and assume the role that was always intended for you."

Once when I was very small, I became very sick. I was vomiting almost constantly until my mother steeped soothing herbs into a tea. My insides seemed as though they would never calm. They burned and swirled inside. My emotions are doing that now. Boku has shown me his true feelings, he is not loyal to me and I do not believe he was ever loyal to my father. He seeks power. My anger mixes with my anxiety. My selfishness fights my responsibility. I choose, and my calm returns.

"No," I say, my head shaking deliberately. "No. I am Chief. You may not have intended this to happen, but it has. I am Chief and as Chief I get to choose when and who to take. You will not take that from me. It is all you have left me."

Boku smiles, a familiar expression. I have seen it many times over the years, whenever my father would counter one of his plans. It is a look of acquiescence, but not surrender.

"If that is what you want."

I move to the sacred stone and lean fully upon it as Boku leaves. I hear his strong steps retreating down the path.

Once alone again I run my hand in the groove that has been worn there by the sacred knife.

Since the beginning, the Mighty One has required that the people shed blood for our defects. Taking a young, innocent ram, and spilling its blood here at this stone to cover our deficiencies, to make us whole and acceptable to him. When I was a small child, mother would console me for hours, trying to explain to me the need of killing the animal, but I never could understand the cruelty, the seeming heartlessness of the ceremony.

Over the years, I have often felt like that young innocent animal, being offered up and tortured for the good of others. I had accepted that my life was no longer my own, but now I have a choice. There is only one choice left to me and I will not sacrifice it for anything.

27 A NEW CHIEF

The celebration passes by as a blur. I raise a knife and offer the sacrifice, praise the Mighty One for his provision, and then we all go back to the preparation camp. Normally the festive mood would cause the people to rush back to the celebration feast, but today, no one rushes, for once we reach camp, the decision for our future will be announced by Boku.

As head elder, it is his duty to proclaim the decisions of the council to the people, and he takes his duty solemnly, standing before all of us with his staff raised high on one side and his stump arm on the other.

"My people, the council has come to a decision. Our great fathers survived the long journey from the forgotten valley, escaping the wars to look for a better land—this land. We have hunted the mammoth, the fleet foot, the wooly one horn, for more moons than any of us can remember." Here he pauses, gesturing at me with his stump. "Our chief would have us leave and seek new lands following the mammoth once again. Some of you agree with her and find the adventure enticing, yet others want to remain where we are. Some wish to look to a new way of life instead of reinstating the old. The elders have thought much and discussed both futures, but we do not feel that we have the right to make anyone's choice and so we have decided that each man will make his own path. If you choose to stay or to go, the choice is yours."

I run my hand through Qim's fur, running deep grooves into the thinned coat, frustration at the duplicity of Boku's statements boiling in my core. The elders do not mind choosing for people, they just want us to believe they are thinking of our good.

"Those who stay and change as our world changes will embrace a new leader. A man of proven skill, a man of responsibility, one that we can all trust, my son, Balek." A gleam of pride lights his eye.

My hand stops in its motion at the mention of Balek. I had assumed that Iruq would be named, but that of course would not be Boku's desire. And so because I did not choose Balek, Balek now cannot choose to follow me.

I look to Balek, whose eyes dart quickly from his father's face to mine, as though he searches me for an answer, an answer that I do not have.

And so with the selection of Balek as leader, the most capable of men, I am now uncertain if I will have any to lead. With such a leader, all may wish to stay. But no matter what others choose, I plan to journey with the mammoth.

I find myself under the great tree. After Boku's announcement there was not much else for me to do. And so I had called Qim to my side and left the gathering. I had to think, to process, to plan the journey.

I must find out who wants to follow me, a woman, into the unknown and then figure out the needed provisions. This should not be difficult. I have been calculating such things with my father since before my testing.

I run my hands through Qim's fur.

"Will anyone follow me?" I ask.

"Of course someone will." The deep voice surprises me.

Balek stands behind me, a bewildered expression on his handsome, yet scarred face.

"I am not sure of that. If I were a man that was to choose between staying with a strong hunter and going with some silly woman, I am fairly certain I know which choice I would make." I stare at the gray horizon.

"Do you?"

"Yes, but I do not get to choose, not anymore." I sink to the ground; it feels cool under me. He comes and sits next to me, and Qim settles between us, a fleshly wall.

"Did you wish to be rid of me so badly that you would strip me of my choice as well, Siira? How could you make me Chief? Did you not know that I would want to follow you?"

"Balek, I did not choose you as Chief. I had no part in the decision."

"No?"

"No, Balek, that decision was the elders'. I was not even there when they made it."

His face twists into a grimace, and he tosses a rock at a low branch, sending a leaf fluttering to the ground. Among the people it is expected to do as our fathers wish, just as I had no choice in my destiny; Balek has no choice now in his. He will be Chief. "I loved this tree when we were young. It was here, I think, that I fell in love with you."

I turn.

"Does that surprise you so much?"

I don't answer.

"I think that I always did, you know, but now it does not matter for you will journey with the mammoth, forever away from me. I shall never see you again."

"You don't love me, Balek. Not really. You will find someone else, someone better."

He runs a hand across the rough bark. "Do you remember that day? It seems so long ago, when I bested you in a fight?"

I nod.

"You sneaked up on me. I was carving there, perched on that branch?" He points at it. "I was making a present for you, a flower. I loved you then. I knew what my father wanted and I accepted it gladly because it meant a lifetime with you."

I wish he would stop, but I can't make him. He continues on but never looks at me.

"You are beautiful, courageous. A fire burns in you that no man can quench. And that is what I love."

"Balek, no more, don't think of it. I am to journey and you are to make your father proud and claim another."

All of the passion drains from his voice. "You are right. Did you ever love me Siira? Was there ever hope? I need to know."

I turn to him, trying to carve his face onto my memory next to my father's face. I raise my hand to the scar, and run a finger down it. "Balek, I do love you." As hope kindles in his eyes, his hand reaches up and covers mine. "You are the bravest, most courageous man of the people, but my love for you is the love that I would have given Siiraq."

His hand drops from mine. "No more than a brother?"

"No, Balek. My love for you is the love of a proud sister, a very proud sister." I lean over and kiss his ragged cheek.

He stands and wordlessly leaves, leaving me alone to my thoughts. I know that I have wounded him more than any grizzly. I hope he will soon recover.

Once the Great Light has disappeared and Qim and I are in the brief darkness of this night, she moves, sniffs the air, then circles to lie down, waiting. I join her on the ground and there we lay until the Great Light is high in the sky.

As I stretch out my arms, yawning away the cares of the night, embracing the challenges of the day, I catch sight of his back from the corner of my eye. Maruq sits with Nal as though he guards me, watching for approaching dangers.

My heart races at the sight of him.

"When did you get here?" I sit up, knowing that I must look rather disheveled, but unable to do much about it. I take the tie out of my hair and shake it out as he turns and answers.

"Last night."

"And why did you not make your presence known then?"

He smiles enigmatically. "You were in conference and I did not want to disturb any farewell that was to be said."

What kind of farewell was he expecting me to give Balek? Heat rushes into my cheeks. I am certain that Balek's feelings are no secret, but the idea that Maruq would think I return them unsettles me.

"The farewell was not one that could not be disturbed, Maruq. It was merely old friends talking."

"Yes, I noticed." His eyebrow cocks in doubt. I remember the kiss I had given Balek and shift uncomfortably.

"The kiss was nothing more than a sister saying farewell to a loved brother."

His eyes narrow slightly before he nods. He stands and calls Nal to his side.

"Why were you looking for me last night?" I call after him.

He turns and crosses his arms. "I wanted to tell you that I wish to journey with you following the mammoth." His voice is cool, the melody flat.

"I am grateful for your confidence, but I am not sure how many will be with us." I mimic his tone.

"There are many who still wish to journey. A wanderlust is something born into man." He scans the horizon.

"Is it?" I feel he wants to leave me, but I want him to stay, to talk with me, to regain the closeness I had felt the last time we spoke. But the distance between us is wide and of my doing.

"Yes, in my home, I had a brother. He was older than I was by many annuals. And he left us to journey down to the warmer forests."

"Did you have a large family?"

"Yes."

"Tell me, please?" I am desperate to shore up the breach that I have unwittingly created.

"There was my father and mother, my older brother, five sisters, and I came last."

"A brother and five sisters? What happened to them?"

His bright eyes cloud, and a muscle in his jaw tenses. "They all died."

I do not ask for any more and he does not offer it. Perhaps one day I will learn what happened, but not now.

A wind begins to blow and my long black hair picks up and tickles my arms, my face, my neck. I gather it into my hand and begin to tie it back.

"Why don't you braid it?" he asks.

"Only women braid their hair."

"Do you want to?"

I am confused by his question. I have never really thought about it. "I don't know?"

"If you ever decide, please tell me." He says, a light melody returning to his voice.

TO BE WOMAN

28 FAREWELL

Nineteen have entrusted me with their future, although I think that Maruq is correct in that they desire to leave more than they desire my leadership, wanderlust apparent in their eyes.

Today, I have taken Qim with me to the Great Salt Water. I need to finalize numbers and plans, as we leave in only two moons and there is much to do. I hold a charred stick and a piece of white bark, scratching marks down, as my father had shown me. The hunts will continue and the abundance will be divided accordingly for each new people group, Balek's people consisting of four times mine.

Part of me is pleased at the number. If I had to lead all of the people, there would have been more workers but also more danger. None of the elders have approached me, and so I believe we will be able to move quickly with our young numbers.

Eventually my mind wearies of figuring food and sleds, wolves and tents, and I sit motionlessly on a rock, as though I am trying to become a part of it. Listening to the waves break on the shore. I study the gray haze; it seems darker today, threatening storms. I try to picture a new sky, perhaps one the color of the flowers of remembrance blooming at my feet, the color of Maruq's eyes.

Grandmother's stories tell of the blue skies of Xerena. The skies of the Forgotten Valley are also said to be blue, but I have never seen them. Our skies vary in shades of gray, either a soft gray, lit with the Great Light or a black as dark as night, but never a peaceful blue.

A twig behind me snaps. Reflexively, I drop off of the rock, as quiet as a cat, flattening my body against the ground, allowing it to hide me. I don't want to be bothered now, nor do I want a fight.

"Siira, little one, where are you?" Grandmother's voice calls, rasping softly like the rush of the water receding from the shore. I spring up from the ground, leaving my anxiety in the grass. I smile, standing erect.

"Oh, there you are, still playing games." She shuffles breathlessly toward me. Stopping and holding her staff, her body shakes as a coughing fit overcomes her. In the last few moons her health has deteriorated rapidly: a hunch in her back that I had never noticed, a shaking of the hand, a slight drooping to her mouth. Sometimes her coughing will keep me awake at night, wondering when I will lose her too.

I rush to her side and take her arm. Her bones feel as fragile as a small feathered flyer. Suddenly, a rock settles in the pit of my stomach.

Soon, she will leave me too.

In all of my preparation, I had not thought of her. Not once. I never considered whether she would stay with Balek or come with me. Not once. And now as I hold her, I fear she will not live to the end of hunts.

I push the thought away and help her sit on the rock. Once Grandmother has settled into a groove, she motions for me to sit at her feet, my favorite spot as a child for storytelling, though I am certain that she has not come with a story for me.

"My child, I need to talk to you of the move." Grandmother's clouded eyes mist. "I do not believe that I can go. I am old and weary. Soon I will be with the Mighty One in Xerena and I would only slow you."

I know that she will say these things, but I cannot control the well of emotion that causes the rock in my stomach to swim, stinging my eyes with tears.

"I know, my child that you would have made special arrangements for me to go, but I do not wish to be a burden." Coughing slightly, she reaches down and gently moves a strand of hair off of my forehead, her thin and dry fingers tracing the line of my cheekbone. "I shall not look forward to our parting, my daughter, so I will treasure the time left us by the Mighty One even more."

I grab her hand and fiercely kiss her palm, and then I stand and run to the salt water. I dive in, finally allowing my tears to flow freely, to mingle with the water, washing my sorrow away, invisibly.

I swim until I ache. Qim waits on the shore for me, running impatiently on the beach. I come out of the water and flop down next to her, trying to soak in her heat. I want to lie there all afternoon, but to shirk my responsibilities now is not an option. There is much work to be done.

I find Pire and Maruq dressing a fleet foot. I outline my plans and needs to them.

"As the only unclaimed hunters of the party, I feel that we shall be required to do most of the scouting on the trip, at least at night. I would prefer that the men stay with their families."

"Yes, my chief, I do not mind that." Pire assures me.

I look to Maruq and he nods, eyeing my wet clothes.

"Good then, we leave with the mammoth."

Grandmother's health continues to deteriorate and now, a moon later, she is laying on her bed, dying.

Natiq and Tiqa tend her daily, giving her the herbs recommended by Tomu, to alleviate some pain and help her rest as she fades into oblivion.

Each evening I come to spend time with her, and, after the first few days, a routine is established. I tell her of the preparations while combing her fine white hair. As I finish, I braid it, lay it over her small shoulder, and place a soft kiss on her cheek to silently say goodnight.

But on this night, she does not allow me to speak; she insists I listen.

"Siira," her voice rasps and her breaths are shallow. I have to lean in to hear her well.

"Yes, Grandmother, I am here."

"Siira, my child, I know that your life has been a struggle and that you have doubts about the Mighty One. Doubts about his purposes." She seems frantic that I understand her, and so I nod.

"But he loves you. He is looking for your good. Remember that, no matter," her voice cracks and she struggles to finish, "no matter what . . . happens."

I lay my head next to hers, closing the distance between us, as if I could keep her close to me. I listen to her rasping breath, I watch her chest labor to rise and fall, and I feel the beats of her heart become sluggish.

"I will try, I will."

Her body relaxes, the air leaves her, and she is gone. I pull back and examine the face that had been with me during every struggle. I am not sure what I expect to see, a lifeless gaze, a mouth agape at having to leave, but I do not expect a smile. I have seen many lifeless bodies, but they were all killed in torturous ways: landslides, earth shakes, and tramplings. Grandmother's death is the first peaceful one that I have witnessed, and if it had been the only one, I would have no qualms about believing the journey to Xerena, for I can see her entering that land in the smile left forever on her lips.

I press a kiss into her lifeless cheek and leave the tent to tell Natiq of my Grandmother's passing and to make arrangements for her death boat.

Now I, like Maruq, am alone. I leave nothing behind me on our upcoming journey.

The day is like the one that sent my mother off on her final journey, for it is drowning us in rain. Perhaps the sky is shedding all the tears that I cannot. I stand stoic and stone faced next to Balek and his father. Now that we are two peoples soon to be parted forever, we both, Balek and I, preside over the death boat.

Although we are all wet and cold, none seems to mind. Even the children feel the loss of our Keeper of Stories.

"She lived a long and blessed life, blessing others with her wisdom and care. Now the Mighty One has taken her to him. She is now on her last journey, the journey to Xerena, a land that she knew so well in her tales, she now sees with her eyes." Balek's deep voice is clear in the rain, carrying his farewell message to all that have gathered. He will be a good chief.

I stand by as every child lays blue remembering flowers onto the wrapped body. Some faces are somber, understanding that Grandmother will never tell stories again; others are serene, even curious, not yet able to comprehend the meaning of the ceremony.

When the children have finished, I take the cord and release her to the Great Salt Water. The boat is slowly pulled out to the water, rocking peacefully, as though someone lulled her to sleep, and not to death. I can bear to watch no more and so I leave and return to my empty tent. I lie down in my bed of furs and curl up into a tight ball. Qim lays at my back, motionless; perhaps she can feel my loss.

I alternate between tensing and relaxing my muscles, wanting to feel something other than the heavy silence of night. No longer will I be kept awake by Grandmother's night sounds, the sounds that reminded me of a wooly one horn, the sounds that I had wished to stifle every night of my life, the sounds that meant she was alive and well and near me. I will now spend my last few nights in the cave alone and in silence. I continue the rhythmical contracting and relaxing of my muscles until I drift into a black oblivion of exhaustion.

29 THE CORRIDOR

I make no goodbyes. I have none to make.

A hum of excitement surrounds my new people as they gather in the preparation camp. Chattering children run in play, cautious mothers recheck their packs and sleds, and reassuring fathers tell the women that they have forgotten nothing.

Maruq checks the harnesses on the wolves that we are taking. Nal and her three children will pull our sleds and two pups will scurry alongside. Maruq is leaving a male and female with their four pups here with Malu. Malu, Kumal's father, has spent much of the hunts training with these wolves, learning from Maruq. He will be able to continue teaching the use to the others.

I gather my personal belongings. A pack holds a day's ration, my token, sleeping roll, and heavier clothing. My blades, meat pouch, and water are secured in my belt. I swing the pack onto my back and slide my throwing stick under the straps on my shoulders. I carry my darts in my hand as a walking stick.

Qim chases her tail in circles around me.

Boku steps out into the bustling group, his staff in his hand.

"The elders wish to send you on your journey with a blessing of the Mighty One. May the Mighty One keep you from harm, may he lead you into safe paths, and may he give you an abundance of food, and strength in trials. May he give wisdom to your chief and bless you with safe passage through the corridor."

I nod to Boku as if to say thank you and then I lead my people past everything familiar: our cave, our meadow, our lives. I refuse to look at the faces of those I leave behind. The people that I love, the people that I cared for all my life, the people I will never see again.

I focus on the path ahead of us, on the new journey. The men command the wolves to begin pulling sleds. Qim is at my side. The women follow, bringing the young.

At the lookout rock, I turn to say a final farewell to the cave, my home. A lone figure stands at the mouth. Unmistakable in his grizzly cape, he stands looking strong and capable, ready to lead.

"Good-bye, Balek, my friend." I say the words into the wind, hoping they find their way to his ears. Then I turn and follow my people.

As the Great Light reaches mid-sky, we reach the mouth of the corridor. I know the valley behind me, having explored it since I could walk, scraping my knees on many of the rocks, finding small animals to hunt in the brush, but always I stopped at the gaping blackness in front of us, the corridor of the mammoth.

At the end of the hunts, the mammoth leave by this cave, disappearing into the black hole during the cold and returning again the next annual. A small herd left through here just the day before and now we follow. I tell the families to rest here, so that I can scout with Qim at my side. Leaving the group, I journey into the unknown, tentatively starting in, listening to the heavy silence. Qim sniffs the air, her ears perk in curiosity.

"Today, we go in." I pat her head.

She turns her head, looking behind us, and her tail begins to wag. "I need a torch." I say to her.

Maruq appears from nowhere, fulfilling my request, carrying torches, silently offering one to me. His expression is carefully masked. I take it and step inside, my curiosity bubbling.

As I walk, the light flickers, illuminating the rough walls and ceiling, as high as any great tree, the walls free of cave drawings, giving evidence to the lack of man travelling this way. The only sound is the soft pat of our feet. The cave is wide enough for a mammoth herd to travel single file. How long is it? I wonder.

"It goes for a half day's journey," Maruq answers my unspoken question.

Turning to face him, I wonder if he reads minds or just logically concludes my thoughts. I nod, and then continue forward, using my darts as a walking stick. I remember then that this corridor is not unfamiliar to Maruq; he would go here with his father.

"How often have you scouted here?" I ask as I watch for dangers.

"Often enough."

"How far have you gone?"

"About a day's journey out of the cave."

"Good." I stop moving forward and turn facing him, allowing a smile to spread on my lips. "You can be lead scout then."

"I would like that." The grin that spreads across his face lights his eyes. I know that Maruq relishes being alone, preferring to scout and hunt with only his wolf.

"Will you need Nal?" I ask, knowing that he is not used to working without her.

He looks back out the corridor. I watch him in the torchlight. His head tilts to one side as he thinks. "No, she is needed elsewhere."

I look down to Qim. "Would you like to take her with

you, so that you are not alone?"

His eyes come back to mine. "No, I do not need her." He ruffs behind her ear, her favorite spot. Qim leans into his hand, a whine of pleasure escapes. "I will meet you on the other end."

Maruq trots off into the darkness. I watch him disappear, his graceful form becoming a bouncing light illuminating the corridor walls until the light disappears around a bend.

"He makes my heart soar when he is near and ache when he is gone."

Qim barks and howls excitedly and runs back down the corridor toward the waiting people. Then she stops staring at me as though to say, "Come on, we have work to do."

I glance into the dark where Maruq has gone and then jog off with Qim. We return to the waiting families. Expectant faces find mine, asking unspoken questions.

"We need to go through the cave. Maruq is scouting ahead. I will lead and Pol and Pire, you will bring up the rear. The rest of you, be attentive to your family. Each family will need a torch for light."

I ruff Qim's ear and watch as the men make torches, wrapping skins that they had soaked in fat around long sticks, lighting them with a few strokes of their stones. Women gather straying children, wiping dirty faces, seating the small ones on the sleds, preparing them for the dark. My people line up like a herd of mammoth, following me into the unknown.

Although no command was given, the families assume hushed conversations in the dark. I listen to Lotik behind me answer sporadic questions from his son, Lomri.

"How far are we going?" The boy's voice asks, piercing the darkness with its pitch.

"As far as we can." Lotik's hushed answer contrasts starkly with the boy's, as much as the firelight from our torches from the darkness ahead.

"What will it look like?"

"I do not know."

"Will there be a cave for us?"

"No, at least not soon."

The hushed conversation diverts me from more somber thoughts.

Finally, we come to the end of the corridor; the hushed voices stopped some time ago. I am sure that the women and children are exhausted, although the men are used to such journeys when hunting.

Tired eyes look to me for direction. It is dark outside.

"We shall make camp in the corridor for the night and continue at first light."

Whispered sighs of relief break from the women, who begin to unroll furs and spread them out next to the sleds. The men release the wolves from their harnesses and feed them. The beasts eagerly gulp down all that is provided and then move out of the corridor, following their noses.

Qim leaves my side for the first time since entering the corridor. I watch her trot alongside one of the males. I watch them all head straight to a crouching figure outside, near a fire. It is Maruq. I smile, and then join the pack, following my heart.

Reaching my hands out to the fire, rubbing them together, I soak in its warmth.

"Siira." He looks up to me from his pot; he is warming some herbs in water. Qim has curled up a span away next to the other wolf. "Do you want me to take the first watch?"

Ignoring the question, I settle down on my heels, as if to draw closer to the fire, but I want to be closer to him. I look at my wolf. She is settled next to the male. "She seems content."

"I think you shall soon have pups of your own." He removes the pot from the flame, blowing on it.

I stare at him trying to discover if he is teasing, but he is not. "Pups." I whisper.

"All things change, all families grow." He sips the water. "Not all families." I say, thinking of my lack; I am alone. He offers me a drink. "Yes, all families."

I look into his eyes. He, like me, has lost everyone; how can he possibly say that his family has grown when the Mighty One has taken so many from him. Confusion floods my mind at his words. I want to run, but I stare at the drink in his proffered hand.

"Yes, you take the watch. Wake me at mid-night." I say, answering his earlier question. And then I stand. Leaving him with the warm drink and the wolves. I go to check on my people.

I assure myself of each family's comfort. There are only four miniature groups, gathered around the four sleds. Lotik is sleeping next to his woman, their four children tangled together in a pile. Sinaq, whose wife died bearing a third child, has wrapped his arms around his young ones, Torsu and Tinaq. Kavok, the oldest among us, lies with his wife, Kora. Their daughter, Korak, who is the promised of Pire, cradles her young sister in her arms, keeping the child warm.

Bela and Pol are both sleeping with their child. They lay on their sides. Pol's arm rests across Bela's shoulder, and Bela's arm hugs the child to her. The babe rests bundled in thick skins that are laced up the front. Straps are attached to the skins so that the child can be easily carried on the mother's back. As I look at her, I can't imagine that it would be comfortable, but the babe is sleeping soundly. I crouch down in front of Bela's babe and study her sleeping in her pack, peaceful, not a care in the world, just as happy here as at the village. Dark, straight locks frame perfect features: a miniature of her mother's mouth, like two red berries, her slanted eyes resembling her father's, dark lashes resting on chubby cheeks. A new beginning for a new generation. I hope it will be a better, safer world.

I find Pire watching close by and relieve him.

"Go, sleep, Maruq will take the first watch." He strides off and lays out a fur not far from Korak's sleeping form.

I lay out my fur near a rock just inside the corridor. Stretching out, I watch Maruq drink, the drink I refused. The peace that seems to surround him amazes me. The pack is all resting, the fire glows softly illuminating the immediate area. Maruq tips his face to the dark sky. He seems to soak in the quiet, to save it for later use, so that if his life becomes chaotic he still has this moment stored to draw peace from.

I do not realize that I have drifted to sleep until Maruq rouses me to take the watch. He stands there with a curious expression on his face, a mixture of pleasure and regret. Qim yips as though to say good morning.

"Ah, so you are to help me then, girl."

I gather my weapons and follow Maruq to the small fire that he has been tending. I settle back down where I had sat earlier, stretching my hands out once again to the warmth. Without a word, Maruq leaves me, followed by his wolves, only Qim stays with me, but he does not return to the corridor. He silently strides farther out, finding a circle of young trees, then turns and smiles. I wonder if he has camped there before. As though he heard my thought, he nods and enters the trees, disappearing from sight like a vision in the night.

30 THE VALLEY BEYOND

I watch over the people as the darkness gives way to the light. My first sight of the valley beyond the corridor does not allay my misgivings about the future. Sheer rock walls stand guard to the valley, which is perhaps fifty spans wide. The walls, capped by snow and ice, jut into the sky, cutting us off from the world. I feel trapped by them. The ground under me is covered in green plants, grasses, and small bushes. Clusters of trees, like the one that Maruq retreated to, are common enough. I wonder what had formed this place and if it led anywhere, or would we journey only to discover another wall opposite many spans away, trapping us here.

I hear the families begin to stir inside the corridor. I gather my nerves, capturing my fears, hiding them deep into my gut. I can't let my people know that uncertainty plagues me.

As the families finish their morning meals, I call the men to me, dividing the day's duties.

"Maruq and Pire will scout. Lotik, Kavok, and Sinaq, you manage the wolves and sleds. Pol and I will guard, at dusk we will set up camp."

Pire grabs his pack, runs a hand down Korak's bare arm,

and joins Maruq, who is jogging off ahead of us. Since we are trying to follow the mammoth to a new home, the scouts must make sure we stay on the right path, constantly running ahead of us and signaling back to guide us through whatever may lay ahead.

By the third day, we are surrounded by trees, tall greenery reaching to the sky. And by the tenth day, the wolves can no longer pull the sleds in a straight line, but we must weave in and out. At one point the forest is so dense we must assist the wolves with their labor, lifting and jostling the sleds by hand to avoid the gnarled roots sticking out of the ground. By mid-morning, I am ready to leave the sleds where they are, but then we would have no supplies.

Qim is harnessed to help another wolf, the father of her pups, pull a sled and I stand at the back with a strong pole, trying to aid it in gliding across a massive root. Sweat is dripping down my face; my muscles are knotted from the strain. I pull something in my shoulder and let out a quiet curse. The sled finally moves past the troubling root, and I lean heavily against my pole. I close my eyes, grateful for the momentary reprieve in my physical exertion.

I hear a low whistle and turn my head in the direction of the sound. Maruq emerges from the trees and the sight of him sends a shiver of pleasure through me. I have not seen him since we left the corridor. If he had messages, he would send them with Pire, who is now helping guide the sleds.

A bemused smile plays at his mouth.

"Did you need something or did you just want to have a good laugh?" I say.

"There is a clearing ahead, about a half-day's journey, or more at the rate you are going." He teases, pointing at my pole.

I smile and wipe away the sweat that is running into my eyes.

"There are several hot pools there. We could camp and rest up for a couple of days, even hunt."

"Maruq, you are my hero." I hear a sound as the sled catches on another root. "Now help me with this sled."

He joins me, placing his hands high on my pole. Without a word, we pull down as a team; it feels natural and right having him by me. With both of us the sled is soon free of the root.

"Pull, pull." He commands the wolves.

I watch the muscles of their hind legs strain under the load and then the sled begins to slide easily away. Well, until it finds another root and we repeat our actions.

I am not certain if it is the thought of relaxing in a hot pool that evening or the silent help of Maruq, who anticipates my every movement, but the rest of the day feels much easier, and my burden much lighter.

I tend to all of my duties, assist in erecting tents for some needed privacy among the separate families, and then make my way to the pool that I had designated for the women. There is still enough daylight left that I don't take a torch along with me.

I hear a soft, sweet laughter coming from the pool. Bela is bathing her child.

"How is the water?" I ask her.

"Ah, my chief, the water is wonderful." The babe kicks and grins at her mother, obviously happy to be free from the constraining pack.

I quickly shed my clothes, hanging my necklace in a nearby bush, and slip into the heat. The water is indeed wonderful. I feel the heat penetrate my tight muscles, releasing stress from the past days. I lean my head back on a small rock and close my eyes. I sigh. "Perfect."

I listen to the quiet around me, a gentle rustling of leaves, the almost imperceptible chatter of bushy tails, a slight crunching of the brown leaves that cover the ground around us.

The crunching sound causes me to lift my head up in curiosity. I search the forest with my eyes.

"Do you see something, Siira?" Bela asks.

"No, I probably just heard a fleet foot or a jumper."

I try to relax again for her sake, but something is not right. I feel we are being watched.

"So, do you like him?" Bela asks, apparently assuming that I would know who she was talking of.

"Who?"

"Siira, I am like your sister. I notice everything."

"Really?" I arch an eyebrow. "And what have you noticed?"

The babe jumps and giggles. "That your gaze is often fixed on a certain hunter and when he is not around your gaze often scans the trees for signs of him."

I swim out to the middle of the pool and plunge down, without answering her, soaking my body and my hair, making it heavy with water. I am done bathing.

I climb out, grabbing my necklace I pull it over my head first. And then I dress quickly as the air has developed a chill. I listen to the woods, waiting for any repeat of the crunching I heard earlier, but there is only the chattering of small creatures and the twitter of flyers.

"I am right then." She says as she climbs out, handing me the naked babe. "You do favor him."

"Maruq is different." I say not wanting to betray the feelings that he stirs when he is near.

"He is a good man." She says as she ties the belt around her dress. "I always pictured you with Balek, but when I began to see you were watching Maruq, I wondered. I noticed that you would sometimes slip away and later I would see you silently sitting with him." She reaches out for the babe, dressing her. "He doesn't speak often. And he rarely joins in with the people. What is it that you find so fascinating?"

I stare at her, thinking, trying to put my feelings into

words. "He is so calm, so certain of things. He doesn't need others approval. He is himself."

Having snuggled the babe into her pack, Bela stands still, staring at me, as though she is trying to digest what I have said, chewing it over in her mind until it becomes mush. A slow, mischievous smile spreads across her face. "And he has amazing blue eyes." She says. And then picks up the child and swings her up onto her back in one graceful motion.

"Yes, he does have amazing blue eyes." I laugh.

We walk on through the trees, making our way back to the camp.

"Are you enjoying the journey?" I ask.

"Well, I have never done this before, so it is quite an adventure." She reaches a hand back behind her and adjusts the pack slightly.

"Does she seem to mind being in that thing?" I point at the pack.

"No, well, sometimes. She enjoys being able to stretch out."

"Have you thought of what you will name her, at her ceremony?" We, the people, don't name our children until they have lived an annual. It is the first important marker on a journey, the naming ceremony. We use the names to honor our family. My name is a combination of my mother's and my grandfather's names.

"Yes, well, I have thought of honoring my mother and Pol, but I don't like the sound of Potiqa."

I laugh at the odd-sounding name. "No, well how about, Nola?"

"Nola," she says the name over, slowly, trying it on her tongue. "I like it. I shall have to ask Pol."

"Well, you don't have to decide yet, there is still another half an annual before her ceremony."

We walk slowly back to the camp, allowing the wind to blow our hair around. Bela stops abruptly and quickly braids her hair, her hands moving swiftly, gracefully in the way that happens only after a lifetime of practice.

I wonder what the people would think if I were to braid my hair. But how would I braid it? If I braid it in one braid as Bela does, it would mean that I am a woman, which I am not; but if I braid it in two braids it would mean that I am a girl, young and innocent, which I don't think I qualify for either. So I gather my hair and tie it in its usual tail, long down my back.

We have rested for three days, enjoying the pools and quiet. The women and children relax and play, while the men replenish our food supply with the kills they bring in. Maruq and Pire have scouted ahead and found the mammoth grazing in a great clearing and so we shall stay here until the herd moves on.

Qim and I take the afternoon to scout, working our way to the edge of the forest and scaling high to the ridge of the rock wall. I stand on snow and ice; all of the world lies out below me, my vantage point unparalleled. The wind gusts around me, sending loose tendrils of my black hair into my eyes.

Scanning the valley below me, I see the forest going on for many spans. I see the clearing where the mammoth are, their lumbering forms grazing. I see a great river shine like a blue cord weaving through the trees. And off at a great distance, I see blue smoke rise into the gray sky. Everything surrounding the smoke is green, the forest seeming to go on forever.

But how can there be smoke at that distance? It does not look like the smoke caused by a great fire, as if lightening had struck and set the earth ablaze. It is very much like the fires of men. But what men? I have never heard tales of men journeying beyond the corridor.

I turn to see what is behind me. White peaks go on, until

they meet a dark blue shimmer. The Great Salt Water. A pain of loss runs in my heart. My home is back there, everything familiar to me is behind me. But my heart is no longer there; I have lost every one that I loved, well not everyone. I think of Balek. He was born to lead. I had always known that without realizing it. The men naturally listened to him and rallied around him. I hope he is becoming the leader that the people need. I hope that he is not pining for me. He must know that wasting time on regret is not what the people need.

"Help him," I say making a quiet petition to the Mighty One, hoping it will be answered.

I crouch down to pet Qim, who has started whining.

"What is it, girl?"

Her ears perk up and she sniffs into the wind, then she growls.

Danger, she smells danger.

Then I see it. A very fresh cat's print, the size telling me that it is a large male. Warily, I scan the area. Maybe I am wrong, maybe, but probably not. I know cats. I place my throwing stick in my strong hand, placing a dart at ready. I begin to track him, for I can't have him finding the camp.

"Get Maruq," I command Qim. She runs off, and I move into the wind, knowing that if the cat is in front of me, he will never smell me coming. The Great Light has traveled its day's journey and is beginning to sink behind the horizon when I find him, a large male blade-tooth, larger than any I have seen.

His focus is on something ahead; my focus is on him. His thick fur shows many battle scars, deep and ragged, including one across his strong eye. He must have fought many a challenging cat for control of his territory, but never one like me.

I must protect my people, and allowing him free range would be dangerous. And so, I decide to go after him.

Removing my pack and jacket, preparing my dart in my

throwing stick, I stand, rushing to him. He turns, hearing my approach. He crouches, immediately preparing to attack. I focus on the kill spot; I throw my dart. It flies strong through the air, speeding toward his neck, but he is not easily taken. He swipes at my dart and knocks it away. It lands in the snow not two spans behind him. He bares his teeth and snarls at me, hissing, as if to warn me off.

He has never seen a creature like me before, and so is cautious, unsure of me. I doubt that I look dangerous to him. I have no sharp teeth, no claws. I am a weak thing. He crouches, approaching cautiously, ears pinned to his head. I ready another dart, trying to appear fiercer than he thinks I am, stabbing at him with it. He bats at my hand. His great claw scratches me. Pain surges up my arm, but I do not drop the dart. We circle around, measuring each other.

Neither one advances. I know that he can easily kill me, perhaps he knows it too. I wait for him to pounce, standing my ground. He leaps high placing his front paws on my shoulders. But before I can maneuver to safety, he knocks me over. I am pinned to the ground. I attempt to struggle but I cannot get out, once again held to the ground by an opponent.

I stop struggling as his claws dig into my shoulders, puncturing my tunic. I concentrate on my breathing, if I am to die, so be it. I look up into his tawny eyes. The fading light of the day reflects red in them. The cat sniffs at me, curious. Then he must decide that I have learned my lesson, for he steps off of me and cries. His cry sends shivers tingling, down my spine, as though insects crawl across every inch of my skin.

Then just as quickly as the confrontation had begun, it is over. I watch the great beast stalk off. He cries out again, perhaps warning me; perhaps calling to others in his family alerting them to the new creatures that are in the area. But what does he tell them? Does he say we are not worth their time or does he say we look like a tasty meal?

I sit up. My shoulders and hand throb in unison.

I hear the snow crunching and a wolf howl. It is Qim. Unsettled by my encounter with the ancient hunter, I try to tell myself that we will just be careful and that will be enough, but I am not certain.

Qim trots up to my side, sniffing me and making certain that I am well. I look into her eyes, and she begins to lick the back of my hand. I wince, pulling my hand away from her.

"I am fine girl."

She whines.

I hear a commotion behind me and turn, reaching for my dart, half expecting the cat. I crouch ready to attack. But from the trees emerges Maruq. He is running with Nal at his side. His bow is in his hand and his pack is on his back as though ready for anything. He is breathing hard. The exertion has awakened a fire in his eyes and given color to his cheeks. I smile, admiring the Mighty One's craftsmanship.

"Siira, what is it?" He slows, stopping a couple of spans away.

"We found a cat." I relax my stance, lowering my dart. Qim runs to him, circling Nal before returning to me.

"A cat?" His eyes examine me, pausing briefly at my shoulders, and resting on my strong hand. He slowly sucks in air as if calming himself.

"I don't think it had ever seen man before. It treated me like a novelty, but I don't think it was hungry or else I wouldn't be talking to you."

"So how did you get that?" He points his bow at my injured hand.

"It's just a scratch." I lift it, thinking to show him how minor the injury is, but as I examine it for the first time, I become lightheaded. Bright spots dance before my eyes. There are three gashes. Each runs from my wrist to the fingers of my strong hand. I can see the cords of my hand move as I move the fingers, slowly testing them. Each works.

Blood seeps out and onto the snow at my feet.

I settle back into the snow, breathing in the crisp air. Qim settle next to me, sniffing at my injury.

"It needs tending to," Maruq says, closing the distance between us.

I try to smile and ruff Qim's ear with my other hand. "That is what she is doing."

Qim licks me again and I wince.

"I think you need better medicine." Maruq's eyes have changed, becoming clouded with emotion. Setting his bow down, he gently takes my hand, examining it. "Move your fingers." I wiggle each one in turn.

"Bela has some of Tomu's herbs in her tent." I fight the urge to give in to the weakness overcoming me. "She can help me, but the cat? We can't let it roam around freely."

"I will track him and we can set a watch, but right now let's get you to Bela's." He takes firm hold of my elbow, setting my injured hand high on my shoulder. "Now, leave it there," he insists.

He shrugs his pack from his back. Opening it, he searches through the contents. I close my eyes, focusing on the wind swirling around my body, taking deep breaths, waiting for my strength to return. I feel long, confident fingers grasp my hand and begin to wrap it in soft skin. A soft gasp of pain escapes my lips. Maruq's hand stills.

"I am fine." I assure him keeping my eyes closed.

Once he finishes with wrapping and binding it, I hear the snow crunch. I open my eyes at the sound. He is removing his belt from around his waist.

"What is that for?"

Without answering he places my hand back on my shoulder beginning to wrap me with his belt, going in circles from shoulder to shoulder until my hand is secure.

"Can you walk?" Maruq asks when he is finished.

"Yes, I can walk, Maruq." My voice sounds stronger than I feel. "The wound is on my hand. You go after the cat."

"First, I will take you back to camp," he says, not fooled by my bravado. He leaves for a moment finding my pack and jacket.

"I am fine; you don't need to help me."

He wraps my jacket around my shoulders, carefully adjusting it, helping me to slip my free arm into the sleeve. I watch him. His hands are trembling slightly.

"You're worried about me?" My head swims, but not because of the injury. I have never really had a man worry about me. My father taught me to be self-sufficient. Balek believed I could do anything. But now here is Maruq, and he worries about me.

"You don't need to." I take his hand, trying to reassure him.

"No, I don't, but I still do." He merely holds my gaze, unrelenting concern clouding his eyes, making them gray. I have seen this look before, the night he came to my tent concerned that I was to fight Iruq.

I get lost in the depths of his eyes for a moment. There is nothing around us except snow and ice, but I still don't feel free to do as I please. The man I choose would have to lose himself to be joined to me, becoming a nothing, an in between. I can't do that to him.

"Grab my pack, and let's take me to Bela's," I say.

31 THE CAT ATTACK

As soon as we enter camp, I send Maruq to alert the men about the cat. I want a guard set on the perimeter at all times. We must be more wary.

I find Bela in her tent tending her babe.

"I need some herbs and dressings," I say, shrugging my jacket off.

"Why?" she asks as she turns from her babe. Seeing my hand strapped to my shoulder, she says, "Oh. And how did you do that?" She begins to rifle through her belongings. She has dressed many wounds. Her father's and brother's wounds make mine look like a small scratch.

"I found a cat."

"A cat?" I hear a wavering in her voice. She turns to me, a pouch of dried herbs in her hand, fear in her eyes. She indicates a pile of furs near the fire pit for me to sit on. "Do you think it was watching us at the pool?" Her voice is a whisper.

I think back. Possibly, it could have been a cat, but not the great cat I faced today. The crunching of the steps was too light. Mighty One was it a cat?

I look at Bela. Fear has found its place in her eyes.

"Well, I can handle an old cat." I slump down, tired and

attempting to appear bored. Qim comes and lays next to me, exhausted.

Bela gives me a bowl of water and a soft skin to clean the wound. I begin to slowly unwrap Maruq's belt from around me. I set the bandaged, throbbing hand on my knee, carefully unwrapping it, and then wipe at the wound with cool water. Waves of faintness wash over me. But I fight them and soon the dried and blotchy scab that had formed is gone and only ragged flesh remains. I play with it, trying to lay it down flat so that it will heal to look as normal as possible.

Bela comes with herbs she has mixed and stewed in a pot. At the sight of my hand, she sucks in her breath. She sets to work packing the herbs into my wound. With each movement she makes, I wince.

"Now for the dressing." She says, beginning to hum. I try to focus on the melody and not what she is doing. When she is finished, I look as though I have a large mitten. It is an unwieldy dressing. I study it. How will I hunt without my strong hand?

"Don't look so worried, my chief, it will heal quickly." Her voice is light and a smile has returned to her face.

"I know." I think of all of the hunts that I have been on, of all of the practicing and training I have done, and this is my first wound. *It should make for a great scar.* Balek's words come back to me. He had said that so long ago. And now, now I know that if he were here he would repeat it.

"Do you want some food?" Her question pulls me from my thoughts. "I need to feed the babe." As though beckoned, the infant giggles in anticipation.

"No, I will wait."

"At least take some herbs."

I nod and absently pet Qim while she fills a bowl with hot water and herbs for me. The babe waits on a soft skin for her mother to feed her. Bela takes some meat powder and puts it in her mouth, chewing it until it is a soft mush. She then takes her child into her arms, settling down to feed her.

"She is old enough for that?"

Bela puts another bit of mush into her babe's mouth before answering, "Oh, yes. She still needs my milk, but she enjoys the mush. And it is nice to be able to feed her something other than me."

Wonder fills me as I watch the babe eat. How does Bela know what she can have and when? Does the Mighty One just give the knowledge out as the mother needs it? Or is it something born in her?

Pire peaks in, his eyes adjusting to the darkness of the tent, and says, "Pol and the others have returned, my chief, and they got a fleet foot. Kora is roasting it. We will have a feast tonight."

"Thank you," I say. He leaves.

"When are you going to perform the joining ceremony? I don't see a need for them to wait any longer, do you?"

No, there is no need. Pire had left his family to follow his promised one and her family. Any more waiting may cause a problem that I don't want to deal with. I have watched them talking together the last couple of nights. They need their own tent.

"I suppose we could do it while we rest here. I shall announce it at the feast."

Yes, perhaps the news of a joining ceremony will overshadow the fear of lurking cats.

Bela begins humming a night song to her child. I recognize it as the one that my mother and grandmother would sing to me.

Sleep, sleep, beautiful child.

I nod to sleep.

When I awaken, the babe is resting, wrapped in her pack, warm and safe and quiet. I lay motionless, mesmerized by the small perfection next to me. Bela is quietly stitching on something.

I hear a rustling at the tent door, someone pushing the flap back with a flourish. I move, pulling my head out of the foggy land of dreams.

"The feast has begun, my love." Pol stands in the opening, grinning ridiculously at his woman.

I push myself up onto my elbows. "For a fine hunter, you certainly are loud." I grumble at him.

His head jerks in my direction, startled at first by my presence, and then he laughs good-naturedly, a contagious laughter. Soon I am smiling.

"Sorry, my chief, I just came to get my woman and child. I didn't know you were still here, resting."

"Well, my love," Bela says, "you have delivered your message; the child and I will join you soon."

Bela stands and looks to me. "Can you watch her for a moment? I will be back." Bela turns quickly, suddenly eager to be out of the tent.

"Where are you going?" I look to the child. She is sound asleep, harmless. But panic rises in me nevertheless.

"I will be right back. I just need to relieve myself." Bela smiles. "It's alright, she is sleeping and if she wakes you don't have to do anything; just let her cry."

I am uncertain and incredulous, but before I can object, she disappears.

I stare at the child as she rhythmically breathes in and out, slow, quiet breaths. I mimic her. She drags in a long, deep breath. I wait for her to exhale, holding my breath along with her. The rhythm skips many beats, as does my heart. A small fear grows inside me as she continues to hold her breath. I release mine, hoping that it will cause her to do the same, but it does not. Is she dead? No, she lets out the air in a long exhale, her lips quiver as she does it. Is that normal? I have no way to know.

I move closer to her, wanting to run a finger along her soft cheek, but hesitate, for I do not want to wake her, to disturb her peace. I raise my uninjured hand. Her pink perfection sharply contrasts against my dark, calloused hand. A sigh escapes her lips, content in the knowledge that here she is safe, wrapped tightly in skins and fur, bound in a bundle, ready to be lifted and carried wherever her parents take her.

The peace is shattered by a screech. I know that sound. A cat has found a victim. A rush of adrenaline surges through me. The cry is close to the tent, too close. I hear the men run past in a fury. They are ready to fight the cat, to protect the people. I feel useless with my strong hand injured and bound.

Men are yelling. A woman screams. A cat yowls. Then silence.

I can't leave Bela's child alone in the tent, yet I must see what has happened. I am Chief; I am responsible. Without another thought I swing the child onto my back. I hear a small grunt, as if the babe says that I am too rough with her. I grab one of my darts with my weak hand. My strong hand throbs, as if to protest its uselessness.

Quickening my steps, I round the tent and pass into the trees. Not far away I see torches and a circle of men. They have slain the attacker. It is the great cat that I had seen earlier. He must have smelled our kill and come to dine. Its lifeless body lies abandoned by the men. They have formed a tight ring around something else. I remember, a woman screamed.

As I draw closer, the men make way for me. I see Pol kneeling, a head on his lap.

No, I silently scream. *Not Bela.*

I am now directly behind him and my steps freeze, like my soul. In front of me, Pol rocks back and forth, silent at first then a base noise coming from the depths of his soul and escaping his lips.

I stare, refusing to comprehend. Trying to maintain a stone face, trying to push my feelings down, and trying to be

Chief. Yet there lays Bela, my friend, my only sister, soaked in her own blood. Long, jagged slashes run across her neck and chest. The blade-tooth had ambushed her. Bela was an easy prey; she had not sensed danger. She had no weapon, no skill in hunting, and so she had died.

I am frozen to my place behind Pol, silently arguing with the Mighty One who allowed such an injustice. I want to scream, to weep, but I am Chief. I cannot grieve her as Pol does.

I walk back to the carcass of the cat. Rage, blind red rage, courses through me, and I thrust my dart into its neck. I hear men behind me. I will my lips to move, my voice to give orders. From far off, I hear myself command them to take the cat, to clean it for use.

"I want the blades," I say, and then I disappear into the night.

32 GRIEF

I run, mindlessly, into the black night, dodging trees and branches. My mind fights the images: Bela playing dolls, Bela whispering secrets, Bela taking Pol as her man, Bela singing to her child, Bela lying in blood.

I can't see where I am going and I don't care. I am weighted down, my light, quick steps replaced by heaviness.

Why? Why punish her? She is innocent. She only every trusted, loved, obeyed. I should be the one punished, not her, but maybe this is punishment.

I scream blasphemous threats into the sky, hoping that the Mighty One's caprice will at last fall on me that my grief will end. I catch my foot on a root and fall. As I fall, I hear another sound, a small gasp. In my grief, I have forgotten that I carry Bela's child on my back. The child's volume grows as comfort does not come quickly to her. The familiar soothing tones of her mother's voice do not calm her. Her cries swell into full-throated screams that mimic my pain.

I stand up; weighted down by a burden I should never have to bear, a motherless child. Stumbling blindly through the thick forest, unsure of how far I am from the camp or how to return to it. I keep moving. Motion means that I am alive, and no matter how much my hollow frame tells me to sink onto the ground and never move again, I cannot. I am pulled along by a need to return to my people, to return the child to her father.

The rhythmic swaying of my walk must have soothed the child for she is silent.

My ears twitch at a slight scrape behind me. Through force of habit, I reach for my blades on my belt, forgetting about my injured hand. Angrily I breathe a curse and grasp one blade. I stand poised in the night, among the trees, ready to encounter whatever comes.

I remember the babe, how can I fight with her weighing me down? Will the Mighty One take me tonight so that I may join the others? I decide to crouch low, waiting for my fate. My heart drums in my ears; my head begins to feel light. I don't want to die now. I must return Bela's babe to her father.

The steps come closer and I see a lean form approaching, weaving through the trees, right in my direction. The slow, graceful motions are unhurried. Maruq is tracking.

I replace my blade and stand, unafraid, yet heartbroken. I long for comfort.

"Siira?" He stops frozen in his tracks, a question in his eyes at the sight of the babe. "Why are you here? Pire told me there would be a feast tonight."

"Bela's dead." I stare back at him, feeling hollow. I have lost so many in my life that the pain should not bother me anymore. Like the callouses on my hands, or my hardened muscles, I should be so accustomed to loss that I no longer ache at it. But I am raw, empty. The darkness is winning, conquering my soul, taking all of my light.

As I stare into his eyes, longing for the comfort that strong arms can give, he steps closer. He opens his arms to me and I step in, accepting his calm. As his lean arms wrap around me, tears build in my eyes until they cannot be contained, and they overflow, like water breaking through a dam.

I nestle into his chest. His arms gather around me tightly, his head softly rests on mine. His warmth melts the ice in my soul, like the heat of the Great Light melting the ice above the high river. I cry, not just for Bela, but for all I have lost.

All of my tragedies flood into my mind, sweeping in great sobs down my body; Pol's wailing with Bela in his lap, Grandmother's serene passing, my father's bloodied form laying in the grass, and my mother's body drifting out to the great water. I am five once again, weeping openly, and being comforted.

As the waves of grief come, I lean into Maruq wanting more of his warm strength.

Finding my voice, I sob into his chest, "Why? Why her?"

Maruq gently kisses my head. And then pulls away slightly so that I can look up at him.

"She is safe with the Mighty One."

I look into the glistening blue of his eyes, he has been crying as well.

"But what of us? Her babe needs her, Pol needs her. I need her."

"The Mighty One will provide." The serene melody of his voice, his calm assurance seems to mock me.

The Mighty One. My blood boils, forgetting its grief at the mention of him. I am tired of his whims, tired of the caprice that ruins my life. I need Bela. She was my friend, my sister. But I can't have her. She has been taken from me.

"Don't talk to me of *his* plans, of *his* love. I don't see it. Don't believe in it." I pull back from him ready to run back to the camp to return the child to her father. The dark sky roars out a grumble.

Maruq catches my injured hand in his, stopping me. "Siira, I know you are in pain."

"Pain?" I spit out the word, and the sky begins to pelt rain down on us. "I am in agony." I shout above the storm. I try to shake his hand from mine, but he is too strong and my hand too weak. "You are hurting me." I say, choking back sobs, hoping that he will release me.

"Then stop struggling."

He pulls me closer. Part of me wants to remain to hear him, to believe as he does, but the other part wants to fight and run blindly into the rain.

"I understand your pain." He looks up to the sky, allowing the water to shower down onto him, accepting it. He lowers his head and I see the pain in his eyes. "I have known it. I have lost more than anyone should."

"Then how can you still trust him, believe him." Another clap of thunder punctuates my words.

He opens his mouth, but before he can answer me the ground shakes.

The violent shaking rocks us and throws me into his chest. Maruq falls backward and we land in a pile. Terror fills me as the ground rolls again. It is as though the solid earth has become an undulating body of water, rising and falling in waves. Maruq pulls me to my feet. I search his eyes. They are calm, determined. "Run." He commands taking my uninjured hand, and I obey.

We run, side by side, hand in hand. We dodge falling trees and rolling rocks. Fixing my eyes on the moving ground ahead of me I try to anticipate the obstacles that are being set before me.

A low moan fills my ears, vibrating off of everything around me. It is not human: the earth moans. I watch as boulders break apart, becoming jagged obstructions. I leap over them, my blood surges giving me extra energy. As I land, the ground shoots me up, tearing my hand from Maruq's. Unbalanced, I drop to my knees. Bela's babe wails in fear. I search the ground below me. Maruq stands and scrambles up the newly formed cliff, climbing back to me. I reach out for him. He takes my hand, entangling my fingers with his, and we set off again.

I let him lead me, not wanting to lose him again. Is this

the shake of Bela's dream? Did we leave the cave in vain? What of the camp? I am their chief, they need me.

Abruptly, I stop running.

"Siira, come on." Maruq tugs on my hand, knowing my thoughts before I voice them. "You can't help them now."

Allowing him to pull me forward, back into motion. We run, but I do not know why. There is no escape. I have failed to save my people, to lead them to a better future. Bela's painting flashes into my mind; the mammoths will not lead their child to safety. No matter what we try, we cannot escape what will be.

The earth shoots up again. I am thrown forward into Maruq's back. We fall, tumbling one over the other. I land in a sitting position. I curl up into a tight ball, pulling my legs into my chest. The babe on my back continues to scream into the storm. Maruq tries to get me up. He tugs on my hand, pulls on me, but I refuse to move. I will stay here until something kills me. I release his hand, but instead of leaving me he sits and wraps me in his arms.

A few more waves of the earth, and the terror is over. The rain continues to pelt us. When I am certain that the ground is once again solid, I pull away from him. He stands and moves away, probably to scout the area.

I shrug the pack off of my shoulders. I try to hush the child, to comfort her with promises I should not make.

"Shh, baby, we will find your father, tomorrow. I am sure he has survived." But I am not sure, I am not sure of anything.

She squeals in terror. I run a finger down her cheek. I begin to unlace her. As I pull her from the pack, she begins to kick and scream in protest. I try to remember how Bela held her to calm her. Clumsily, I settle her into my arms. Pressing her against my body, sheltering her from the rain, I begin to sway back and forth. I attempt to hum, but refuse to sing.

Grateful for the distraction of a helpless child, I begin to soothe my nerves, convincing myself that my earlier promises were true. Maruq and I survived, surely others did as well. The rocking motion works like a sleeping concoction my grandmother gave me as a child. Soon the child is sleeping. Exhaustion washes over me and I know that I must secure the babe back in the pack.

I gently place her back and begin to lace her tightly. When I begin to pull the lace tight, I notice a dark object on the ground. It must have fallen out of the pack. I finish lacing her and then retrieve it. It is a small wooden rattle, one that is carved for babes to entertain them.

I study it and soon realize that Balek had made it for her. A final gift in the hopes that he will be remembered. I run my fingers over the carving of a great grizzly . Pain stabs me again. I have lost so much.

Was Balek able to save the others? Or are we all gone, everyone but me and the babe and Maruq.

"Why?" I sob, as I tuck the rattle back into the pack.

Maruq returns.

"I will watch." He says settling against a fallen tree. I lay down and curl around the child in her pack. Exhaustion takes over and I begin to fade to sleep.

I am Chief. I repeat to myself over and over, like the beating of the dancer's drums. I am Chief, I am Chief. The rain beats along with the rhythm. I am Chief, I am Chief. And yet, of what, I don't know.

33 SHARING

Morning light streams through the leaves above me, waking me. I blink into it, trying to remember why I feel empty. The memory returns too quickly. I sit up. Maruq and the babe are gone.

I stand, searching the broken landscape for movement. The trees above me stand askew, shooting out of the jagged ground at odd angles. Other trees are toppled on top of each other or splintered. Abrupt rock walls rise where the ground was level just the day before. The world looks as though it was shaken by a great hand and broken up into uneven pieces. Even if I could discern the direction of the camp, I don't know if I could make it back.

After last night's fit of motion, everything is silent. I remember the moaning sounds and contrast them with the peace of the moment; it is as contradictory in my mind as a cat lying peacefully with a curly horn.

I search around me, frantic for any sign that Maruq will return. I spin in small circles. Then I see it, next to a fallen tree Maruq's pack, a small pouch and a water skin laying on top of it. I relax at the silent message. He would have me eat. I sink down and grasp the water skin, gulping mouthfuls of liquid, but it is not refreshing.

I think of all that I have lost, all that was left behind. I do not have my pack. I do not have my throwing stick or my darts. I do not have my bed. All I have are my clothes, my cuff, and my tokens.

Maruq has everything. His pack and weapons were on him when he found me last night. I look about me for the bow and darts.

"He would have taken those with him," I remind myself.

I grab up the meat powder pouch with my uninjured hand, placing it on my bandaged mitten. Balancing it precariously there, I use my first two fingers to work the pouch open. There is a hollowness in my stomach that I hope will be alleviated by the meat powder in the pouch, but I really don't believe the feeling is hunger. I pinch at the pulverized food and put it on my tongue. Its dryness soaks up any moisture that the water had provided, leaving my throat even rougher than before.

Before I eat my fill, Maruq returns with the babe on his back. He looks almost unaware of her weight, as though he carries nothing more than his regular burden, his sleeping roll, his weapons, and food.

He holds up two dead jumpers on a cord. He must have shot them while out.

"I see that you have been busy," I say, and then pinch more meat powder and drop it into my mouth.

He smiles.

"How are you this morning?" I ask.

Gingerly, he feels the back of his head. He must have hit it during the great shake. "Sore."

He sets the jumpers down in front of me. Shrugging the pack off of his back, he swings the babe. She giggles from the exhilaration of the motion.

"Are you going to do something with those?" I nod at the jumpers, my voice hard.

"I thought we could roast them before we set out."

I nod in assent.

"I caught them, you cook them," he says, a playful gleam in his bright eyes.

"I am Chief." I say in no mood to play.

"I have the babe." He swings her again, causing more giggling.

Setting down the pouch, I catch the pack with my good hand. Tugging the babe to me, I cradle her against my chest.

"Not anymore."

He shrugs and takes the jumpers. Crouching down, he takes a blade from his belt and begins skinning the kill.

"Did you find anything out there?" I gesture behind him into the trees.

He pauses momentarily as he answers. "No, I found nothing, not even Nal answered my calls. But I didn't go very far. I thought we could search together."

I realize then that I hadn't seen his constant companion with him last night. "Where was she?"

"I left her with Kavok. He was scouting near the pools."

I study him. He slices down the jumper's jacket in one long fluid motion. Turning it over, he strips it. Nothing in his movements seems agitated or disturbed in the wake of the turmoil. Somehow he still manages to have a calm and relaxed demeanor.

The babe in my arms starts to nuzzle against my chest. She works her mouth as though there is something there for her. I stare down at her in dismay.

"I think she wants milk," Maruq says. Having skinned the first jumper, he works on the second.

Yes, Bela's babe seems not to notice that I am not her mother; she does not yet understand the loss. But she will soon; she still requires milk. Meat powder mush will have to suffice for now, but she still needs milk, her mother's milk.

"I could find a mother fleet foot," Maruq says, reading my mind again. "I spotted one last night before . . . I found you." He begins a small fire near a fallen tree. Skewering the jumpers with a thin, sturdy twig, he lays them across two piles of stones. He sits down across from me, reclining against the tree, watching the food roast. I watch him. His serenity seems misplaced in these surroundings, under these circumstances.

"If we are able to find the fleet foot, then what, latch her to the animal?"

Maruq's laughter fills the heavy air with a bright melody. "No, we make her a drinking sack from my extra water skin. I have suckled orphaned wolves that way, I am sure it will work for the child."

He is right, I remember seeing Natiq nurse a babe the same way once when the mother was gravely ill. I had even done something similar with Qim.

Qim. Where is she? Did she survive as I had? I try to remember when I saw her last. But then the babe begins to whimper, a soft distressed noise that begins to grow.

Since I cannot fill her stomach with milk, I lay her on the ground next to me and reach into the pouch again. I begin to chew the powder as I had seen Bela do yesterday. Was it just yesterday? The babe's cries demand that I meet her need.

"Patience," I manage to say through the mush.

I see the rattle and shake it in front of her. She reaches out her long fingers for it. And I hand it to her. She grasps it and pulls it to her mouth.

Since I cannot hold her and feed her the way her mother did because of my injury, I lie down next to the child and feed her. Eventually, she has her fill and drifts to sleep, clutching the grizzly claw rattle.

I sit up and find Maruq watching me. Our eyes meet, he smiles, setting senseless flutters free in my stomach. And then he looks at the meat that is roasting.

Unsettled, I pull the tie from my hair, planning on simply smoothing my tangled mane before retying it. I lift my hand and run my fingers through it. And then I realize that I can't bind the tie with only one hand.

"I could braid it for you." Maruq says, smiling.

I harden myself. I have just lost Bela and possibly everyone else and Maruq teases. And so I stare hard at him, while I gather it in one hand and twist it around and around until it is a long cord. I yank it into a loose knot. It won't hold for long, but it is all I can do.

"We lived in mountains across the Great Salt Water." His smile has vanished and a sad serious expression has replaced it. "My older brother had left us long before that day, and so only my father and I could take the herd to graze in the high brush. We left my mother two days before. She was beautiful, long, dark hair braided down her back, bright blue eyes, and a mouth that easily smiled. I can still see her watching us from our small home as we walked up a path into the mountains.

"The days were long and still. My father was constantly checking everything. He was as jumpy as a jumper, any sound seemed to alarm him. I didn't understand why, until we returned home, or where home was supposed to be." He shifts his position, as if the memory still pains him.

"The home that I once knew had been washed away; the land was wiped clean like sand after the water has rushed back out. Our small homes were flattened. Bodies were strewn on the shore carelessly abandoned. I found Kara's body tossed carelessly behind some bushes." He blinks back tears that are in his eyes. "Tara and her two daughters were in their flattened home, her husband's body was floating near the shore. Qitar, one of my baby nieces, she was three annuals. Her hair used to shine in the sun, as she would run laughing away from me. My father found her body by the boats. My mother and my other sisters and their families we never found. My people were all gone. In one afternoon the great water had taken everything."

He turns the jumpers. "It took us three days to burn the bodies, sending them to the Great Father."

I watch him as he speaks. Except for the grief, so

apparent in his voice and features, he seems calm, peaceful. His movements measured and steady.

"Father chose to go in search of a new people. We repaired a boat that had belonged to my eldest sister's man and set out across the water, always keeping land in sight. Xin, my father's wolf, did not like the boat much, and so we soon abandoned it and walked. When we found your people, we praised the Mighty One."

I eat up every morsel of information he gives me, wanting to know him better, wanting to understand how he can still trust in the Mighty One. Unconsciously, I lean forward, eager for more.

"I am not certain you remember that first annual we were with you. I felt awkward and out of place. I did not speak your language and those that were my age were not inclined to teach me. And so I watched and stayed with my father. It was your father that taught us much about your ways.

"When an annual had passed and we were to endure the testing, both my father and I could communicate easily with anyone we wished. I had already passed a similar challenge among my people when I was twelve, and so I had no qualms about taking a fleet foot on my own."

He stands and takes the jumpers off the fire. Coming over to me, he sits and hands me one of them. I toss it back and forth between my mittened hand and my other hand to cool it down.

"I remember. You came back to the cave the earliest of any man I had seen. I was impressed." My voice sounds more normal, less stern.

He raises an eyebrow in question.

"Truly, it impressed me, as did your token."

"A fleet foot impressed you?" Maruq says.

"Yes. You and your father were new to us. I would have thought that you would seek to impress the men, to gain favor and acceptance. But instead you returned with no flourish, no story."

Maruq bites his meat, chewing slowly, thinking. "But your friend Balek came back with a grizzly, and a most impressive story."

"Well, yes, Balek had been trying to impress me." I grimace, remembering how he had almost died. "But you," I look into his eyes, "you only did what you wanted. With no thought of anyone's opinion. I admired that. I have always had to concern myself with the opinions of others, but you are free."

Gazing into my eyes, he says, "You don't have to try to impress people, the Mighty One has gifted you greatly, my chief. You are an amazing person."

His words stir me, soothing some of my hurt.

We finish the meal in silence.

"Shall we do some exploring then?" He stands and kicks dirt into the fire.

I nod. We have used enough of the day storytelling. I need to find my people, if there are any to find. Standing, I pick up Bela's babe in her pack. Swinging her onto my back, my hair gets caught under a strap. I grunt as my mittened hand gets tangled in my mass of hair and the pack. I struggle, pulling my hair free, trying to free my strong hand.

"No wonder the women braid their hair," I mutter, adding a soft curse.

"Let me." Maruq reaches behind me, grasps my thick hair at the base of my neck, and gently works it free. "You may want to do something with it or else the babe will pull on it."

"What exactly do you suggest?"

"You could braid it." A gleam in his eyes. I assume he is trying desperately to lighten my mood.

I hold up my wrapped hand.

"Or cut it."

I scowl. With my hand incapacitated, the suggestion has some merits, but I am unwilling to cut it.

"Or," He says turning to his pack. He digs around in it, and then with a flourish he pulls out a long wide cord. He returns to me. His long fingers gather my hair in his hand. I feel him wrapping the cord around my hair. Binding it. He wraps it almost all the way to my waist.

And then he drapes the thick tail over my shoulder. "Good?" He asks.

I smile at him. "Thank you."

He nods and then turns to gather his belongings. We scale several small jagged hills, newly formed by the earthshake. Hiking up and across, scrambling down and over. The peaceful forest that I had gazed upon from the top of the mountain no longer exists. I wonder if anything still exists.

34 A FALL

A sheer cliff rises before us, shooting about ten spans into the gray sky. I am positive that this was not here the day before when I scanned the valley from the top of the mountain. It must have been formed by the earthshake.

"We will have to climb."

I look from him to the dressings on my strong hand.

"You could wait."

"No. I will be fine." I protest. I am incapable of waiting while he climbs. I quickly unbind my hand. The herbs have changed my hand. It is slimy and greenish looking. I work my hand, opening and closing it. An aching, pulsing pain spreads from my hand up my forearm. The newly healing skin threatens to break open.

"Are you certain?" Maruq has been watching me, concern in his bright eyes.

"Of course." I harden my voice and my resolve.

He swings the pack off of his back and sets it down, searching for something. "Here, at least let me bind it with something." He holds out a thin leather cord and a scrap of something else.

I hold my hand out to him. He lays the scrap on the wounds and wraps the cord around my hand. I try moving my fingers again. It is much easier.

"Thank you."

As he nods, the muscles in his jaw move, tightening as if he is forcing himself not to speak, to object.

I head for the cliff and stretch high trying to reach a root that is sticking out.

"Wait. Let me carry the babe."

I glare at him, at the implication that I cannot climb with the babe.

"We can trade." He offers me his pack.

I assent. He is right. I am injured, and if I carry the babe I may kill her if I fall. My people's needs must come before my pride. And the babe needs to get to her father. I take his less precious, although just as heavy, pack, and begin to climb.

I stretch up and try for a root. I am not able to keep up with Maruq. My hand is much weaker than I had thought it would be. I have to compensate, using my weaker hand to hold more of my weight as I pull up and dig my feet into the loose earth. Pulling and digging in, I climb.

About halfway up, I have to rest. Sweat rolls down my neck and back, my hand aches, my grip is starting to weaken. I look up to see that Maruq has made the top. He stands looking down at me. A frown on his face, a wrinkled brow and tightly drawn lips, express his concern. I watch his fingers flutter over his bowstring.

"Do you need help?"

"No!" I take a deep breath, and then reach for another root. I curl my fingers around it, but I feel my hand slip. I scramble trying to regain my hold, but then I lose my footing. I watch as Maruq's lips part to make a noise, but I never hear him. I hear, rather than feel, the impact. I see red and purple lights dance before my eyes and then my world goes dark.

"Siira, Siira, wake up, please wake up." The pained voice pulls me from my dark hole. "I shouldn't have let you try it."

I know that voice.

"Please, Great Father, don't take her. Let her wake up."

I don't want to leave him. I force my eyes open and squint at the light, blinking. Maruq's face is directly in front of mine, I see tear stains that have run down his dust covered cheeks. Tears for me float in the blue depths of his eyes. Uncontrollable warmth spreads through me.

He loves me. The thought forms slowly. And I try to speak, but I cannot.

His arms encircle me, pulling me to his chest. He presses his cheek against mine, as he rocks me back and forth, continuing to plead with the Great Father. The motion makes me dizzy and disoriented.

A grunt escapes my lips. He pulls me back, staring into my eyes. "You are alive." His whispered exclamation brims with joy. I rest my head on his shoulder. And he holds me gently, but firmly, as though afraid to hurt me.

As I become more aware, I feel a throbbing pulse in my head, sharp pains in my ribs, and dull aches along my spine and leg. I fear that I have broken something.

"What . . . happened?"

"You fell. I thought you were dead."

"Me? Dead? Not yet." I try to take a deep breath, but it hurts.

"Easy. Start slowly. Does it hurt when you breathe?"

I nod.

"Anything else hurting?"

Everything hurts, but I try to feel beyond the overall pain, to find the sources of the pain. I pull myself away from him, out of his arms, rolling my head from side to side, gingerly testing my neck. I straighten and bend my back. It is only bruised, probably from the pack that I landed on. I move each joint and muscle in my legs; they all work. Then I try my ankles. The ankle on my strong side feels swollen and tight inside my boot.

"My strong ankle." I say, becoming dizzy. "And my head."

Carefully, with Maruq's help, I slide out of the straps of the pack. Using it as a cushion for me to lean against, I close my eyes and let him examine me. His long strong fingers probe my hip. I flinch, squeezing my eyes tight, as he finds a new bruise. His hands continue down my leg, and then my knee. One hand remains on my knee and another gently rests under my calf. He methodically lifts my leg, bending and straightening it. I try to relax, to just allow him to search, but my body is aching, throbbing with every movement. I long for the black oblivion so that he can finish without my feeling it.

Satisfied, he releases my leg and squeezes my ankle. I wince, gasping slightly, squeezing my eyes shut until I see colors swirling in the blackness of my mind.

"There?" He asks, his voice thick.

Without opening my eyes, I nod.

Maruq doesn't say anything else. He simply removes his hands from me. As the pain ebbs, I open my eyes. He sits hunched next to me, staring at my booted foot. His head is tilted as though he waits for instructions. Bela's pack is still on his back.

"Is it broken?" I ask, referring to my ankle.

"I don't know, but you can't walk on it right now."

"What are we going to do?" I can't climb, but I need to know if there are others. "The babe needs her father."

He doesn't answer. Instead he scans the area around us. His eyes look to the cliff, which is no longer an option, at least not for me.

"You could go on without me." I say, voicing the only option the babe has.

He gazes over my shoulder, as though he hasn't heard me, but I know that he has for his eyes are alive with emotions and thoughts.

"Please, I can take care of myself." I rest my hands on his arm.

He looks at me. "I can't leave you here alone."

"But the others," I say, "you can find them and then come back for me."

"And what if there are no others?" He covers my hands with one of his. "We need to stay together."

I don't argue. I can't, there is no other path to take.

We move, slowly, my strong arm wrapped around his waist for support. Each movement sends fire throughout my body; sharp needles jab across my ribs with each breath. I need a distraction, but all I can think of is the others. What has happened to them?

"If they live, we will find them." His voice soothes my thoughts.

He is right, we will. He has taken all of the burdens because I can't. He carries Bela's babe on his back, his pack is in his strong hand and I lean heavily on him. All I can manage to help with is his bow and darts.

Maruq stops and places his fingers over my lips. I find the motion pointless since I have not spoken since we started moving in this direction. I look at him and he points. I follow the gesture and see a mother fleet foot and her babe grazing not ten spans ahead of us.

I let go of Maruq and slip down onto a rock behind me. Setting his pack down, he silently slips the babe from his back and onto the ground at my feet. I grasp the straps, holding the babe upright with my weak hand.

He loosens his belt. Taking it in both of his hands, stretching it tight between them, he moves to the mother fleet foot. If he can but catch her, one good thing will have come of the day.

She does not see him until he is three spans away, but

instead of fleeing she gazes at him curiously. He slowly raises his hands, palms out, his belt going slack. Never losing eye contact with her, he walks, creeping closer. She tastes the air with her tongue and returns to her grazing.

Maruq makes his way to her side, laying a gentle hand on her back. She lifts her head and curiously turns her head to examine him, but finding no threat she again returns to her meal. Maruq wraps his belt around her graceful neck and secures her to the tree.

It is a miracle. We have a fleet foot.

Maruq reaches down and grasps some of the grass that she has been munching on and holds it out to her in his open palm. She nuzzles it and begins to eat. He offers her babe some green grass in his other hand, whispering words to them that I cannot hear.

"Now you shall have milk," I tell Bela's babe.

She whines. I pull the meat pouch from my belt and begin to chew a piece of dried meat. Turning it to mush for her, I try to feed her but she spits it right back out.

"I think you had better milk the fleet foot soon. She is refusing the mush."

With long easy strides, he returns to us. Searching through his pack, he flashes me a lopsided smile as he pulls out his extra water skin and a wooden bowl.

He leaves us, returning to the captured mother.

As he works, I feel useless and decide to make camp. I look around and find level ground behind me. Grasping his pack, I drag it to me. I untie his bed roll, and shake out the folds. I lay it out, crawling on all fours, wincing with every movement, but choosing to ignore the pain.

It is a large well-worn grizzly skin. I long to lay on it and sleep, to dream of days that are gone forever, but I have more work to tend to.

I crawl over and lift Bela's babe out of her pack. She kicks and squirms, rolling onto her stomach and then pushing onto her hands and knees. She rocks wildly back and forth, babbling angrily, as though she chides me for my ineptness at caring for her.

"I know." I tell her agreeing with her complaints. "You need your mother."

As I speak with her the child stops her complaining and cocks her head, listening to me. "I was to lead you all to safety, but I have failed."

I continue to talk, telling her my complaints like I would have told Qim. "What would have happened if I had agreed to Boku's demands, if I had joined with Balek?" I crawl closer to her, finding her rattle. I shake it.

"Would Bela and Pol have stayed? Would we all be safe?" She coos and rolls onto her back, her arms and legs wildly kicking as she jabbers, reaching for the finely carved grizzly.

Maruq returns with a skin full of milk. He settles down, easily lifting her into his lap. He hands the skin to her, showing her what to do. Quickly she understands and drains the skin of its warm contents, eagerly filling her stomach. Before she is finished she falls asleep, but continues to suck on the sack.

"What did Boku demand of you?" He asks.

I blink at him surprised. I did not think he could hear me. "He wanted me to join with Balek." I say, holding out the carving, as if the artist himself were in my hand.

Maruq's brilliant eyes blink back at me, his eyebrows knit together. He stares at the rattle. "Why didn't you?"

I know why I didn't want to. Maruq had just told me that he wanted me. I had begun to hope in that dream. Balek was like a brother, whereas Maruq was like a promise of love. But the words to explain catch in my throat and I only stare at him for a long moment.

"How much meat powder do you have?" I ask, dropping the rattle on the fur.

"Only what is in that pouch." He answers allowing me to escape an explanation for now.

"We will need to forage."

"Tomorrow," he says, laying the sleeping babe down.

"Do you think I was foolish?" I ask, wondering now that I know he heard what I said to the babe.

"I think that you need to focus on the blessings."

"Blessings?"

"You are alive. The babe is alive. And we have milk."

"Come on let's get some sleep." He scoots down next to the sleeping child. Stretching out, he closes his eyes, and soon his breathing is a soft rhythm of sleep.

I lie down, trying to be as still as possible, not wanting to disturb either of them. My ribs burn with fire, my ankle throbs in harmony with my hand. My head is foggy, but not in a sleep-inducing way, more in a way that means I cannot find sleep. I cannot drift peacefully into dreams. I can only worry, worry about my people, worry about my wolf, and worry about the future.

Be strong, rise to the challenge, and continue where you are right now. Try to see the good. Grandmother's rasping voice echoes in my mind. She had said those words to me so long ago when I had complained after my first hunt. She reminded me that I had saved lives that day.

The good. I roll my head toward the sleeping babe. Bela's babe. She is alive. Pol and Bela would have left no matter what I did, they wanted to leave before I suggested anything to the council. What would have become of the babe if I had not been here? *She would have died with her parents.*

To give my child, my daughter, a chance at life, I would risk anything. She had said. And she had.

35 GIGGLES

I hear a rustling in the brush, and pull myself from sleep. Forgetting where I am and what has happened, I sit up too quickly. Pain rises, sending a cry up my throat, but I stop it before it escapes and alerts the intruder to my presence.

I look around for Maruq, but he has taken the babe and gone somewhere again. I am alone. I know that if I call out he will come, for he cannot be far away. But I can't bring myself to do it. The bush rustles again and I reach for my blades. I need better weapons. My token blades are not much good against a grizzly or a cat.

My muscles tense, as my heart pounds, loud in my chest. My tawny eyes are fixed on the bush. A forked tongue flicks out catching a flying insect. I relax. It is only a serpent. I watch as it comes out from the low brush. But it is unlike any serpent I have ever seen. For it has wings, featherless wings. It flicks out its forked tongue again, tasting the air around it.

I gaze in wonder. Its skin shines in the early light. My stomach protests at being empty and I wonder what it would taste like. Casting a glance at the dwindling supply of meat powder, I decide that I would not mind trying a new flavor.

The only weapons I have will not work for killing this creature. I look about. My eyes find five smooth stones beside the grizzly skin not two hands away. Sucking in air as I reach over, I gather them to me. And then I take careful aim at my oblivious victim. I launch one at him and the rock stings the side of his head, stunning him. I send a second rock to make certain that he will stay down while I crawl over to him.

Won't Maruq be surprised that I will have a meal waiting for him?

Grasping the creature around the neck, I twist until I hear the familiar crunch. Using one of Maruq's blades, I slit him down the belly and set him aside to allow the blood to drain while I make a fire.

Just as the meal is ready, I hear Maruq's familiar whistle. It reminds me of the day he gave me Qim, and I wonder again about my friend. Did she survive the earthshake? Loss and guilt course through my veins. I have lost everyone that meant anything to me, my friends and family, and it is all my doing.

"Think of the good." I remind myself, tears threatening my eyes, sobs choking my throat. But I push them down and fix my stone mask as Maruq appears from behind a tree, smiling. The babe is on his back, his bow slung across one shoulder and his dart pouch across the other. In his hands is a pouch full of something.

"I found a berry bush." He holds the pouch out to me. The berries resemble fireberries, but they are black.

"I have never seen these." I grumble.

"We had them at my home, they are delicious." As though for emphasis, he plucks one out of the pouch and tosses it into his mouth.

He is doing it again, trying to make me smile. "Obviously." My voice is flat.

Maruq raises an eyebrow and shrugs.

"Have you ever seen such a creature?" I ask, pointing to

the fire.

He moves closer to examine it. "Not one so small."

"Really?" My interest is piqued.

"And I have never eaten one."

He sets his weapons down on the bed roll and shrugs off the babe. She is sleeping. He crouches down and takes the flying creature from the spit. Breaking off a leg, he sucks on it.

"Different, but good."

I take a leg and test the meat.

"Good? It tastes like old cat." I toss the remainder to him.

He smiles and shakes his head, as though I am a choosy child. I snatch his berry pouch and begin devouring his morning's labor. I believe the trade is fair, his labor for mine.

"Did you find any signs of our people, our camp?" I ask, hope brimming, but I try to hold it in.

"No, the earthshake has so changed the terrain that I cannot find any of the landmarks I had noted while scouting."

"We are lost then." A stone sinks in my stomach.

"Not lost, just misplaced." His lopsided grin lightens his eyes.

I toss a berry at his face, leaving a black stain on his fine cheek.

The babe starts to wiggle and squirm, her face contorting into large yawns. Maruq takes the milk skin from his belt and, leaving his meal, begins to care for her.

"I can do that."

"I don't mind caring for Giggles, she reminds me of a niece I had once."

I remember the story he shared and try to remember the name of the three year old his father had found dead, but I can't. "Giggles?"

"Well, I had to call her something."

"But Giggles?"

As though to show her approval, the babe pulls the skin from her mouth and smiles, giggling up at Maruq, her caretaker.

"She likes it."

I hum a disgruntled note at him. "I think I should care for her, though. I can't do much else with my leg like this."

"Are your ribs well enough?"

"I caught that creature, didn't I?" I snap at him, tired of being an invalid.

"Yes, well, we shall see. You can start by feeding her while I pack up." He hands Giggles to me and the milk skin. Holding her is painful, but I manage her.

I watch her finish her meal while listening to the bustling of Maruq around me as he gathers all of our belongings.

"All packed up. Give me the babe and we can be off."

I oblige, knowing that there is no way for me to carry her.

"Oh, and I found you a staff." As if from the air, he produces a sturdy staff, smooth and free of bark. I reach out and take the gift from him.

A smile plays at the corners of my mouth. I can't remember the last time someone looked out for me. It was always assumed that I could do everything. If I needed a staff, I would have needed to find it and strip it for myself. "Thank you." I say, pushing myself up to stand in front of him.

A muscle in his jaw tightens and he turns, walking to gather the fleet foot and her babe.

We travel keeping the Great Light on our weak sides in the morning and strong sides in the evening. Maruq sets an easy pace, leading the mother fleet foot, carrying the babe, the pack, and his weapons. I feel useless, staggering along with my staff. Then as we make camp on that first night, it begins to rain.

Maruq makes a tent out of the grizzly skin, but when we awaken the next day it is still raining. And it doesn't stop for the next three days.

Each day we continue on in the rain, making little if any progress, never seeing any signs of our people. I am exhausted, injured, and heart sore. I need a place to stay out of the rain. A place to get warm and heal.

Just as I am about to collapse, I see it. "Maruq, up there." I point, a small cave about halfway up a hill that appears untouched by the recent earthshake.

Without comment, Maruq turns and makes his way up to the cave, leading the fleet feet. I follow slowly, step by step, forcing one foot in front of the other. About five spans up the hill, I can do no more, I must rest. Holding the staff, I sink to the ground. I lean my head against it, closing my eyes. The rain pelts cold against my drenched body cooling the aching fire that begins in my injured side and radiates out to my fingers and toes, beating on my skin like the distant drums from my past.

I can't make it. I have no more strength in me; it has ebbed out like the blood from a kill over the past few days. Like my people, my will to live is gone.

I hear Giggles. Maruq must have made it to the cave. He will need to tie up the fleet foot and begin a fire. I need to stand, I need to make it to join them, I must, but I don't think I can.

Sobs start from deep within me, so deep and strong that I cannot breathe or catch my breath. With each sob, my ribs shoot pain through me, but I can't stop. I want to melt into the ground, to fly away on the wind, to leave this world and its grief. To find Xerena.

I feel strong arms around me, lifting me up. I lay my head on a solid shoulder and continue to cry. He says nothing; he just carries me to the cave and sets me next Giggles, who is laying on the ground kicking at the sky.

He leaves me and I hear the noise of flints hitting together. I see sparks fly out from his hands. One lands on some dried grass and smoke begins to rise. I drag in a ragged breath. Maruq leans forward and blows on the smoke until a small flame bursts into sight, a tiny light in the dark cave. He puts twigs onto it, encouraging the flames growth. Within a moment, I can feel the heat reaching out to me, warming my wet, cold body.

Maruq returns to me and gathers me into his arms like a child. Carefully, tenderly, he lays me near the fire. My sobs have stopped and I am left empty, except for the heat created by Maruq's care.

I hear him tending the fleet foot and then return. I hear him pick up Giggles. Out of the corner of my eye, I see him settle next to me by the fire, feeding the babe. I hear a contented sigh when Giggles has had her fill. I watch the fire dance.

"It is my fault, you know." My voice surprises me. It is hollow and dead.

"What?"

"That we are the only ones left, that they are all dead. If only I had stayed, if only I taken his offer."

"To join with Balek?"

I nod.

"Would that have prevented the earthshake?"

"No."

"Would Balek have chosen a different path than you, keeping us all in the valley?"

"I don't know. Maybe?" I stare up at the black ceiling of the small cave. The smoke from the fire has started to curl and find an escape through a hole in the far corner.

"Would you be happy then, as Balek's woman?" His voice sounds tight, as though saying the words pains him.

I look down to my hands. My strong hand is healing, three ragged scars forming. I think of when Maruq had bandaged my hand, of when he had cried over me at the bottom of the cliff, of all the little moments that I had shared with him. "No, but happiness is not something that this life gives."

"That is not true."

I look at him. He stares into the fire, cradling Giggles in his arms.

"Happiness is something that most people don't have the courage to pursue." He takes a deep breath, eyes trained on the flickering flames. "You are strong and courageous; you can find happiness, just don't give in to the sorrow, the regret. Tomorrow dawns a new day with hope. You are here, Giggles is here, and I am here. Others may have survived. Keep the hope and happiness will come." He turns to me before finishing, "I know."

36 RAIN

The next morning I wake with a start of pain, as though someone has jabbed me with a blade. I moan. It was no blade, but Maruq's elbow in my injured side. I shift gingerly away and closer to Giggles, who is awake and cooing. I watch her, fascinated. Other than that first night's wailing she seems oblivious to what is going on. I want to be her.

I look past her to the cave beyond, examining it in the early purple light. It is small, a mere fraction of my old home. The floor is even, made of smooth stone. In the far corner there is a cistern worn into the floor, a hole directly above, the one the smoke escaped by. I watch as rain pours through it and into the cistern. I wonder if the Mighty One put it there, or if a man had. The walls are free of any drawings, but there are evidences of man, for a fire pit has been ringed in the middle for warmth. And a small stack of dry wood is nearby. It will make us a nice home.

Giggles whines; she is hungry. I look at Maruq's still-sleeping form and decide to tend to her myself. I look around for the milk skin. It is easily within my reach, but it is empty. Carefully, so as not to disturb Maruq, I slide out from under the soft skin that we are sharing. I struggle to my feet, making my way to the mother fleet foot who is tied just

258

inside the cave entrance. Her graceful neck stretches down and she begins to pluck at the bits of grass growing just outside. I need to milk her, something I have only seen the women do.

As I limp toward the docile beast, she lifts her head. Staring into her serene eyes, I try not to excite fear. I have never seen a fleet foot when it is enraged, but I have heard that they can be fierce when provoked. I don't want to provoke her. I have enough injuries now.

I settle down next to her, running a hand gently down her neck and leg, letting her know that I am no threat. She begins to lift a front leg.

"Easy."

I reach under her, preparing to repeat the motions that I have only seen from a distance. I let out a disgruntled hum when I realize that I forgot the bowl. I don't want to go back to get it. My ankle is burning, my ribs are on fire, but I must. I lean back, breathing slowly; I close my eyes to gather strength.

"Need this?"

I open my eyes. Maruq stands above me, Giggles laughing in his arm. He holds out the bowl to me with the other. I take it, relieved.

"Yes."

I place it under the mother, and then reach up to start milking her. I pull on the teat; but nothing comes out. I try again and again and only accomplish annoying the animal, and frustrating myself.

I feel him crouch down behind me. He sets Giggles down, handing her the empty milk sack to chew on. He encircles me with his arms, his hands cover mine, and he begins to pull and squeeze, showing me how to properly milk her. I watch as his capable hands move in their slow motion over mine.

"Pull and squeeze." His breath tickles my neck and pleasure sweeps through my body. His hands stop and without letting go, he says, "You try."

I try to focus on my hands, try to mimic his movements, but all I feel is his nearness.

"Good." He says when I have filled the bowl.

"Since you don't need me," he whispers in my ear, "I am going to scout around see if I can find some food." He stands and I feel alone.

I turn handing him the bowl and he helps me up. Giggles still sits chewing on the sack. I bend to gather her up, but my ribs argue with me.

"Here," He takes her back to the fire ring. I fill the sack with the milk and join them.

"I won't be long." He picks up his dart pouch and slings it across his back. Putting his bow over one shoulder, he turns and walks to the entrance. I watch his graceful movements, his lean form moving effortlessly. He stops and turns, fixing his gaze in my direction. He grins.

"I shall keep the fire going." I assure him.

"If you need me, whistle." He leans a hand against the cave wall. "You do know how to whistle, don't you Siira?"

"Yes, Maruq, I know how to whistle." I say and ease myself down next to the babe.

"Pity, I wanted to teach you." A playful gleam lights his eyes and his grin broadens. He pushes off of the wall and disappears from my sight. I can't imagine why he would want to teach me to whistle, until I pucker my lips to practice.

I give the milk sack to Giggles and hum trying to calm the pounding in my heart. Soon, she has had her fill and drifts to sleep. I become restless. I cast my eyes around the small cave. The cistern is full and so I decide to fill our water skins. Grabbing my staff, I make my way to it and plunge the skins down, waiting for the air bubbles to stop before pulling them back up.

I stand and limp back to the fire, stoking it with a couple of logs. I check on Giggles, she still sleeps. I glance at the entrance. The rain has grown stronger, coming down in sheets. I hear rumbling thunder and see a flash of lightning. I begin to worry about Maruq.

I need to keep busy. Searching for something to do, I grab a long stick and begin to turn it into a torch. When I have finished, I use the fire to light it and stand to take the torch to the entrance. A light to bring Maruq home. Worry clouds my mind again. How many of my loved ones will never again come home? *Please, let me have Maruq,* I beg.

I limp back to Giggles and the fire. I stare into it. And wait.

Near night fall, I hear a low whistle. My pulse races. He has returned.

When he enters, he shakes the water from his head, showering the ground around his feet. "I have set some traps, but until the rain stops I am not sure that anything will be caught. I did, however, gather more berries." He holds up a sopping-wet pouch.

"Too bad we don't have a pot, I could conjure a stew." I smile, pleased at the sight of him. It is good.

"Actually," he says, taking long strides and moving to his pack, "we do." He digs in it for a while.

Is there anything he is not prepared for?

"No, not much," he answers my unspoken question.

"How? Did you?" My mouth stumbles over the words as I try to make the question that is bouncing around in my mind come out.

"How did I what?"

How did you read my mind, how do you answer me before I speak? I want to say, but I feel foolish.

"How did you know that we would need a pot?" I ask.

"Siira, I always carry a pot." He grins and I join him.

The sky pours out rain constantly. It has been over a moon since we left the corridor. And half of it has been spent in the rain.

As I watch our cistern fill, I begin to think of Grandmother's stories of the Old Man in the box. Has the Mighty One decided to join in my grief, and drown me?

I can do nothing, there is nothing to do. Back home the cold weather brought a time of preparation, but here, although we have things to prepare, we have none of the supplies. And so I sit and stare outside.

I miss my old cave with its cavernous interior, one that I had explored and found secret places in. This cave's only secret is its previous owner. At times I try to imagine who had lived here before us. Who had stacked the supply of dry wood? I imagine a traveler long ago, someone like me who had lost everything.

Maruq spends his captivity carving. He is not as talented as Balek, but he is good. He carves a toy for Giggles, a fleet foot. A stirring stick for the pot.

One afternoon, I sit near the entrance, watching the gray outside, a wall of water falling from the clouds, washing away all scars of the earthshake.

"The world is cleaned, refreshed; it is made new." Maruq comes up behind me, seeming to quote words from a time long ago. He appears his hands hidden behind him.

"Close your eyes."

I readily comply.

"Open them." He holds my staff out to me. I take it and examine it in the torchlight. He has carved creatures into it, matching the design on my cuff. Below them a lace is wrapped creating a hand hold.

I run my hand over the carvings. "It's beautiful." I say, breathless, overwhelmed by his gift. "How do you do it?"

"With a blade."

I smile, "That is not what I meant." I look out to the rain.

"I have watched you lose your father. I have seen you

weather the storms that the Mighty One gives you. The ridicule, the false charges, the grief, and yet you still have peace, faith, even trust in spite of it all."

"And you do not?" The melody of the question somber.

"No. I have lived even though all those that I love have died. I want to believe that the Mighty One wants my good. Grandmother told me he did. Father said that the Mighty One gives us what we need to do what we are called to do. And yet I have lost all my people. I am no longer Chief. I am no longer friend. I am no longer daughter. How do you still trust in the Mighty One?"

Several silent moments pass. I shift uncomfortably and begin to doubt that he can answer my question.

He kneels in front of me and takes my hand, running his thumb across the scars.

"Because of his promise."

"What promise?" I raise an eyebrow.

I try to think of a promise that the Mighty One has made, a promise that has not been broken. But in all of Grandmother's stories, I can think of nothing.

Maruq releases my hand and settles onto the ground next to me. Taking up some rocks, he tosses them one by one outside, punctuating his story. "When I was very young, I would huddle scared in the corner of our family home during any storm. The thundering and lightning frightened me a great deal. I asked her why the Great Father was angry with us, why was he frightening me, what had I done? She stroked my hair and told me a story. I believe I have heard your Grandmother tell a version of it." He looks up at me with his calm blue eyes.

"About the Old Man that was hidden in the box. In my mother's tale, the Great Father kept him and his family safe, guiding them to a safe landing. When he came out of the boat, he offered thanks to the Great Father. And the Great Father in return made a promise, a promise that every time he would cause it to rain, to cleanse the earth and make it new again, he would cause a bow to be in the sky. The bow would remind him of his promise, and so he would give man another chance.

"I remember that my mother told me that whenever it rained and I became scared that I was to trust the Great Father. And after the storm had passed, to always look for the bow. I always did and I always found it. And so the Great Father has remained faithful from that time until this. So I believe him."

He looks outside at the rain falling. "You know, I am still frightened of thunder and lightning, but I know that after every storm the bow will appear."

37 A PROMISE

The next day the rain stops. I make my way to the entrance and look for the bow. Just like Maruq had said, a beautiful array of colors sweeps across the gray sky. I smile, allowing the beauty of the sight to soothe my aching soul.

He keeps his promise, again. I look back into the cave. Maruq is digging in his pack, searching for something. "You were right." I say limping back to him.

"About what?" He stops his searching and looks up at me.

I point at the entrance. "The bow. It's there." For the first time since Bela's death, my voice sounds light, full of hope for the future. "The Mighty One, the Great Father, he didn't forget."

Maruq's eyes search my face, as though trying to find something there. Whatever it is that he looks for he must not find it, for he stands coming to me to make a better examination. He stands within arm's reach, his eyes clouded in doubt.

"I need to hunt." He says.

I blink back my surprise, and fight the panic that rises. I don't want him to go. What if he never comes back?

"We need meat, Siira. For half a moon now, we haven't

265

had anything more than the berries and herbs I gather. I must go."

My emotions crash like a wave on the shore. I want him to stay or take us with him, but I know that both are impossible.

"Siira, I will return." I look up to him, doubting his words.

He steps forward closing the distance between us. Taking my hands, he looks into my eyes.

"Do you remember that night at the edge of the cave when we threw pebbles?"

I nod.

"I told you that I had asked for you, that I wanted to claim you as my own. And although I was just beginning to know you, your father gave his permission for reasons I don't understand. And then he named his price."

I really don't care what my father said. I would freely give myself to him if only he would stay longer, and wrap his arms around me, sharing his peace. "So what was my price?"

"He asked for a promise." He looks down at our hands. "I was to promise to never make you something you are not." He smiles at me, his sweet lopsided smile. "I have spent the last few annuals since losing my father getting to know you, learning to understand you. Now, I think I can say that I do. And you are many things, but you are no coward."

"No?" I don't feel brave. I feel vulnerable.

He shakes his head. "You always rise to the occasion, no matter what is required of you, whether a big strong hunter challenges you to a fight, or an elder tries to force you into something you do not want to do."

It was true. I had not backed away then, but then I had not lost everything.

"You will rise again. I know it. As surely as I know that the Great Father kept me alive all those years ago so that I could find you." He reaches up and traces a finger along my forehead, moving an errant strand of hair from my eyes.

A rush of joy, like the exhilaration of soaring through the air, twisting freely until I land firmly on my feet, runs through me at his words. I see a new life in his bright eyes, shimmering with multicolored hope, like the bow that arches through the gray sky.

Yes, I have lost everything, but that loss has given me an opportunity to become what I have always longed to be. Myself. In his eyes, I see that I only need to be myself. He expects nothing more of me. He only wants my love, a love that will match his. I lift my chin accepting the new challenge ahead. "How long will you be?"

"I don't know. I hope no more than two or three days, but you know how hunts go." He releases me and turns to his pack again.

Yes, of all the women that the Mighty One has made, I understand hunts better than any. And now I shall learn what it means to be a woman, for because of my still mending injuries I must wait in the cave with Giggles until he returns.

I watch as he finishes gathering his needed supplies, carving his image into my mind. His thick honey-colored hair, his strong jaw and chiseled features, so perfect that he could only have been formed by a master carver, his bright blue eyes, so full of love and peace. As he stands to leave, I know that I must tell him one thing before he goes.

"Maruq," I manage only to say his name, before emotions overwhelm my words.

He comes to me. Taking my hand, he runs his thumb across the scarred skin. Gathering me into his strong arms, he lays his head atop mine. I breathe in his scent trying to imprint it into my memory alongside the carving of his image.

"When I return, Siira, will you become my woman?"

Tears overflow my eyes. I look up at him. "I would like

nothing better."

The joy that lights his eyes reaches into me, lighting my soul. He bends down and kisses me. A long kiss full of promise, sealing our words, entangling our souls. I never knew how much I needed him until that moment. His assurance and serenity, his patience and love have become my life line. He has kept me from sinking into despair by his mere presence.

He pulls back, breaking the kiss. I reach up longing for more of him. But wisely he retreats.

"Not yet, my love. Not yet."

I nod.

Maruq removes his token from his wrist, and slides it down over my hand. I stare at it, loving the promise of the gesture. He will return to me.

I release him, allowing him to leave, to go find us provisions. But I know that time will pass slowly, torturing me until his return.

Giggles cries having awakened. I bend to pick her up, a slight gasp leaving my lips as a small pain runs through my ribs, reminding me that healing takes much time. Cradling her to my chest, I speak softly, "I have a surprise for you, Giggles. I shall be Maruq's woman. When he returns, I will no longer be Chief. I am just a woman."

A woman. Maruq's promised one. No longer is there a need to pretend to have no emotions. No longer must I push everything down, freezing my feelings, being stronger than I am. I am free to be what the Mighty One has made me. A strange peace settles on me as I think of it.

Everything is new with this life before me. A joy wells inside me at the prospect, a joy that casts out my fear and grief. And yet as I look down at the babe in my arms, a pang of remorse runs through me. How can I be so joyous in the wake of such pain?

Giggles tugs on something that is around my neck. I look down to see what it is. In her hands, she plays with the beaded necklace that Bela had made for me so long ago, a present for before my testing, to bring me luck. I stare at the beaded flower pattern, blue remembering flowers gathered into a small bunch.

Giggles smiles and begins to gum it.

"No mouth." I tug it from her, searching for her rattle or fleet foot toy. I see the fleet foot and set her down. Bouncing it in front of her, enticing her to take it, she grasps it and begins chewing on the end.

Removing the necklace up and over my head, I contemplate it in my hand. *I never said goodbye.* Not to Bela, not to Pol, or Pire, to Kavok or Kora. They are all gone without a farewell. But how am I to say goodbye with no death boat, with no Great Salt Water, with nothing.

The beautiful necklace is all I have left of my people.

The fire snaps and crackles, its red glow needing tended. Another fire comes to memory, another farewell. When I became Chief, Boku had burned the token of my father. Now as I become a woman, as I leave my old life behind, I would burn another token, Bela's gift.

I move to the small flames. Stoking it, I prepare myself for what I must do. I remember each face, faces that I have known my entire life. Kavok speaking with his wife before a hunt. Sinaq sleeping with his children near. Pol smiling at Bela. Bela singing to her babe.

I let other faces come to mind. I had made no good-byes when we left for the corridor because I couldn't afford the emotions, but now I can. I see Kumal and his sister little Malukim. I remember Iruq, my challenger. I see Natiq, like a second mother to me. Balek's strong handsome face comes to my mind. My heart aches for him, my friend and my brother.

I hold the necklace out, letting it swing softly. And then I drop it into the flame. The soft skin cord shrivels in the heat, releasing small tendrils of smoke. The medallion burns around the edges slowly smoldering, like my grief. Tears begin to stream down my cheeks as the gift burns. "Goodbye."

I hear Giggles moving to me. I grab her up, clutching her to me. "I promise you this, my friends, she will not forget you. She will live and remember, for as long as I have breath, I will keep the stories alive."

38 JOINED

The days pass. Two, three, four.

I keep busy, telling myself that I know what the hunts are like. I milk the fleet foot and feed Giggles. I fill the water skins from the cistern. I make a fire. I set out some of the berries to dry. I walk to the entrance and look for Maruq. I go to Giggles when she cries. I tell stories. I pace, back and forth; I try to calm her fears and mine. I even begin to adorn the cave with the bright, clean flowers that I find in the forest.

"He is fine," I tell Giggles as she gums her toy. "Why, once I tracked a fleet foot for four days before I had a clear shot." I bounce her on my knee. A thought comes to me. "How would you like a swing?"

She smiles reaching for my cuff, apparently done with her toy. She watches the firelight gleam off of it, running her fingers over the creatures engraved there. I remember doing the same thing when my father wore it on his wrist, but he never took off the sign of his leadership, and so I do not. Not because I am clinging to my position as Chief, but because I am his daughter, the last of his line.

I pull off my token belt, sliding one of my blades in its sheath off of it. I check the latch and then hand her the blade. She gums the handle.

I set her on the grizzly skin and set about making a small swinging bed for her. Gathering sturdy twigs that I angle into peaks, a small skin, and some cord Maruq has left. I soon fashion a usable, if unsightly, swing. And soon she is rocking gently back and forth, her eyes fluttering open and closed as she tries to fight sleep, but eventually she is breathing in and out in a rhythm that tells me she has succumbed to the inevitable.

"Go to sleep, Siira." I tell myself. "The night journeys more quickly when your eyes are closed."

And so I stretch out on the furs, imagine Maruq's warmth just behind me, and join Giggles in slumber.

When I open my eyes, the Great Light has not yet begun its journey across the day sky. I reach behind me, hoping to feel a strong body there, but Maruq has not returned.

I have not had to wait for a hunter to return in so many annuals that I have forgotten how to be patient. Even as a child I could run to the meadow or set traps of my own, always staying busy. Balek was always ready to do anything to stay busy, anything that kept us from waiting with the women.

But now I have no choice, nothing to occupy me, except my aching injuries and my worries.

I check Giggles and she is still sleeping, but I know that she will be hungry when she awakens. And so I limp to the mother fleet foot. Milking her, while she eats, filling the bowl with warm milk. I watch the steam rise from the bowl, curling through the air. A cold wind blows from the entrance raising bumps on my bare arms. I have no jacket.

I look at the grizzly skin that Maruq has left and wonder if I could manage to make a jacket from it and still leave enough to keep warm. If Maruq is successful, we will have a new skin to prepare. I smile. It will at least give me something to do. But as I walk back to the skin, I realize that I do not have the skill to make the jacket.

I had only ever learned to make boots. Grandmother and the other women made the jackets, and leggings and tunics. I think of the great cape they had fashioned for Balek. Malukim's natural talent to look at a skin and see the possibilities, but I can't even imagine how to cut this skin for a simple jacket.

Giggles begins to stir and I put my plan aside. I fill the milk sack for her with the warm milk. She grabs it as soon as I hold it out to her, pulling it to her mouth and sucking. She is so eager, so full of life, full of hope and promise. Worry does not cross her mind. She expects to be cared for, oblivious to all her loss.

I settle on the floor, sucking in a breath at the pain that is constantly with me, I pull her into my lap, cradling her in my crossed legs. She kicks her legs playfully as she drinks; her bright eyes aware and alive with life and love.

A noise outside of the cave draws my attention to the entrance. Rocks skittering down the hill, the crunch of soft steps. My heart begins to race. Maruq has returned at last. My hand flies to my hair, it is loose and wild. Soon I will be able to braid it. Soon, I will be a woman, Maruq's woman. My new life will begin.

But the face that I expect to see peeking in, smiling, the face of my beloved, does not appear; instead it is a muzzle, a wolf's muzzle. A new hope is born in me.

"Qim?" My whispered question filling the cave.

She has found me. After more than half a moon, she has returned.

As she comes into view, I am filled with joy; a friend I never thought to see again has found me. She lopes over to me, miraculously free of any injury. "Good girl. I have missed you." She whines, nuzzling my hand, my shoulder, almost knocking me and the babe over onto the floor, causing me to suck in air at the dull ache in my side.

"Sit."

She obeys just as eagerly as ever.

"Are you hungry, girl?" I ruff the fur around her ear, her soft warm fur. She barks, a quick, excited bark. Oh, how I have missed her. "Yes, well, all I have are berries." I look around me and see the milk bowl. "I know." I catch up the milking bowl and settle Giggles into a sitting position next to Qim.

Giggles reaches out a curious hand to her fur, and Qim turns her head, sniffing at the small hand. I go to the mother fleet foot and milk her until I have a full bowl.

Setting the creamy warm liquid down in front of Qim, she sniffs at it then begins lapping noisily. I notice that although Qim has been on her own her stomach seems to bulge. And then I remember the pups. I remember that Maruq had said that soon there would be pups, but how soon?

I hope that Maruq will come back before I need to learn to

deliver babes.

When I can find nothing else to do because Giggles is fed and sleeping again, the fire is blazing, the water skins are full, I begin to mope. I rub Qim's ears, talking to her of everything that has happened since I saw her last. Telling her of my fall, of finding the cave, of Maruq's love for me and mine for him.

I look into her eyes and wish that she could tell me her tale. She settles down, resting her head on her paws. She yawns and closes her eyes.

"Yes, it is late." I lay down and she takes her position at my feet, the way she had at my family tent. Comforted, I drift to sleep.

I sit in a boat, rocking gently. Giggles is curled in my arms, sleeping. Maruq sits in front of me paddling. We are leaving going somewhere, but I am unsure of where it is. I look around me and we are on a giant body of calm silver water. There is no wind, no waves. It is peaceful. On the shore I see mammoth grazing; there are hundreds of them. I look up and see a brilliantly blue sky. Xerena. The word whispers through my mind. I open my mouth to speak, but something behind us startles me.

I wake.

The noise, almost as though a heavy beast is stomping outside of the cave, is coming from outside. Then a deep, rumbling laugh floats to my ears. I shift on the furs, reaching out a hand, checking the babe. She swings in her bed. My eyes adjust from fuzzy sleepiness to sharp clarity. Qim is in front of me; her ears are pinned back and her mouth is snarling. I reach for my staff. My useless tokens lie under the furs. As I wish for a throwing stick and darts, I turn.

A massive head peers at me from the entrance of the cave. Thick, curly red hair covers his features, except for pale eyes alive with curiosity. Well-worn wrinkles at the corners of them crinkle as his mouth curves in a broad toothy grin.

He ducks his head entering, standing to his full height. His fiery hair brushes the cave's dark ceiling, a height that I may touch with my staff if I extended it as high as possible. He is at least three spans tall, and a span broad. I had thought Balek large, but next to this monstrous man, even Balek would appear but a child.

Fear grips me. I crouch down, ready to attempt an attack if he proves unfriendly. But I know that I am not well enough to defeat him if he is.

His curious eyes glance over me and Qim, who is still growling, and scan the cave, taking in the full cistern, the small pen for the animals, and the flowery arrangements. He reaches out his massive hand and picks up a wilting flower, twirling it between his finger and thumb.

His pale eyes eventually return to me. My muscles tense and my heart pounds as I hold his gaze, my stone mask in place once again. He raises one of his bushy eyebrows, as though to ask a question. I must seem as strange to him as he does to me. I crouch down pointing my staff at him, my long mane wild and loose to my waist, a young child playing next to me, an obviously protective wolf growling at him.

He speaks, probably voicing one of his questions, but his words are incomprehensible. They growl and bark at me. I shake my head, trying to communicate to him my lack of comprehension.

He speaks again, this time more slowly, but it doesn't help. I do not understand his barking. He smiles, patiently as at a child. The wrinkles around his pale eyes multiply, as he grins raising his empty hands as if to show that he means me no harm. I release my staff laying it back down. I settle into a more relaxed position, but my senses stay alert.

He makes no move to come closer. I am sure that he probably wants to warm himself and drink from the cistern, but instead of coming in, he sits down in the entrance, apparently unwilling to alarm me. He cups one hand and scoops the other up to his mouth. I watch as he repeats the sign several times. I realize that he is asking after food and so I toss him the pouch of berries. He smiles and laughs; the rumbling laughter makes him seem less formidable, more like a jolly giant than a menacing monster.

I pick up Giggles, she has begun to demand food. I begin to plead with the Great Father for Maruq's quick return.

"Sit." I say to Qim, tapping the ground next to me. She gives a warning growl to our visitor, and then sits, never taking her eyes off him.

I settle Giggles next to her, making sure that the babe has her rattle to occupy her while I milk the mother fleet foot. I grab the bowl and my staff, making my way to the animals. I try not to limp, holding my head high, my shoulders erect. I do not want to show him any weakness, give him any opportunity to do us harm.

I quickly fill the bowl and return to the grizzly skin. I fill Giggles milk sack and hand it to her. I settle back down. I know that he has been watching me, weighing my every movement. His smile has vanished, his brows are now knit together, deep furrows crease his forehead. He is trying to work something out, but I do not know what.

After a while, he decides to try to communicate again for he opens his mouth, uttering the absurd barking and grunting noises.

I shake my head.

And then he points to himself and repeats two sounds over and over.

"Val-dr, Val-dr."

Hoping that he is telling me his name, I repeat him. "Valdr?"

"Ya." Then he points to me.

"Si-i-ra," I say.

"Siira," he repeats and nods. Then he points to Giggles. I tell him her name and he repeats it, until satisfied. Then he leans his head back and closes his eyes, falling asleep.

Calm settles on me, my nerves quiet as I watch his large chest rise and fall in the shallow rhythm of sleep. I fill my lungs with air, blowing out the anxiety that the meeting had created. I stand and move to stoke the fire.

My stomach complains, wanting food. I see the pouch of berries discarded next to him. He has emptied it. I need to gather more, but I cannot. For my giant visitor has blocked the entrance with his massive sleeping body. I will have to wait for him to wake up.

Moving back to Qim and Giggles, I settle and study him. He wears heavy furs that cover him from his neck to his wrists to his trunk-like thighs. His hairy legs are bare except for heavy, furry boots that are wrapped around his calves with lacing, much in the fashion of mine. I stare at his booted feet. They appear to be the length of my arm and as thick as a log. He could easily smash my skull or anything else he stepped on, so large and heavy they are.

I look about him for weapons. He has no blades or darts,

although I doubt that he needs any. But I do see a massive club leaning against the cave wall. The club is about as big as me, both in height and width. The fact that he can apparently swing it about wielding it to do harm, frightens me.

Where is Maruq?

As Valdr sleeps, I quietly tend to Giggles, feeding her, playing with her, changing dirty rags for cleaner ones. I even milk the fleet foot in an attempt to fill my stomach with something. As the Great Light begins the final stages of its journey across the sky, I begin to plead with the Mighty One, the Great Father for Maruq's quick return.

I settle back into the furs, Giggles in my arms. Valdr stirs rolling. He must have journeyed far to have needed so much sleep.

Then I hear Maruq's whistle. I impulsively lean forward. My heart races, I don't know what to do, I have never had a need to respond to his approach, to warn him, but somehow I must alert him to the monstrous man that is sleeping, blocking my way to him.

As Maruq's whistle sings in the air a second time, I see Valdr stir again. His pale eyes blinking open, orienting himself, he looks about him. Once his eyes rest on me, he seems to remember where he is.

"Siira?" his deep, guttural voice asks.

I nod and point outside. "Ma-ru-q," I say at the sound of another merry whistle.

He nods, as though he understands me. I stand, picking up Giggles, nestling her in my arm. I take the staff in my strong hand, and I purposefully walk over to Valdr. He seems to grow larger the closer I get. Holding my ground, pushing my fear down, I gaze up at him and tap the side of his leg gently with my staff.

A patient grin spreads across his face and he draws his legs up and out of my way. I hear Qim jump up from the furs. Eager to go to her master, she runs out ahead of me now that the way is clear. Squaring my shoulders, I walk out of the cave.

I work my way down to the base of the hill. Maruq emerges from the trees, carrying a large fleet foot across his shoulders. At the sight of him healthy and handsome, I wish to run to him, to wrap my arms around him and cover him in kisses, but I cannot. Valdr is watching.

Qim makes it to him first, jumping and yipping. A smile lights Maruq's eyes. "Qim, good girl." I am certain that if his hands were free, he would pet her, and wrestle.

"Surprise," I say, now standing in front of him. The babe in my arm giggles and reaches out for him. He leans forward and nuzzles her stomach with his face. The action causes her to squirm and laugh. I have to concentrate hard to hold her, my ribs rippling with pain.

"I have a surprise for you, too," he looks at me with joy dancing in his eyes. And then I see some movement behind him. The branches of the trees swing and lift up. A black head comes into view. It is Pire, carrying a string of jumpers. I am overwhelmed, but my surprise is not finished for Korak appears, carrying her sister, Sanq, who sleeps on her shoulder.

Joy bubbles in my soul like an overheated stew spilling out and over the sides of a pot. A burning desire to run and jump and fly from rock to tree rushes through me, but I must content myself with a smile that is too large for my face and happy streams of tears that I feel on my cheeks.

"Pire, Korak! Are there others?"

"No." Maruq shakes his head. "The earth swallowed the rest of the camp. Pire and Korak watched it happen and then ran just like us."

Three of them. Three had survived. That is more than I thought. I push down the sadness and think of the joy.

Korak rushes to me, and then her words spill forth. "My chief, I never thought that I would see any of my people again. I thought that the Mighty One had punished me for some unfaithfulness by taking everything, and then we saw Maruq. He told us of you and the babe and I thought that perhaps all was not lost." She continues to ramble on for a while longer. I listen as she releases all of her anxieties and hopes. "I am so glad to see you, my chief."

At her constant use of my title, I grow uncomfortable. I have given up my leadership position and I don't want to pick it back up. I don't want to worry about others, to take on the responsibility.

"Korak, this is a new family, a new people, a new life. I am just Siira. Please, I am no longer Chief."

She sinks down onto a nearby log, sucks in a deep breath. I feel that she was hoping for some kind of normality, and I have just told her that her old life is entirely gone. She begins to cry, anew. At the sound Sanq, who is no more than seven annuals, wakes. She wraps her arms around her sister, attempting to comfort her.

I let her weep, not knowing how to comfort her. As Korak's crying lessens, her sister's grasp loosens. Sanq searches her sister's face. A slight smile from the young girl is rewarded by a nod from her sister. She slides off and moves away to explore a little, but not too far away. I watch as Sanq constantly looks back to check on her sister's position. I decide to give Korak something to occupy herself with and hand her Giggles.

I know that I have made a wise decision when Korak's expression mirrors Giggles smile.

"I need to talk to Maruq. Can you keep the babe?"

She nods without looking away from her.

I work my way down to Maruq and Pire, who stand at the base of the hill, dressing their kills. The fleet foot is free of his skin, tied to a tree, and draining. Both men squat over the jumpers, freeing them of their small coats.

"It is good to see you, Pire," I say as I approach, interrupting whatever discussion they were having.

"The Mighty One be praised," he responds.

I nod. "Yes."

"Where did you find them?" I ask.

"They were wandering just above that ridge that you fell from."

"You fell, my chief?" Pire looks up at me, honest surprise in his eyes.

"Yes, Pire," I put a hand on my injured ribs, "as impossible as it may seem, I fell." I smile, trying to still the nervous fluttering in my stomach. "You did a good job taking care of your promised one. I think I know of a fitting reward. How would you like it if we had an official joining tonight?"

Pire's eyes become large and the excitement makes his voice quiver. "Yes, my chief, I would like that. I would like that very much."

"Good then, and Pire, I am no longer Chief. I have no people to lead."

"You have us."

"In truth, Pire, I no longer want to lead." My admission to this hunter is more difficult than I thought it would be. He stares at me blankly, almost as if I am barking at him in unintelligible words. "The responsibility is too great for me and I desire a different role in our new family, our new life."

Pire looks at me. His previously busy hands, still. His expression twists in confusion, as he tries to work out what I am saying. The men probably thought that I wanted to lead, wanted to follow my father. After all, that is what they would want. Only I knew the truth. That all I ever wanted was what I could not have until now. The freedom to be me, to love a caring man, to be loved by him.

Maruq grins and taps Pire's shoulder with his blade drawing his attention. "She is to be my woman."

Pire's dark eyes dart back to me. A look of incredulity washing over his face. "Really?"

"Really." I nod earnestly.

Slowly Pire's expression changes, a small crooked smile across his lips. "Ah, so it will be a double joining."

"Yes, a double joining." I repeat.

"While you were gone, Maruq, we had a guest," I say delivering the message that I had come to deliver.

"A guest?" His blade stops in its work.

"Yes, a very large guest. He is waiting at the cave." I can tell that Maruq is trying to understand me, but I am being cryptic. "This is something you need to see to believe." I reach out my strong hand to him. He drops the jumper. Looking at his hands that are covered in blood, he turns to his water skin and pours the cleansing liquid onto them. He runs his hands on his leggings in an attempt to dry them before taking mine.

Valdr no longer sits dozing, stretched across the opening; he sits on what seems to be a small stone under him, but I know its true size. His broad grin beams as I return with Maruq. As we come closer fear again stirs in my stomach. I feel Maruq tense as we approach. He steps in front of me, placing himself between me and Valdr, instinctively protecting me. I don't object.

"Is he safe?" He whispers back to me.

"So far, but he doesn't speak our language. All we have been successful at communicating is our names and that he was hungry."

As if he is trying to work out a puzzle, Valdr stares at Maruq, examining every piece of him from his head to his boot. He points one of his large fingers at Maruq and then looks at me. "Ma-ruk?" He asks.

"Ma-ru-q," I correct.

He nods and smiles again. His teeth gleaming. "Goot." He then growls and barks at Maruq good-naturedly, making hand signals at the same time.

"I think he wants to take us to his home," Maruq says, apparently better at interpreting signs than I am.

"Do you think it would be safe?"

"He seems very friendly, and he probably has food and provisions there."

"Alright, but tomorrow. Tonight we have a celebration." I squeeze his hand.

Valdr looks between Maruq and me, seeming to be very confused by what is going on. As Maruq attempts to convey my message to Valdr with hand signals, I stand patiently quiet, stilling the fears inside me.

Maruq signals to Valdr to follow him. "He can help Pire and me with the roasting." Valdr stands, rising to his full height, towering above us like a great tree.

My insides melt at the sight of him.

Maruq nods his head down the hill and Valdr begins to saunter in that direction. "I think he would terrify Korak and Sanq, so you bring them to the cave to help you." He says.

I nod, agreeing completely.

Maruq pulls my hand, drawing my attention from the departing giant and back to him. "And you need to prepare." He runs a finger across my forehead, down my face and to the back of my neck. A shiver of pleasure runs down me. "I missed you." He leans in and places a tender kiss on my lips.

Desire leaps inside me. "And I you." I lean into him and show him how much. When he pulls away, I am breathless.

"So," His bright eyes sparkling with a fire from inside him, "will you braid your hair?"

"Maybe." I tease, making my way down the hill to fetch the others.

I hear Maruq's whistle outside the cave.

All is ready. Korak and I have spent the time washing and preparing as best we could. Gathering flowers, adorning the cave and ourselves. I do not know how I look, but Korak is beautiful. I feel awkward and unappealing next to her. She is everything a woman should be.

Her skin soft and smooth, her hair shining in its long braid with the flowers plaited in it and wreathed around her head. Her dress, although worn, hugs her curves, attesting to her femininity.

I wear my tunic and leggings with my tokens fastened around my lean waist. My cuff shines on my muscled arm. Korak made a wreath for my hair. She helped me to tame my wild mane braiding it, long down my back. When I tried the task, my fingers proved to be unwieldy. I am certain that instead of beautiful I am a strange creature, still half one thing and half another.

Qim trots in, her ears ticking in motion, taking in every sound, Sanq playing with Giggles by the fire, Korak chattering at me. She can probably even hear the pounding of my heart.

The men appear at the entrance together, but I only have eyes for one of them. His eyes, intense and brilliant, reminding me of the remembering flowers. Everything that we have faced in the last few annuals comes rushing into my mind. Then he smiles, his easy lopsided grin and all of the hopes for the future fill me. "We left the fleet foot to smoke overnight. Valdr says he will watch it."

Qim nudges my hand. I kneel down and pet her. She sniffs at the flowers adorning my hair.

"How soon will the pups come?" I ask rubbing her stomach.

"She was spending a lot of time with Maq before we began our journey, but I would guess, another half-moon or so."

"Maq?" I say not knowing the name of the male wolf that had stolen my wolf's fancy.

"I was hoping that they would breed. The pups will be good."

I smile, shaking my head. "It seems that we are all moving forward."

"How shall we do this? We no longer have a chief to perform the ceremony." The voice is Pire's.

I turn. "I suppose that we can give our vows, just as if my father were here. We can bind you and Korak, and then you can bind us." I point at the jumpers. "Our small feast will follow, but as for going to separate rooms for the night, I don't have any idea." I shrug, trying not to appear disappointed.

"Let the men worry about that." He says. "It has always been our part."

I nod, recalling the separate rooms at the large cave.

We all gather near the fire. Maruq and Pire spit the jumpers over it, so that they can begin to roast. Qim lies at my feet.

I remember the joining I performed last annual at Sacred Point. Pol had stood nervously waiting for Bela and I had officiated. But now they are gone. So much can happen in only one annual, thirteen moons speed by causing so much change. And now I am no longer a man, no longer Chief; I am a woman, joining with the man of my choosing.

Maruq stands next to me, taking my strong hand in his. He nods to Pire, who begins to give his vows to Korak. I hear him without hearing him. I watch as he pledges to Korak, promising his life-long faithfulness, without really seeing it. I am too focused on the warmth of the callused hand holding mine.

Pire finishes his pledge and Korak begins to speak. Her sweet voice a jumbled melody in my mind. In only a few moments I will be pledging, promising to Maruq, making a vow. Panic rises. Will I remember what to say?

Korak's voice stops and expectant eyes focus on me. Maruq holds out a cord to me.

Releasing Maruq's hand, I take it and then wrap their hands, "I bind you to each other with this cord, as you have bound yourselves with your words." I say and then turn back to Maruq, my stomach churning with nervous excitement.

Maruq takes my hand. His melodic voice, calming me. "Siira, I will be your man, protecting and providing for you; understanding and loving you until death takes one or both of us.

I will be a good leader for our family as we make our way in this life given to us by the Great Father. This I pledge you."

I gaze into his eyes, open my mouth and hope that the words come out. "I will be your woman, serving and honoring you until death takes one or both of us." I say without faltering, I recite the pledge of our people. "I will take care of our family in the way prescribed by the Mighty One, teaching our ways to any children in order to keep the traditions of the fathers. This I pledge you."

I am focused completely on my man, hearing nothing else, only aware him. And then I feel Pire bind our hands. I hear him say the final words. And then Maruq steps in and places a kiss on my forehead, another on each of my cheeks. And then gathering his arms around me, wrapping me into warm security, he covers my mouth with his. I am his. As if we two are the only ones in the world, the only ones in the forest, in the cave, I return the kiss.

A shrill cry brings me back to reality. I pull back from him, reluctant. Maruq takes Giggles from Sanq. Raising her high into the air, tossing her softly, catching her in his arms

"Patience, child, we will feed you."

Warmth fills my soul, contentment that I have never before known. I smile at him. This is my man, my child, my family. Tonight we will feast, we will love, and tomorrow we will leave for a new home, following a new friend. The future shines brightly before me, multi-faceted and multi-colored.

ABOUT THE AUTHOR

Serenity K. Orr resides in Northeastern Nevada with her family. She is a graduate of Pensacola Christian College. She has a passion for literature and history. She divides her time between her family and her faith. She enjoys serving in her local church, hiking in the nearby mountains, sketching, painting, and writing.